BLOODLINES
OF ATMOS

THE STORY OF JACE
BOOK 3 - REDEMPTION

J. P. EDGAR

BLOODLINES OF ATMOS
THE STORY OF JACE, BOOK 3 — REDEMPTION

ISBN: 979-8-88653-024-7

Melange Books, LLC
White Bear Lake, MN 55110
www.melange-books.com

Published in the United States of America.

Cover Design by Ashley Redbird Designs

In loving memory of William "Brush" Edgar

PROLOGUE

THE FIGHTS WITH HER BOYFRIEND GREW MORE FREQUENT. ALMOST every day, in fact. It didn't matter to her, though. Deep down, underneath his bulging muscles and tough exterior, she knew he loved her. After all, even the best relationships had their problems.

Her taxi pulled up in front of her house late in the evening, the sudden push of the brakes prodding her fresh bruise against the door. She held back a wince as she pressed her hand on the keypad, entered a tip for the driver, then exited the vehicle.

The taxi pulled away, and she stood still. Fear stopped her. Fear of what she would come home to.

After a breath, her eyes drifted toward the painted yellow and pink mailbox and the words "Hastings" in big, bold letters. This was her house. Well, her daddy's. And she wasn't going to be afraid of anyone who might be inside.

After those reassuring thoughts, Ms. Hastings walked over the stepping stones that led from the street, through the grass-hilled yard she needed to mow, to her front door. She put her hand on the knob, waited a moment to hear the click of the lock, then opened the door.

She took a few steps in the dark and quietly closed the door behind her. Without making a sound, she snuck over the hardwood floor to the living room. There, buried under dirty and oily hair that covered his face, shivering, sweating, and reeking of alcohol, was her childhood friend.

She sat in an adjacent chair and stared through the pale moonlight at how much he had grown. She shook her head. How could someone so brave and strong be reduced to a homeless drunk? That's when her eyes glanced toward the strange-looking backpack at the side of her couch. She had never seen a bag like that before, nor the unusual fabric he had on under his ripped, bloody, and grimy clothes. It was almost impossible to get him undressed.

Though she wanted answers, she respected his privacy and decided not to go through his backpack. She stood up to check on the glass of water and pills on the coffee table. They remained untouched. Again, she wondered if she should call an ambulance. "Tomorrow," she mouthed. "If you don't wake up by tomorrow morning, I'm taking you to the hospital."

After a sigh, she adjusted the blanket on her guest. That's when she noticed that some of the moisture on his face wasn't sweat, but tears. He was crying.

Her heart almost gave out as she let out a quivering breath. "What happened to you?"

Knowing he wasn't going to answer, she stood straight and navigated through the front room in the dark to make her way to the bedroom. After a long and rough day, a deep soak in a hot bath would calm her nerves. It had indeed been a crappy night, and she had a test tomorrow.

—

The next morning, Ms. Hastings turned off the alarm on her wrist PC, got out of bed, and went to her bathroom. She washed her face, then wiped away the splashed water from the mirror to look over her features. Her eyes went to the roots of her shoulder-length pink hair as she grabbed a few strands for inspection. It was time for a new color.

"What do you think? Yellow?"

As if hearing an answer, she brushed back her hair with her fingers and exited her bathroom. "Six problems. Six problems." She paused, thinking about the acronym she and her study-buddies came up with. "PROC PIt.—Prevention, reversal, omission, commission, principle, incorrect transactions." She didn't take long in her closet as she picked out a long-sleeve yellow shirt, more to hide her bruised arms than any other reason, and bright green pants. All the while, she kept repeating "PROC Pit" and some other acronyms while she got ready.

Afterward, she made her way downstairs, her thoughts going from education to music, when she heard her footsteps making a particular beat. She smiled and made a grandiose landing on the bottom floor—her head down and eyes closed, her fingers trilling the air as if she were playing the notes from her head on a piano, then turned her attention to her unusual guest.

There he sat, face buried in his hands, weeping.

Her mood soured.

Before she took a step forward, she noticed a broken lamp on a pile of vomit on the floor next to the couch, and a small blood trail going toward the kitchen. And out of all of that, the water and pills remained untouched on the coffee table.

She slowly approached, still wondering how he wound up collapsed on her lawn. "I can't believe it's you." She knelt in front of him.

His puffy red eyes stared at her while he blinked away the tears. Then he squinted, gave a sniff, and his expression changed from sorrow to confusion as he visually scanned her. "Claire?"

She nodded, sat next to him, and put an arm around his shoulder. He fell into her arms, sobbing all the while.

————

Jace eventually passed out in her arms. She gently put him back on the couch, covered him in her favorite fuzzy tan blanket, then began to clean up the mess he left behind.

After bandaging his feet up with a medkit in the hallway, she went to the kitchen, following the thin trail of blood, to grab some paper towels. She gasped, seeing all of the cabinets, the fridge, and the freezer wide open. It looked as if thieves had ransacked the entire place. She glanced behind her at Jace. What was he searching for?

Knowing she could ask later, she grabbed the paper towels and began to clean up the vomit. When she got it under control, she picked up the broken glass, noticing a rather large shard covered in red. Was this how Jace hurt his foot?

Jace bolted upright, gasping and looking around in alarm.

Startled, Claire put a hand on the couch, ready to stand and assist her guest. "Are you okay?"

"What?" He turned to stare at her with fright and confusion.

A moment later, she decided to ask him about his injury. She lifted the bloody shard of glass from the floor.

His eyes went to the shard, and a look of recognition washed over his face.

Not getting any answers, Claire tossed the shard in the glass pile, then sat in the seat next to the couch. "Not exactly the reunion I imagined." She grabbed the water from the coffee table so he could get hydrated.

Jace laid back down, resting his head on the armrest, and stared at the presented drink. "Do you have anything stronger?"

Her eyes popped wide in surprise. "Oh, no. No more alcohol. You're already sick."

He raised a hand to decline the water.

"Drink."

Jace diverted his gaze.

At first, Claire grew angry. His stubbornness was getting under her skin. Then she noticed the pain in his eyes and the tears that formed, and her anger quickly transformed into genuine concern. She had so many questions but decided patience would be her best bet. She sighed, put the water back on the table, and sat back to sit quietly with her friend.

———

After messaging her professor from her wrist PC to explain the situation, Claire was relieved she could reschedule her test. That also meant she could digitally unplug from the world and work on Jace's health. His recovery was her focus.

He slept all day. And as the night fell, Claire wondered if Jace would wake up at some point and destroy her house again. So she blew up an air mattress and slept on the floor for the night.

Her uncomfortable sleep was interrupted by a scream. She sat up and whipped her head to Jace, who clenched the blanket and panted.

"Are you okay?"

He began to get up, but his balance was shaky at best.

Claire stood and got in front of him. "No, no, no." With barely a nudge from her hand, Jace collapsed back on the couch. "Where do you think you're going?"

"I need a drink."

"Here." She reached for the glass of water.

Like a stubborn jackass, Jace began to stand up again.

"I said no, damn it!" She pushed him hard. He fell flat onto the couch.

"Get out of my way!"

"Make me!" Claire pressed a hand against his chest.

Jace growled in pathetic rage, and he grabbed her arm. Shortly after, he went limp again.

She gave an exhale and stood straight. "Don't make me handcuff you."

He huffed and rolled over, putting his back against her, and curled up in a ball.

Her heart beat furiously, but she took a step back from Jace to calm down. She scanned the room, thinking of how to stop him from getting up and doing something stupid while she slept or when she was in class. That's when she remembered her freshman year and riding her bike to and from school. She went into the garage and took off the oversized cable and lock from her bike. Then she gathered some chains and other cords she could lock together. Eventually, she created some contraption that was long enough to get to and from the bathroom, and that she could lock. After a brief inspection, she nodded in approval.

————

Every night, Jace would wake her up with some scream or yell, like a child waking up from a nightmare, then curling back into a ball and crying himself back to sleep. Though he always angrily declined the water, eventually Claire began to wake up, or came home to, an empty glass. And gradually, the terrible nights were replaced with constant shifting and moaning. Until one night, he slept through the whole night, and she was able to get some much-needed rest in between taking care of him and her classes.

After school, not having time to cook due to her study group later that evening, Claire grabbed some takeout. She took a cab home, went inside, and began to make her way to the front room. She paused, though, as Jace stood near a wall in her music room and stared at a picture. How could he have gotten into that room? That's when her eyes went to the floor and at the unlocked chain. Her attention returned to Jace, and she put the bag of food on the ground and stood beside him. She remembered when her friend took the picture. It was at a birthday picnic in the park with her music class, and her parents flanked her as she held her new cello.

"My parents. Well, adopted parents."

Jace didn't answer.

She went back to the entryway and grabbed the bag. "They're assholes, but I love them. They gave me the life I have now, and I'll be forever grateful."

After removing the takeout boxes, Claire went to the kitchen for some dishes and utensils. She returned, balancing a couple of lemonade glasses on the plates.

Jace continued to stare at the picture.

"They're divorced now. Maybe eight years ago." She put everything on the coffee table and continued to prepare the food. "I hated my father. Still do, I guess. But..." She pulled up a chair. "I love him, no matter what."

Jace didn't move.

Claire decided to change the subject to something lighter and to something that involved him. "Hey, do you remember that food fight we had in the hiding space?"

Jace's head slightly turned. She had his attention.

"I tossed something at Jess, and she threw back a piece of meat." She smiled at the memory from years past, absent-mindedly dishing out some food. "It took us hours to clean all the food just so we didn't get ants. When we finished, we were a mess." Her gaze went into the nothingness of memory as that day came into her mind. "Jessy had those potatoes down her shirt, and you had gravy in your hair. And we never told you, but we kept joking about it." She chuckled and let out a deep exhale. "I bet I was a mess, too." She set aside one box of food and grabbed another. She gave a brief pause as her eyes locked onto the sauce-covered chicken and decided to provide Jace with the time he needed. "You don't want to tell me what happened? That's fine. Some day, you have to stop living in the past and work on your future. Don't think you're the only one who had a tough life."

She heard Jace whisper, "You're not the only one."

"What was that?"

An alarm went off on her wrist PC. She glanced down at it to see the time and the words, "Your ride has arrived."

She thought she had more time. "Shit!" She stuffed her face, frantically chewed, then washed it down with large gulps of her lemonade. "I have to go. Study group tonight." She tossed on her favorite pink sweater and opened the door. "I'll be a little late. I have to go to the store. Don't get into trouble." And she left him behind.

On the way to the taxi, her wrist PC dinged. She climbed in the cab and looked at the message. At that moment, stress and anxiety tightened her chest, and she found it a little difficult to breathe. Her heart pumped harder, and her vision began to tunnel toward the message on her screen, "From Harold: Where have you been?"

CHAPTER ONE

JACE STARED AT THE MOUND OF HAIR GATHERED IN THE SINK AFTER he shaved his beard and cut his hair. To him, that hair was a symbol of his pure and unbridled hopelessness. To him, shaving his face was like shaving away his shame. At least that's what he told himself.

He wiped the condensation from the mirror and took a long, hard look at what he had become. Through the mist from his hot shower, he stared at his five and a half foot tall frame, seeing the scars and injuries from his previous life and the unknown months of worthless pity that overtook his very soul. Though his body was still toned from the years of exercise and combat, he was unhappy at the pudge that began to develop in his gut, hiding his once immaculate abs.

After splashing water on his face to get him to focus once more, Jace gave himself another inspection. His hair was slightly longer than usual, parting over his right eye and hanging loosely just below his ears. But even with a different hairstyle, Jace still saw his old life in the mirror and remembered the countless horrors he was responsible for.

Jace bounced up and down, wiggling his fingers and flailing his arms to his side. He needed to get his heart pumping. He needed to feel alive, but his eyes ultimately focused on the hair in the sink once more. His mind went toward the decisions that led him to this point, and what The Order turned him into: a terror against the Evolved, the hunter, the slayer, the killer. He thought about how The Order worked to protect mankind. They were the heroes of humanity. They were…

"Liars." Jace clenched his teeth and balled his hands into fists as the anger swelled inside his chest. Liars who used summoning circles to bring forth creatures from unknown places to kill innocent people. Liars who used and manipulated people to fight the "evils" of the Evolved.

Subtle memories of the brainwashing echoed in his mind and began to fuel his rage. He violently shook his head, swatting the memories and emotions away.

Not all of the Evolved were evil. How could they be when his sister, the sweetest person he had ever met, turned out to be an Evolved? If only he could have seen past the blue aura, if he could have fought against the waves of emotion and hatred, if he could have swum through the waves of anger and prejudice, he would still be happy.

His eyes returned to the mirror, and he stared at himself once more. He saw himself in his old life—a life of death and blood and horror.

"You're not the only one who had a tough life," Jace said, echoing what Claire, and Brittaney many years earlier, told him. "You have to stop living in the past and work on your future."

As he continued to stare deep into his own eyes, he wondered how long he aimlessly wandered. How many weeks or months were lost in alcohol and self-loathing? How much time with Maya was lost?

Maya.

That centered his thoughts, and he focused on her.

Jace leaned forward and glared at the reflection once more. It was time for him to mend his mistakes. He knew who he was. Now it was time to be who he wanted to be - Jace, loving older brother to Maya, and her protector from the dangerous and chaotic world.

Feeling the tips of his fingers clench the sink, Jace took a renewed breath, inhaling the calming steam from the shower, and began to relax his muscles. He could see the mental image of his old life shed from his reflection, slowly turning to the person he stared at in the mirror and at the person he wanted to be. Feeling renewed, he took another deep breath.

"Don't worry, Maya. I'm coming."

———

His eyes opened in the pitch black when he heard the muffled, angry, and distressed voice of Claire from outside. He sat up and listened to try and make out the conversation.

"No. I'll explain later."

A deeper tone replied, but Jace couldn't make out what was said.

"Just go. Please."

Jace stood and walked toward the door, just in case the heated conversation escalated. A moment later, tires screeched, and the door opened, letting a cold breeze fill the room. Claire entered, but gasped and a bag fell from her hands. Jace's heightened reflexes effortlessly caught the bag before hitting the ground.

"Shit." Claire reached her hand to the wall and turned on the lights. "You scared the hell out of me."

Jace stood up, holding the groceries in his hands.

She visually inspected him, probably noticing the change of clothes and the grooming, and grinned. "There's the badass I once knew."

Jace lowered his gaze, feeling a great deal of shame and embarrassment. That's when he noticed a bruise on her arm. Was that always there? He didn't question it, but instead began to say what he originally wanted to say. "I'm sorry. I didn't mean to treat you so poorly."

For a few moments, Claire didn't reply. Then she wrapped Jace up in a hug. It lasted many, many heartbeats, letting the negative emotions wash away.

After, she held Jace at arm's length. "It's fine. I forgive you." She smiled and took the bag from his arms. "But you'll have to tell me what happened some time." She set the bag on the coffee table. "Like, how in the hell did you end up on my lawn?"

"Well, I..." Jace blinked, then looked at the door. "I really don't know."

"That's a lie." Claire leaped back onto the couch. She brought the folded fuzzy blanket to her face and smelled it. "Did you... wash this?"

Jace nodded.

She sniffed the couch. "And this, too?" That's when she began to look around the front room. "You cleaned yourself up, and you cleaned my house?"

Again, Jace nodded.

Claire smiled with a huff and shook her head. "You're looking much better. Amazing, really." She patted the cushion next to her, prompting Jace to approach and take a seat. "So tell me."

Jace took a moment to consider the question. He wondered what he should say and how detailed it should be.

"Come on, come on. Spit it out. It can't be that hard."

Jace cleared his throat. "Well, I... I've been looking for you and Jessica for years. At least to get some questions answered."

That seemed to perk Claire up a little. "You know where Jessy is?"

Jace shook his head. "That's the strange thing. She vanished the same night you were adopted."

"Vanished?" Claire's expression grew solemn. "That bitch wouldn't leave you."

"No, she wouldn't. And she didn't. At least I'm sure she didn't. I think Sanctuary took her, or something like that."

Claire brought her hand up to stop Jace. "Wait, wait. You mean Sanctuary, *the* Sanctuary for Orphaned Children, took her away from you?"

Jace nodded.

"That's ridiculous."

"Is it?"

"Yes." Claire crossed her arms in defiance. "That place is renowned and respected. Why would they do something like that?"

"Let me ask you this—why are there records of your adoption but nothing on her? At all."

"What do you mean 'nothing'?"

"As in, she never existed."

Claire paused for a moment, her crossed arms slowly relaxing.

"And your file was buried. I had to have a friend who, uh..." Jace stammered as his mind once again spiraled toward the past.

"A friend who..."

That brought Jace back into the present. He blinked a few times to regather his thoughts. "I had a friend... who helped me find a bunch of people from Sanctuary. A real wiz. Probably the smartest guy I've ever met. He said they were hiding you from me."

"Oh, really?"

Jace nodded. "Yeah. Brittaney is brainwashed. Jessica is missing."

"But here I am."

That gave Jace pause. Indeed, there she was. His sweet, dear, colorful, and chipper Claire back in his life once again. He looked away, deep in thought.

"I'm sorry, Jace. That seems a little farfetched."

Jace sighed. "Yeah, it does. Regardless, my old acquaintance found you for me."

"I'm sure if you really wanted to find Jessy, it'll only be a matter of time."

After a couple of heartbeats, Jace nodded to himself. "Yes. I will find Jessica."

Claire smiled and leaned back on the couch to get comfortable. "So tell me, what happened after I left?"

"After you left?" Jace looked at Claire, then ran his fingers through his hair. He took a moment, then smiled. "You first." He gestured to the picture he stared at on the wall.

"Deal. I gotta get a drink first. You thirsty?"

Jace shook his head.

Claire got up and went to the kitchen. "You did the dishes, too?" A minute later, she looped around to grab the picture with more than a little spring in her step, then returned to the couch, half a glass of lemonade in one hand, the framed photograph in the other. She hopped over the armrest, careful not to spill her drink, and presented the picture. "Darrel and Monica Hastings. They're my adopted parents. They're good, wonderful people who changed my life. I'm so lucky to have them."

She went on about having a seemingly normal life after the orphanage. He learned she was an aspiring musician who would go to some music college, but arthritis prevented her from pursuing that course. Then she told him about going to school to study business, economics, and sociology, and she was in her last months before graduating.

Jace looked up toward the vaulted white popcorn ceiling. "And the house?"

"My parents. I'm daddy's little girl."

Claire's good life made Jace genuinely happy for her. After meeting with Brittaney and learning about her apparent memory loss, Jace had feared that Claire and Jessica would have had the same outcome. But seeing her having such a happy, normal life with no apparent memory loss gave Jace hope about Jessica and how things will go when he does find her.

"But that's enough about me," Claire said after taking a drink. "It's your turn. What happened to you after I left? You still got that killer body." She slightly cocked her head and eyed him suspiciously. "Please tell me you're still not getting into fights."

Jace didn't immediately answer.

Claire's face went from curiosity to a hint of disappointment. "You are."

"Well, kind of. Not really. W-well..." Jace took a moment to consider his answer. What should he tell her? Would she understand? "It's hard to explain."

"So explain."

Jace half-smiled and shook his head. "You haven't changed a bit."

"Nope. So, entertain me."

After a slight chuckle, Jace began to tell his tale - about how Jessica vanished, how he met another friend only for her to disappear as well, and about his little sister.

Claire beamed with happiness. "You have a little sister? When do I get to meet this little angel of yours?"

Jace's expression grew solemn as he diverted his gaze.

"Jace? She's not dead, is she?"

"No." Jace gave a long, drawn-out sigh. He knew she wouldn't give up. Once she wanted something, she kept at it until she got it. That's how she always was. That's when Jace decided to give her a little more detail. "There's more to the story. A lot more."

He continued his tale, starting with his time in the orphanage, and the many battles he fought at that time. With hesitance, he told Claire about Brian and how the two partnered up in his war against the unnatural. When he talked about how a demon killed his family in a car accident, he grew silent and stared in the distance. Memories of broken glass and screaming flooded his mind. His heart sank when he realized he couldn't remember what his parents or his sister looked or sounded like.

"So things got a lot worse after I left."

"Yeah." Jace blinked a few times, then turned his attention to Claire, who stared intently at him.

"But you're here now. You survived. That's a good thing, right?"

Jace nodded.

"What else?"

He was at some problematic and touchy points in his life's story. Instead of talking about the gangs, the slave ring, or the abandoned military housing incident, Jace jumped forward to after the orphanage and his life in the military.

"You're a soldier?" Claire smiled. "Yeah, I can see you doing that."

"More than a soldier, actually."

"Oh?"

Jace nodded. "I was recruited into special forces. And that got me into..." His voice trailed off into silence.

Into?" When Jace didn't answer, Claire pressed, "Into what? Got you into what?"

After a few more heartbeats, Jace gulped and let out a quick exhale. "The Order."

Claire sat up in her seat. "Wait, really? That group or army or whatever that fights The Evolved?"

Jace nodded. "Yep. That's them."

"I thought that was some myth or something."

"Nope."

"That's amazing!" She plopped back into her chair in surprise. "I mean, they always sounded so fake, like some sort of government propaganda for morale, or whatever."

How did she coax him back into the conversation? Though he didn't want to discuss those details in his life, he found himself mentally stagger to find an answer. "They're not a part of the government. They're... something else."

"So what did you do?"

That simple question threw Jace into deep, horrible memories. One, in particular, surfaced where he executed a child because she glowed blue, all because he couldn't see past the blue glow. He thought about when he razed towns and villages, and how he wiped out entire generations of families because they weren't human.

An overwhelming sense of guilt quickly built in his chest, and he found it difficult to take a breath. "I... I've done so much."

Claire, apparently sensing his distress, gave Jace a comforting hug. A single tear dropped from his cheek onto her shirt. "Shh, it's okay. I know you're a good man."

Jace shook his head, slowly regaining his composure and controlling his emotions. "You wouldn't say that if you knew what I've done."

"Don't say that. I know you're a good man, and it's what you do that defines you."

Jace broke the hug and got to his feet. "Then I'm a monster. Only monsters do what I've done."

"Maybe." Claire stood and put a hand on his arm. "But maybe it's time you did something about that. You know, right the wrongs. That kind of thing."

That gave Jace pause.

"So, what can you do? What can Jace do to make him and his life better?"

"I don't know. I don't think I'll ever be able to fix my mistakes."

"Where can you start?"

Jace looked confused at Claire and gave her question some thought. Every time his mind started to go through the memories of his horrible past, the touch of Claire's hand on his arm would yank him to the present, allowing him to focus.

"Now, what is the first step?"

Though it wasn't the first step, Jace figured it would be the ultimate step. "Maya. I have to find Maya."

Claire smiled. "There we go."

Jace slightly nodded, which grew more animated as that

decision reinforced his confidence. A plan started to form in his head. First, he'd have to seek out Erica.

He paused at that thought. Erica. Just the thought of her made his heart skip a beat. Maybe she could be his first step. However, with how they parted ways, maybe she didn't want anything to do with him. Still, he had to try.

Claire's response broke him out of his thoughts. "And when you do, bring her over. I'd love to meet the little terror's sister."

Jace's face twisted in mock anger. "I'm not little."

"Yes, you are, you little brat."

After a moment, the two smiled and hugged once more.

"By the way," Claire said as the hug broke. "I've been meaning to ask. How did you get out of the chain?"

CHAPTER TWO

CLAIRE AND JACE STAYED UP ALL NIGHT TELLING EACH OTHER stories and reminiscing about days long past. When birds chirped outside, Jace went to the window to peer out at the dawn. The dark sky hinted at a tint of blue as the morning quickly approached. When he turned around, he noticed Claire had fallen asleep on the couch.

He considered his next move. The renewed feeling and a determination he hadn't felt in so long pulled at him, telling him to start his trip. He wanted to see Erica again and begin his journey to get Maya back in his life.

Unable to contain the eager feeling, Jace put the fuzzy tan blanket over Claire, stuffed his armor in his backpack, slung it over his shoulder, then left the house as quietly as possible.

As he walked over the stepping stones through the mowed and freshly watered grass down to the sidewalk, Jace paused, looking from side to side. At that moment, Jace realized he had no idea where he was.

Claire's voice came from behind, "Leaving without a goodbye?"

Jace turned to face Claire, her freshly dyed yellow hair a mess, as she stood in the doorway in her pink spaghetti strap top and hot pink shorts. "No," Jace answered. "Not goodbye."

"Then what would you call this?"

He approached, giving his long, lost friend a warming smile. "A, 'I have to go get my sister, so I'll be right back.'"

She smiled in return and gave Jace another hug. "You'd better." She pointed down the road. "That'll get you to the bus stop. Follow the road two blocks, then turn left at the stoplight. It's about a quarter-mile down just outside the shopping center."

"Thanks."

"Oh, before you go..." Claire padded the air, went back into the house, then came back a minute later. She extended her hand to give Jace a white envelope. "I noticed you're not chipped, so you'll need some money. This isn't much, but it'll help."

Jace raised his hand to politely decline. "Thanks, but I'm okay. I still have plenty of money."

"You do?"

Jace nodded as he took off his backpack and grabbed a wad of cash.

Claire's eyes went wide in surprise. "Holy shit!"

"In fact, I should be paying you." He began counting.

"Oh, no you don't. You don't owe me... anything." Her words trailed when she diverted her eyes. At that moment, Jace heard a loud engine and tires lightly screech as a vehicle pulled up in the driveway. She whispered, "Oh shit."

Jace turned as a dark-haired man shouted from the driver's seat of the yellow and red, restored classic truck, "Claire, what the hell?" The man exited and aggressively approached the two, slapping the hood as he walked around. He inspected the hit. "You'll be in trouble if I dented this."

The guy probably stood over a foot taller than Jace, but what caught his attention more than the size was the jacket he wore over his barreled chest. It was dark gray with a white and yellow

24

"DH" embroidered on the left sleeve and "12" on the right sleeve. Jace wondered if the guy was stuck in his high school days.

Claire called out in a weak and unsteady tone over Jace's shoulder, "What are you doing here, Harold?"

Her tone seemed odd to him. She sounded passive and weak and not the strong and confident woman he spent so much time with.

"Is this the guy?" Harold pointed to Jace as he continued to walk toward them. "Is this him?"

Claire moved around Jace to intercept Harold. As if unsure of herself and scared, she said, "I don't know what you're talking about."

Seeing the aggressive posture, Jace wondered who this person was, and why her manner suddenly shifted. "Claire?"

"I knew something was going on!" Harold stopped three paces away and pointed an accusing finger, his hand trembling in rage.

She peered back at Jace, but she had a look in her eye. "It's okay."

"I knew something was going on. No wonder you didn't reply." Harold slightly rocked side to side. "After everything I've done for you. After all I've given you. What I've sacrificed for you. And with this punk?"

"Please, go home, Harold. We'll talk late—"

"We'll talk now!" His face began to turn red, and his lips pressed tightly together. "We were supposed to go places."

"We—"

"Shut up!" Harold's jaw muscles visibly tensed as he gritted his teeth. "Shut your whore mouth!"

Jace couldn't believe his ears. How in the world could anyone treat Claire with such disrespect? Feeling the tension in the air, Jace rubbed his thumb and fingertips together to get a feel of the environment and calm his nerves. He took a deep breath, ready to intervene, but Claire's outstretched hand gave him pause. Though he could see her lightly tremble, he respected her wishes, remaining still and quiet behind her.

"I know, and I'm sorry," Claire said. "But we need to talk later."

Harold's hand whipped around, slapping Claire across the cheek. Immediate rage shot through Jace as she gave a muffled screech and staggered a step back.

Harold raised a hand to slap Claire again, but Jace pulled her back, making a second slap hit nothing but air. Jace then stepped forward, putting himself between Harold and Claire.

"It's your fault," Harold growled. "You bitch whore."

To Jace's disbelief, he heard Claire say, "I'm sorry."

Claire's strange injuries started to make sense. And though he wanted to lash out and utterly cripple this bastard who dared lay a threatening finger on his dear Claire, he continued to respect her wishes. "You're done here. Leave while you can."

Harold clenched his trembling fists. His eyes were wide open, almost as if they'd fall out of his skull. Every exhale had a hint of spit seep out of his gritted teeth.

Was this guy on drugs? Or maybe he was an Evolved? It didn't matter to Jace as he stood fearless between Harold and Claire. But with his posture and demeanor, and seeing the aggressive stance and building rage, Jace knew precisely how things would turn out. "Now."

As predicted, Harold threw a punch at Jace. He ducked the attack and took a step back, reaching back to feel for Claire. Being that Claire seemed concerned or worried about the guy, Jace decided to go easy on him.

"Stop it!" Claire cried out. "I'm sorry."

That made Jace look back in surprise. What would she have to be sorry about?

He brought his attention back to Harold almost a little too late as another punch blind-sided him. He raised a shoulder and deflected the blow.

With Claire behind him, he couldn't take another step back.

And he dared not move to the side to give Harold a clear shot at his beloved friend. But Jace knew this guy's type—violent and raging, pressing their strength against anyone to get the upper hand. That meant he could go after Claire to get to him. Because of that, he decided that getting her to safety was his priority.

When Harold began to lunge forward, he leaped to the side with the punch to catch the arm, planted his feet against Harold's chest, and flipped him over as he fell. Harold flew over Jace, landing on the grass, and slid down to the sidewalk.

Jace got to his feet and turned to Claire. "Get inside."

"You're dead!" Harold called from behind.

Claire clenched her chest, and her eyes were wide, frozen in fear. She wasn't looking at him, but at Harold.

Knowing he didn't have much time, Jace put a comforting hand on her shoulder. "Please."

Her trembling ceased, and her eyes shifted to look at him. "Don't. He's dangerous."

To try to give her some assurance, Jace smiled. "It'll be okay. I promise. Remember who I am?"

Claire nodded, her face breaking from the fear into a slightly enlightened look and took a couple of steps back to be near the front door.

With her in a safer spot, Jace turned and evaluated the environment - wet grass on a slope, stepping stones, Harold's stupid truck parked in the driveway half a dozen paces away to his right, bushes and a fence to the neighbor's to his left. That's when he noticed some people peeking out of windows, which told Jace he didn't have a lot of time. With that in mind, he put his focus on the piece of shit that hurt his friend.

Harold's face beet red with rage as he looked at his grass-stained jacket. "You're dead meat." He took off his jacket and threw it on the grass, then glanced at Claire. "This is your fault, bitch."

"No," Jace said as he stepped in the way of his glare. "This is all me." He waved the potentially drug-filled rager on to divert his attention.

Harold didn't hesitate, and he stormed up the hill to begin his barrage. Jace ducked, dodged, bobbed, and weaved the slow attacks. Even as he focused on his defense, Jace kept his attention on his footing, and on the still-wet grass. One slip and he could be in trouble.

After a quick sidestep, Jace inspected his opponent. He heaved and trembled, huffed and panted. Since he was far too strong for any choke or limb-lock to work, fatigue and morale would be his battle plan. With the heaving chest, Jace thought he was already half-way there. "Are you done?"

Harold gave a wild and poorly balanced punch.

Guess not.

Jace grabbed the wrist, pivoted his hip toward the tall and muscular man, and flipped him over once more on the grass.

He rolled over, smashing his fists in the dirt, and glared at Jace.

Though Jace's anger grew inside of him, he made sure his composure was kept, and he stood calmly and confidently over his attacker. "Are you done?"

After a growl of fury, Harold charged, staying low to go after his legs.

Jace took a leaping step back to avoid the charge and swatted away a few punches. Then Harold went for another grab. Jace's foot unexpectedly slid back, and Harold gripped Jace's backpack. Harold pulled Jace toward him. Jace went with the movement, twisting to break the grab. He rolled over his shoulders on the grass toward the driveway.

Harold gestured to Claire. "This is your fault."

No longer being in between Harold and Claire, Jace had to get the berserker's attention. He took a step toward the truck and open-palm-pounded on the frame a couple of times. "Hey!"

Harold's head whipped at him.

"Focus on me, okay?" Jace grabbed the side mirror and adjusted it.

"You..." Harold stormed over toward Jace.

That worked better than Jace had expected.

"You're dead meat. When I'm through with you, Claire will—"

Jace had enough. Knowing he wouldn't leave Claire alone, Jace decided to teach this guy a lesson.

When Harold was two paces away, Jace ripped off the side mirror and underhandedly tossed it high toward Harold. Harold's eyes went wide, and his gaze followed the high-flying mirror. With the attention away from him, Jace made his move. He stepped in and gave a one-two kidney punch. Harold tried to counter-attack, his fist glancing off Jace's shoulder, and Jace replied with a punch to the ear, followed by a knife-hand to the neck. To gain some distance, Jace kicked Harold in the gut, leaping back with the hit.

Harold leaned forward, holding his side with one hand and his neck with the other.

Jace took a breath to control his mounting anger. "I think you're done here."

After a growl of protest, Harold stood up straight and lunged once more.

Out of patience, Jace laid into him, giving two vital hits for every one miss from Harold. The neck, the knee, solar plexus, and kidneys were all prime targets, with blows to various parts of the face so he wouldn't soon forget the message.

Harold collapsed to the ground. His face was a bloody mess, and he gasped for breath, and he clenched his side and knee in pain.

Jace knelt in close to Harold. When Harold began to resist, Jace grabbed the guy's shirt and pulled him closer. "I said you're done here." Jace picked up the mirror and handed it to Harold. "Now take your fucking mirror, get in your fucking truck, and drive the fuck off. Or I'll have an ambulance do it for you." He stood up and took a step back.

Harold almost fell flat on the grass as he got to his feet. He opened his mouth to speak again, but Jace's feigned step forward had Harold flinch in fright. Jace knew every ounce of illusionary dominance Harold thought he had was gone after that flinch. Without another word, Harold got into the truck and started it up. He paused to glare at Jace, wiped his bloody face with the back of his hand, pulled out of the driveway, then sped off with screeching tires.

Feeling confident Harold wasn't going to do anything rash, Jace took a calming breath, then turned to check on Claire, only to find she had already walked over to him.

Jace looked at her red cheek. "Are you okay?"

"Yeah." She touched her face with her fingertips.

"How in the world did you end up with that guy?"

"I... I don't know." Her shoulders slumped as if in defeat. "He used to be so kind and nice. He even gave up a football scholarship for me."

Jace couldn't believe her story. How could someone like her be put into a situation like that? Figuring she needed some comfort to help ground her after such an intense situation, he put an arm around her shoulder, and the two stared toward where Harold drove off. "He's gone now."

"He'll be back. He always comes back."

That didn't make Jace happy. He had to help her, but he had a feeling the police were on their way. Jace grabbed the high school jacket, and a wallet fell out.

Claire walked up and grabbed the jacket. "He'll definitely be back for this." She stepped on the sidewalk and stared down the road.

Jace picked up the wallet and looked inside it. He stared at the driver's license for a bit, then took it out of the plastic holder and pocketed it. Then he stood next to Claire and presented the wallet. "Here. Give these to the police and have them hand these over to Harold."

Claire grabbed the wallet. "The police?"

Jace nodded. "They should be here any minute." He turned to Claire. "I'll be back. And when I do, I'll have Maya with me."

She nodded. "Will you be alright?"

"Me? I'll be fine." His eyes went to her swelling cheek. He wanted to tell her what to do, but he figured Harold had already ordered her around enough. "Do you think you can go to a friend's or your parents after the police leave?"

"I... Yeah."

Jace smiled. "Good. I'd feel a lot better knowing you were there."

She returned the smile.

He turned his head down the street toward the bus stop, which is also where Harold drove off. "I have to go. But I'll be back."

"You'd better."

Jace returned his focus to her, nodded, and the two hugged. "I promise." When the hug broke, he gave her one more smile, then ran toward her backyard.

"Wait, where are you going?"

As Jace leaped over the fence, he called out, "To the bus stop."

———

After visiting the apartment complex's office, Jace grabbed a brochure with a map and wandered around a bit. When he saw the truck pull up and park in a parking space, Jace went to the shadows, and he waited.

Late in the night, Jace confirmed the apartment number on the brochure, then began to climb, using ledges and lips to haul him higher and higher from the ground. When he reached the third floor, he grabbed a tool from his backpack, picked the balcony lock, and snuck into the dark apartment.

He waited a minute, letting his eyes adjust, and he listened. Heavy, rhythmic breathing emanated from the side room.

Slowly, methodically, he navigated his way through the dark, avoiding the various exercise equipment strewn all through the room, grabbing the jacket from the hanger while shifting his feet until he stood next to the bed. He turned on the lamp on the nightstand, and Harold's eyes bolted open.

Jace glared down at Harold's bruised face.

Before Harold could do anything, Jace smothered Harold's face with the jacket to muffle any screams, then punched his teeth. The jacket hardly muffled the cries that came from Harold as he quickly sat up.

With the distraction in place, Jace leaped behind Harold and wrapped an arm around his neck, leaning back to block the flow of blood and oxygen from Harold. With the element of surprise, Jace knew choking Harold out would work.

Harold's screams turned into gurgles as he struggled, futilely grabbing at Jace's arm.

Jace brought his lips to Harold's ear. "I want to make sure you understand where I'm coming from."

Harold twisted, and the two fell off the bed. Though Jace figured the downstairs neighbors heard the thuds and crashes, he held firm to his hold. He leaned back, fighting the strain and fatigue in his arms. Just as Harold's arms began to go limp, Jace removed his grip and stood up. Harold choked and rolled to the side, and Jace gave a hard kick with his steel-toed boot to Harold's abdomen. Immediately, he curled forward and fell to his side, struggling to get a simple breath.

Jace stomped on Harold's knee, then knelt in front of him as he curled up in a pitiful ball. "You and Claire are done." When Harold lifted a hand, Jace punched him across the jaw. "Do you hear me? Done."

The worthless man stared up, tears and blood mixing in his hands.

"If you go near Claire again, if I hear you touch anyone else like that again, I'll come back to visit you." He took out Harold's driver's license and showed it to him. "And next time, you won't get off so easily." Jace leaned in close. "Do you want to see me again?" When there was no reply, Jace smacked the nightstand with the palm of his hand, making Harold flinch. "I said, do you want to see me again?"

Harold shook his head. "N-no."

"If anyone asks, was I ever here?"

Again, Harold shook his head.

"Good." Jace tapped Harold's forehead with his driver's license, stood up, then unplugged the lamp.

Hearing Harold gasp in the dark, Jace moved quickly and quietly out the door, through the room, and out the balcony door, even going so far as to lock it again, before climbing down to the ground level. Keeping to the shadows, Jace left Harold broken and alone in his apartment. Next stop, the bus station.

CHAPTER THREE

TURNING CORNERS WITH SCREECHING TIRES AT HIGH SPEEDS, gripping wing joints on the back of humongous flying monsters, jumping out of aircraft, and falling through the clouds, none of them caused Jace as many problems as simply riding in a bus. With the stuffiness and cramped space, every bump made his stomach churn. Nothing stopped Jace in his tracks faster than his motion sickness.

Jace's grip alternated between tight and loose on his sickbag as he took deep breaths. Since he couldn't see the horizon ahead of him to alleviate the nausea, he closed his eyes and focused on his next step. Immediately, his mind took him back to a bar, and an overdressed woman and her dyed blonde hair that never seemed to reach her roots. Jace smiled as he mentally took in the scent of vanilla that always accompanied her. She was his first step in rebuilding his life.

A particularly nasty bump in the road broke Jace out of his thoughts, and an acidic burp built up in his throat.

A withered old voice shifted Jace's attention from another trip to the bathroom. "Don't worry, dear. We're almost there."

Jace clutched the bag once more, then looked to the passenger. Next to him sat an older woman with short, white hair, glasses, and a string of pearls around her neck. If those were real pearls, why would she be riding a stinky, crowded bus?

She put her hand on his arm. "Have you tried that fancy shot for your motion sickness?"

After a moment of confused blinks, Jace shook his head.

"They say it cures it." She shook her head and leaned back in her chair, putting her hands in her lap. "I don't believe it. Never trust the government. Crooks, they all are. Crooks. And this 'Order' thing that's always on the news, crooks." She raised a pointed finger. "They're up to no good."

Jace considered her ramblings for a moment. "Maybe."

With the reply, she sat up and turned to face him. "Did you hear they're building some fancy 3D advertisement thing that is supposed to scan your eyes? Lasers. That's how they get you."

One conspiracy after another. Jace's gaze returned to the back of the seat and focused on the problem at hand.

Regardless of him trying to ignore the ramblings, her persistent babble broke through Jace's thoughts. "And those ID chips in people's hand, they're tracking you. They know where you are, what you're buying, and how to advertise. They're listening in. An invasion of privacy. I don't trust them, I tell you." She seemed to settle down and leaned back in her chair. "That war of theirs is nothing but hogwash." That seemed to ignite her enthusiasm, and she leaned forward again. "Who says we're at war? Not the people. No, no." She pointed at nothing. "They do."

Jace sighed. The woman's mindless ramblings did have a point. There was no official war, but something was going on. He didn't know or understand what their plan was, but it didn't matter. Not anymore.

"I knew tons of those 'Evolved' and none of them gave me no trouble." The woman leaned back in her chair. "They're good people, just like us."

That gave Jace pause. If they were, in fact, "good people," were all of his actions more akin to a villain rather than a hero? He was ashamed of his actions before, but that thought made him feel so much worse. The grumble in his stomach churned more bile, but it wasn't motion sickness that time. It was of pure, unbridled shame.

————

The small airplane landed in the familiar airport as the end of his first step drew closer. He stepped onto the chilly tarmac and stared at the nearby mountains just as the morning sunbathed the peak in yellowish light. For many steamed breaths, all he could do was stare. No matter how warm the temperatures or what time of year, even in the closing months of summer, those mountains always had snow. Mixed feelings swelled in Jace's chest - feelings of anxiety, rage, sorrow.

As to not dwell too deep in his emotions, Jace turned his attention to the surroundings. Though on a different side of the airport, he stood at a node where The Order's members met regularly. Knowing members and officers were given the freedom to do what they wanted to, Jace lifted the collar on his jacket and slightly hunched and left the airport, hoping no one would recognize him. He figured it was more of a precaution than to keep out the biting chill. And he knew some of the officers he talked with seemed unpredictable and unstable, especially if they went along with The Order's plans of murdering countless innocent lives.

A man in an old green wool sweater and a brown cap took a step toward Jace. "Need a ride, sir?"

Jace paused for a moment to scan the area. Usually, The Order sent limos to the airport to give their members fancy and luxurious rides up the mountain. Granted, he hardly ever accepted those rides, preferring to walk to clear his mind and to take in the scenery. He wondered if the cabby was trying to lure him into a trap. After noticing more than a few cabbies parked alongside the curb and inspecting the car, he decided it was what it seemed - a cab.

He gave the man a nod.

"Is that all your luggage?"

Again, Jace nodded.

The cab driver opened the back door. "Alright, get in. I'll turn on the heater so you can get nice and toasty." He didn't hold the door open but got in the driver's seat to start up the car. Jace couldn't help but look around once more before removing his backpack and getting into the cab.

After a few seconds of silence, the cab driver adjusted the rearview mirror. "Hand on the pad."

Jace took out a couple of bills from his backpack. "Uh, cash."

"Cash? Alright. Where to?"

"The city. I don't know the address, but I know the location." He handed the guy some money. "Is this enough?"

The driver scoffed and took the bills. "More than." He folded the bills and tucked them in some inside pocket, then drove off.

———

"Alright, here we are."

The cab pulled up to the building Jace directed the cabbie to. A single glass door in between two wooden pillars that led to a dark purple awning seemed to be the only real entrance. People were able to enter and exit the building after swiping the back of their hand on some sensor to unlock the door. And though he immediately thought of a half dozen ways to gain entrance to the secured facility, Jace couldn't help but pause as he stared out the window. What was he going to say to her? What was she going to do? It wasn't like they left on the best of terms. The last time they saw each other, he said he quit and left her behind.

Those questions and more swam through his mind, and his nerves got the best of him. Jace froze, feeling the initiative and motivation wane.

Then it occurred to him that she may be on her work rotation and may not even be home. He tried to think about how long she'd be at work, wondering what he should do next. Was it a week? Two weeks? He cursed to himself for not considering that simple yet important detail. Hell, what if she didn't live there anymore, or what if he got the wrong address? That meant he couldn't rely on waiting outside to watch and wait. Not only that, but a stranger lurking for hours or days outside the building would draw unwanted attention.

So watching the apartment was out.

That's when he remembered what she always did after her work shift. "Hey, do you know where a nightclub is near here?"

"A nightclub?" The cabbie leaned toward the windshield. "It's still daylight. Not sure they'll even be open."

"Doesn't matter." He stared out at nothing, remembering the dress she wore on their drive. "The place needs to be rather popular and caters to those who dress nicely. So maybe a higher class."

"Huh. Alright, let me think. Oh, I think I know where you're talking about." The cabbie put the car in gear and drove off.

* * * *

A massive bronze-looking statue of a lion sat near the corner entrance with stairs, columns, and water fountains surrounding the front door. High mirrored windows shot up into the sky, framed by blue and purple neon lights. Holographic advertisements for some band he never heard of played over people passing by the overhanging archways. Not a speck of trash littered the streets, and the citizens that strolled by seemed to be in upscale attire.

Feeling satisfied with the nightclub's style and location, Jace paid the cabbie a nice tip and stood outside the building. It was indeed a nice location. Learning his lesson from when he first found Brittaney, he inspected himself, deciding he needed some new clothes before trying to enter the club. New clothes and a hotel room.

He leaned into the cab. "Hey, one more thing."

"Shoot."

"Where is there a hotel and a tailor nearby?"

———

Every night for over a week, Jace would arrive at the club at the same time and stay until the club shut down for the day. He sat at a two-seated table in a corner with a good view of the main and side entrance so he could watch the people enter and exit. Lasers, smoke machines, and loud music filled the massive room. Sometimes, performers would play on stage, gathering massive crowds that filled the structure up to capacity.

At first, he had to stand in line to get in, only getting entrance after paying a nice tip. Eventually, the bouncers would let him skip the line as they'd wave him over once they spotted him exiting a cab when he pulled up to the curb. After a few days into his surveillance, even the bartender would be prepared for Jace's visit, having a glass of orange juice and some cut-up fruit waiting for him at the bar. And the servers would keep his fruit bowl full and his drink glass filled throughout the nights.

Though he could be considered a patient man, ten days of sitting and waiting in loud, headache-inducing music started to wear away his spirits. He ignored the numerous side glances, the apparent nefarious dealings he spotted in the dark corners of the room, the drug use, and the occasional fight on the dance floor. High class or low, people were all the same.

Jace gagged on his orange juice when she finally walked in,

flanked by two of the bouncers. One of them removed her gray fur coat, revealing a deep red dress with laced black webbing, and went to the bar. The other escorted her to a booth. After the bouncer removed the three guys that occupied the booth—Jace couldn't tell if it was through force or if they offered the seat willingly—the man wiped down the table, and she sat down. Almost immediately, the first guy returned to the booth with a drink, then they let her be.

Now that was service.

During his entire recovery, aside from Jessica and Maya, she was constantly on his mind. And now she was close, and it was time to move on to his next step—go and talk with Erica. He still had a problem. What would he say? And how would Erica react? She repeated time and time again that she didn't date soldier boys. But he was no longer a soldier. He was a civilian, like her.

That settled it. It was time to act.

Jace went to stand, or he tried to. He found his rapidly pumping heart made his legs unwilling to obey his hesitating commands. After a swallow of his drink, he tried again, only for his will to falter. He couldn't move. Not by any unnatural means, but because he couldn't mentally gather the courage.

For the next few hours, Jace could only watch Erica from his shadowy table. She had gotten drinks, went dancing with people, got more drinks, and returned to dancing. She seemed to be having fun, and he didn't want to ruin her night, much less her life.

Jace sighed and finally got to his feet. But instead of walking toward Erica like he originally planned, he put some cash on the table and went out the side exit, making sure she didn't notice his leave.

The loud thumping dulled once the side door closed behind him. He stood at the curb, noticing the lack of traffic in the late night. No parked cars. Not even a cab. He took a deep breath and watched the white plume burst from his lips. He whispered to himself, "What now?"

Someone else exited the side door behind Jace, and their heels clicked on the concrete.

He didn't want company, so he turned to leave, deciding to walk to his hotel. Or he was about to when a gentle breeze wafted the subtle scent of vanilla in his nostrils: Vanilla and alcohol.

He stood perfectly still in mid-step as Erica stopped next to him a few feet away. She didn't say anything but lit up a cigarette and stared into the night.

He didn't know she smoked.

She took a drag from the butt, blowing smoke into the chill night, then sniffed the air. From the corner of his eye, he could see her lightly shifting back and forth.

No one said anything.

Jace put his foot down and stood up straight. Options and ideas shot through his head—go and talk to her, walk away, return to the club, climb a building. Every thought was a stupid one at that moment. And all he could do was just stand there.

Erica broke the silence after another drag from her cigarette. "You, you waiting on a cab?"

"Uh..." Jace cleared his throat to process her voice that broke through the ringing in his ears. And though the tone made his heart skip a beat, the slurring made him slightly smile. He knew that slur. She was drunk. "No."

Another awkward pause.

Jace cursed to himself in his thoughts for not being able to say more than 'no.' All of the time and energy, all the long days and money spent, that was all he could say? He clenched an angry and disappointed fist in a pocket.

"You ain't going to find one. Not this late, anyway." She took another drag. "You have to call them for a pickup."

Jace paused, blinking a few times to consider the situation. "If, uh... If that's the case..." He cleared his throat, making sure he faced away from her. "What about you?"

"Me? I'm fine. I'm fine. I just need to walk it off."

Jace almost looked at her in concern. The last time he heard her this intoxicated, she toppled over him and they fell through a fence. Not only that, but he didn't know the neighborhood, and it could be dangerous. "Alone? At this time of night?"

"Yep." She took the last drag from her cigarette and dropped the butt in the gutter. "Everyone around here knows me, and they all know better." She turned and started to walk away. "Good luck getting that cab."

Jace couldn't let her walk alone in the middle of the night. He knew her apartment was too far away to get home at a decent time. And even though she seemed to have a confident air about her, albeit a drunk and staggering air, the memory of the last time they left the bar with her intoxicated plagued his mind. He couldn't let her walk off like this, and he took a few strides to catch up to her. "You shouldn't be out here alone. At least let me walk with you."

She lightly looked back and called over her shoulder, "Look, you're obviously not from around here. So let me give you some advice and don't follow me."

"Look, you're not—"

Erica turned and pointed a finger at his chest. "You don't get it." Her voice trailed to silence, and her eyes went wide. "H-... But y-.... The mission... My m...." Her eyes rolled back, and her legs gave out.

Jace caught her mid-fall. "Shit," he whispered. For a moment, he considered his options. Then he scooped her up in his arms and carried her off into the night.

———

Jace watched the sunrise out of his hotel window the following morning. Again, he had Erica passed out in his bed. After paying for her dress to be express cleaned, Jace picked up some comfortable clothing, general sundries, and headache medication for Erica, and left everything in the bedroom. He knew she would have a hangover when she awoke.

After the sun finished breaking the horizon, Jace started to work on breakfast, slapping some bacon in a hot pan. A minute later, he heard a thump from the bedroom. After a couple of heavy and rushed footsteps, the bedroom door slammed open.

There stood Erica, hair a mess almost naked from the night before, staring wide-eyed at him.

Jace gulped. Once again, he could feel the words choke in his throat. "Uh, good m—"

"You..." She took a couple of steps forward, her eyes never leaving Jace. "You're alive."

Out of all the questions and scenarios that Jace thought of, her thinking he was dead never came to mind. "Alive? Why would you—"

"I thought you were dead!" She crept closer. "I heard there was an attack at the hotel you stayed at."

"Oh, that?" Visions from that nightmarish day flooded his mind. His gaze broke, and he stared off into the distance, only seeing the face of those he killed. And the blue around his beloved sister. He shook those memories away. "No."

The two stared at each other with only the sizzle of the bacon to break the awkward silence.

"Why am I almost naked?" She gestured to her body. "And why am I sticky?"

"You barfed...on yourself last night."

Her brown cheeks tinted red in embarrassment. "I did what?"

"So I had your dress cleaned, and I got you some comfortable clothing for the day."

"You what?"

"Um..." Jace nervously cleared his throat and flipped the bacon, using that action to buy him some time to figure out a response.

Erica didn't say anything else. She turned and went to the bathroom, closed the door, and turned on the shower.

"Shit," Jace muttered to himself. This wasn't going anything like he had planned. After losing his appetite, he took the pan off the burner and sat on the couch.

Eventually, the shower turned off. After some more time had passed, Erica exited the bathroom, dressed in the clothing Jace had gotten for her. She held up the bag of dirty laundry. "Deja vu."

"You want me to make you some breakfast?"

"No. I want answers." She sat on the couch next to Jace.

Nothing how he had planned.

"I thought you were dead. Do you have any idea how much that affected me? How tough this past year has been?"

That made Jace wonder if things were going better than he initially thought. "I didn't mean to..."

"The Order thinks you're dead, so you're free from them. Free to live whatever life you wanted. So what the hell are you doing here?"

On one hand, she seemed not to want Jace around. However, being mere feet away from him, he detected some hint of... something in her eyes. Some sort of hidden emotion or something he couldn't make out. He shifted nervously, trying to form a sentence beyond a simple "I" and "uh." Then he took a deep breath, deciding just to say what he wanted to say. "I came back for you."

That seemed to catch Erica by surprise, as she lightly recoiled. "Me?"

Her reaction didn't give Jace any more confidence. Still, he clung onto the hope of that mystery that she kept inside if there was indeed a secret. "Yes, you. My life has been a wreck this past year, and you were constantly on my mind. I figured since I was no longer a 'soldier boy,' we could..." Jace continued to try and read Erica's posture and figure. Feeling like it was hopeless, and he was making himself look like a fool, he stood up.

Erica got to her feet and blocked Jace's path. She lightly leaned forward with suspicion in her eyes. "We could what?"

All of his training on how to read people, figure out their personalities by their posture and expressions, figure out what they're thinking from their eyes, all of it was useless against Erica. He couldn't read her. He kept getting mixed signals from every direction, making him doubt every word that came out of his mouth. But she seemed to have that little hint, a little bit of bait dangling out, just waiting for Jace to reach out and take it. "We could continue where we left off."

"And where was that?"

"Well..." Jace ran his fingers through his hair. "I thought we had something. Like a spark, but we couldn't do anything because I was enlisted."

Erica crossed her arms and stood defiantly in front of Jace. "So, what do you want?"

"I want you to come with me. Come with me away from The Order."

"And what about my career? My research? My life's work? Have you given any thought about that?"

He felt the bait dangle closer to him, which gave him a hint of confidence in his reply. "We could build a life anywhere we want away from The Order. You can do your research in private."

The two stood in motionless silence from one another. He stared into her eyes. She stared back into his. Again, he tried to read her expression, her posture or attitude. What was she thinking?

Jace was about to sigh and give up before Erica lunged forward, pressing her lips against his. He couldn't move for a couple of heartbeats, then embraced her and returned her kiss.

CHAPTER FOUR

JACE AND ERICA LIVED MOSTLY A VAGABOND LIFE, GOING WHERE THEY pleased and doing whatever they wanted. On some days, Jace would put them up in decent hotel rooms where they could relax and treat themselves to a comfortable bed, hot showers, excellent meals, and gathering supplies for their life on the road. Most of the time, they traveled in random directions, exploring the wilderness, swimming in lakes and rivers, and isolating themselves from the civilization around them.

Eventually, they found themselves on a cliffside overlooking a still lake. Jace held Erica in his arms under a sleeping bag after an evening of passion, and they stared up at the night sky with the crackling of embers from their dying campfire piercing the peace of nature.

Erica let out a sigh.

"What's wrong?"

"It's..." She paused a moment before sitting up, letting the stars from the late summer night cast her naked body in an enticing silhouette. "We've been out for almost two weeks. What's the plan?"

"The plan?" Jace sat up with her. A gentle breeze over his bare chest gave him a mild shiver as the warm summer days were giving way to the autumn season. "What do you mean?"

"Come on." She gestured toward the two oversized backpacks next to them. "You know we can't live the rest of our lives like this."

Though he had dreams of finding Maya and Jessica again, he didn't know how. And for her to question their livelihood after their peaceful time together made Jace wonder what she really thought. "Well, what do you want?"

"Besides chocolate pudding?" She plopped on her back.

Jace laid beside her, putting an arm over her chest so he could look at her. "Besides chocolate pudding."

"Maybe...stability? Living like a couple of hobos is nice and all, but I think I want to get back to work. I spent my whole life learning how to help the world."

"You want to go back?"

Through the moonlight, he saw her glare at him. "What makes you think that? No, I'm talking about other ways I can help people."

After a moment of silence, Jace laid next to her, putting his arm around her shoulder. She tucked the sleeping bag back up over their bodies.

"Let's start with this. You mentioned your friends. What's her name? Jennifer?"

"Jessica?"

"Yeah, her."

He sighed. "I can't find her. The orphanage has no record of her."

"Okay, what about that girl you did find? Brittaney?"

"Yeah, I found her. But she has some strange memory loss that I can't figure out."

"Well, maybe I can. I *am* a doctor."

That realization sparked interest in Jace. "You are!" He sat up and looked at her. "Do you think you can help her?"

"Well, maybe. Though memory manipulation isn't necessarily my specialty." She rubbed her chin. "Do you know where she is?"

"I do."

"Then let's go there."

"I don't know. The last couple of times I visited, things got a little..." Jace rubbed his eye while he thought of a good way to put their last reunion. "Awkward."

"Awkward? You didn't sleep with her, right?"

Jace chuckled. "No, no. I did almost beat up her dad."

"Her dad?" Erica sat up. "Why would you do that?"

"Well, he kind of came at me with a bat."

"And why would he do that?"

Jace shrugged.

"Okay. Then what?"

"Then I told her how to get ahold of me and drove away."

"Wait, let me get this straight. You visit this girl, threatened to beat up her dad, then you give her your com number? If that's how you pick up women—"

Jace playfully nudged her before putting his hand on her leg. After a moment, he sighed. "We can give it a shot."

"Let's head out tomorrow morning."

"Okay." Jace lightly pushed Erica to her back, and he laid on top of her. "But for now, how about we take advantage of our last night under the stars?" He kissed her softly at first, then with more passion after each heartbeat.

———

Two days later, the cab Jace and Erica rode pulled up in front of Brittaney's house in the late morning. When he reached into his bag to grab some cash, Erica put a hand on his arm to stop him.

"You've been paying for everything. At the very least, let me get this." Before Jace could protest, Erica put her hand on the glass panel.

Not giving it another thought, he grabbed their bags and exited the vehicle, extending a hand to help Erica to her feet. The cab drove away, and the two stood on the sidewalk for a long moment.

Erica glanced from side to side down the street. "Are you sure this is the place? All the houses here look the same."

Jace inspected the area, noticing the well-trimmed lawns and the cookie-cutter structures painted in similar colors—white, off-white, or gray. Being that no house stood out from one another, he understood Erica's initial doubt.

He handed Erica her backpack. "She has dogs."

Her eyes widened, and she gave a slight smile as she put on her backpack.

Jace led her around the lawn to the entryway. When he knocked on the door, two dogs barked from beyond the closed portal.

Erica went to the side window and peered inside. Two black and white dogs barked and put their paws against the window. Erica smiled and put her hand against their paws. "Aww, who's a cute puppy? Who's a cute puppy?"

"She isn't home." Jace turned and walked off the porch before looking up at the sky. "We have about five hours before she gets home. Are you hungry?"

That got Erica's attention. "Starved. Let's go."

———

Later in the day, Jace and Erica returned to Brittaney's house. The open garage door gave Jace a clear view of the same car he saw from the last time he visited. His eyes went back to the door, and he paused, wondering once more what he should say once she opened the door.

"What's wrong?" Erica approached and stood beside him.

"I... I never know what to say."

"I wouldn't worry about that." Erica grabbed Jace's arm and pulled him up to the house, where she knocked on the door.

The dogs barked.

Erica continued, "You didn't have a problem earlier today."

"That's because I knew she wouldn't be home." Jace then took a moment to consider their appearance. Apparently, he didn't learn his lesson, regardless of his consideration, before seeing Erica. The first time he showed up at Brittaney's house, he wore old and dirty clothes, and she immediately dismissed him. It was when he returned with a decent casual suit that she listened and paid attention. Now, he and Erica stood in front of her door, and they both wore dirty shirts, shorts, sandals, and big hobo-looking backpacks.

A muffled command silenced the barking animals and indicated her approach. After a click and a shimmy, the door opened up.

Jace stood slightly behind Erica and stared blankly at Brittaney. She appeared as if she just got off work. She looked tired. Her blonde hair seemed to have been tied back in a no-nonsense manner at the beginning of the day, but strands escaped the bind to give her a slightly frazzled look. She hadn't even gotten a chance to take off her high heels or remove her dark gray business coat.

Erica held out a hand. "Hello. My name is Dr. Patel. I'm a friend of Jace, who tells me you have some sort of memory problem."

Brittaney's eyes went from him to Erica, to her extended hand, then back to Erica. Her expression didn't seem happy or convinced. "He told you that?"

Erica nodded, but she kept smiling, retracting her extended hand. "Yes. But more importantly, I'm here to help."

"I don't need help."

Erica gazed up and around, as if inspecting the house. "Of

course you don't. You seem to be doing quite well for yourself. But it isn't your current life that you need help with."

"Look, miss—"

"Doctor," Erica corrected.

"Doctor. Right." Brittaney took half a step back. "I don't have time for this."

Erica raised a hand. "No, no. You seem to be quite busy. But if you could indulge me for just a moment." She pointed a single finger. "One, do you feel like you have a keen sense of your childhood? If so, how clear is it?"

Brittaney glared. "I don't have to answer any of your questions."

Erica raised a second finger. "Two, do you get dreams or nightmares about things you swear are memories but awaken to realize those memories aren't there?"

That gave Brittaney pause.

Erica continued her count. "Three, do you feel like your recent memory feels more real than your past memories?" After another moment of silence, Erica continued. "Four, are there times you feel like you're dreaming, even though you're awake?"

Again, no answer.

Erica licked her lips. "Five, do you mind if we come in? I've been on my feet all day, and I'm parched."

Brittaney eyed Erica and Jace with more than a little suspicion, but her gaze seemed softer than the last time Jace spoke to her. After a long moment, Brittaney took a step back to invite them in.

The door shut softly as they walked onto the hardwood floor. The room had a vaulted ceiling and a plush looking L-shaped couch thoughtfully placed around a nice coffee table with a decent-sized television against the wall.

Brittaney gave a brief high-pitched whistle, and the two dogs walked into the back room. She gestured to the couch. "Have a seat."

Erica smiled. "Thank you."

As Brittaney walked to another room, Jace and Erica removed their bags and sat down on the plush sofa.

Jace leaned over to Erica to whisper, "How do you know all that stuff? I thought this wasn't your specialty."

"It isn't. I made all that stuff up."

That made Jace's eyes widen in surprise. "You were bluffing?"

Erica gave a slight shrug. "Hey, it got us inside. Didn't it?" She shuffled through her backpack for a notepad and a pen.

Brittaney approached, set down a couple of coasters on the coffee table, and set down two glasses. Afterward, she sat in a seat across from them, crossing her arms and legs, giving a defensive and closed-off posture. "I'll give you five minutes, starting now. Then you have to go. And if I see either of you two again, I'll get a restraining order and press charges of harassment and slander."

Erica took a sip of the drink. "Mmm, this is delicious orange juice. Tastes fresh-squeezed. Did you make this yourself?"

Brittaney narrowed her eyes. "Four minutes, forty-five seconds."

"Straight to business. Alright then." Erica set down the drink and leaned forward, pen in hand. "As I said, my name is Dr. Patel. I'm a fully licensed and well renowned medical professional specializing in cellular engineering and medical theory."

Brittaney tapped a finger against her arm in frustration.

"Jace told me about a friend who had apparent memory loss, and I decided to visit you in person to discuss your symptoms."

"I have no symptoms."

Erica shook her head. "No. At least not that you know of. What do you do for a living?"

"Assistant District Attorney." Brittaney's eyes gazed at a clock. "Four minutes, ten seconds."

"Oh, nice." Erica jotted down some notes, writing a lot for what seemed to be a simple question. "Good. For a lady as young as yourself to have the job that you do, I'm betting you're rather intelligent and have a pretty sharp memory."

Brittaney nodded, her posture still in defiance.

"And I'm betting you could remember a lot of what you read. Probably almost everything, word for word. But you can't remember anyone in college."

Though the reaction was subtle, Jace noticed Brittaney's eyes widen a little.

"And I also bet..." Erica took another drink. "You remember every name of every teacher you've ever had. I'll even go so far as to bet you don't remember your childhood friends, though you know you had them." She put her pen to her pursed lips. "No, let me back up a little." She pointed the pen at Brittaney. "I bet you *do* remember them. All of them. Their full names, birthdays, everything. I'd even go so far as you remembering their eye colors." She slapped a palm over Jace's eyes. He almost reached up to move her hand when Erica continued. "But do you know what color our eyes are?"

No answer.

"I mean, if I'm right about your memory, you should know by now. You've been staring at us for a while now."

After a couple of seconds with no answer, Erica lowered her hand, allowing Jace to see once more. Brittaney's posture seemed to have loosened a little, from tense shoulders and back to a little more relaxed. Like she thought hard about what Erica had said and forgot to keep them taut.

"Dave..." Brittaney spoke in a stern, monotone voice. "Dave has brown eyes. His birthday is on August 14th. He is now 26 years old. Christian has brown eyes as well. March 28th. 25 years. William, blue, January 2nd, 26 years."

Erica wrote in her notepad. "Sounds like my theory is right on track."

Brittaney slapped a hand on the arm of her chair. "Now, hold on there. Doctors informed me that I have a photographic memory that—"

"Failed to work in the short-term?" Erica pointed to the other room where the dogs went. "Do you even know the color of your dog's eyes?"

"Brown."

"They both have brown eyes?"

Brittaney nodded.

"Like I said, failed to work in the short-term."

Brittaney jolted to her feet in frustration. "Are you serious?"

Erica nodded. "Yep. Because one of them has blue."

"No, they—"

"Go take a look. And if I'm wrong, we will get out of here, and you'll never see us again."

After a moment of glaring, Brittaney walked toward the back room.

When they were alone, Jace leaned close to Erica. "How do you know one of the dogs has blue eyes?"

"Because I saw them when we were here earlier. Most dogs have brown eyes, so I guessed she'd say brown if she didn't know. Give her a hint of doubt. Make your claim creditable."

Footsteps approached. "Your five minutes are up. Now, if you please..."

Jace twisted around to see Brittaney standing before the front door, her arm extended to invite them to leave.

Erica took another drink and grabbed her backpack, then approached Brittaney. Knowing his last chance to help his friend quickly came to a close, Jace followed, putting on his bag and following Erica.

"It was a pleasure to meet you." Erica reached in a pocket to produce a card, handing it to Brittaney. "Call me if you'd like to continue our conversation. My com number is on the back. Thank you for the drink and for seeing us on such short notice." Erica grabbed the door handle.

Brittaney stared at the card. "Wait."

Erica paused.

Jace stood motionless, wondering what was going on.

Brittaney's voice seemed a little choked. "How do you know all of this?"

"Like I said, medical theory is one of my specialties. I worked with enzymes that attached themselves to specific parts of human DNA and enhancing the human genetic code. Jace's story intrigued me. And with your apparent memory loss, I see I'm right." She turned back to the door and reached for the handle once more.

"Wait!" Brittaney quick-stepped to get in front of them, slapping her palm against the door. "What do you mean you're right? What proof do you have?"

Erica shrugged. "None. But you know deep down that I'm right."

Brittaney's eyes wandered as a hint of fear broke her usually stern gaze. "What if... What if you *are* right? What can I do?"

"Not kick us out, for one."

Brittaney's eyes went between Jace and Erica, as if she were trying to figure out what to do.

Erica put a hand over hers. "Brittaney, you're important to Jace. Important enough to ask me to come to talk to you. And since you're important to him, you're now important to me."

Brittaney eyed the two of them for a long, long while.

"At least let us talk openly about your memories, and we can see where things lead."

After a pause, Brittaney let out a deep, defeated sigh.

Jace gazed at Erica, who continued to look at Brittaney with empathy. She seemed to have an idea about what was going on. Perhaps she could help his long-lost friend. Perhaps she could provide him with suitable answers to the ever-building questions. And those thoughts gave Jace something he hadn't felt in a long time—hope.

CHAPTER FIVE

INTO THE NIGHT, ERICA AND BRITTANEY TALKED WHILE JACE SAT back to keep out of the way. With Erica making things up as she went along, she was very convincing, even making Jace wonder if she was an expert in memory manipulation. Deep into the evening, Brittaney called it a night and led Erica and Jace to a guest bedroom. She even showed them a full-sized bathroom they could use to get cleaned up, which made Erica happy.

Jace slept his usual few hours before he woke up. He carefully got out of bed, making sure he didn't wake Erica up, stood in front of an open window, watched the sunrise, and listened to the chirping birds. He always felt at peace so early in the morning, seeing nature arouse with the coming of light just before the swarm of civilization took over the lands.

The groggy voice of Erica sounded behind him. "Hey. Don't you ever sleep?"

Jace turned and approached. "Not since I was a kid."

"What time is it?"

He sat on the bed and kissed her head. "Maybe six."

She groaned, stretched, then sat up and propped herself up

against the headboard. Her hair poofed outward in every direction, the outcome of going to sleep immediately after a shower.

Jace crawled over Erica to sit next to her and put an arm over her shoulder for a hug. "So, what do you think?"

She rested her head against his shoulder. "About what?"

"Brittaney."

"Well, I can't do anything without my lab. And I need more data."

"More data?" Jace considered that for a moment. "Well, if we can find Brian, I'm sure he could help you."

"Brian?"

"Yeah. We basically grew up together. He's been helping me for years."

Erica gently nodded with a deep yawn, leaned against him, and talked in a daze, like she had fallen asleep against his shoulder. "I'd like to talk to everyone you grew up with. I could do some tests and maybe get some answers."

Answers would be nice. Jace decided she needed more sleep. He dragged her back to bed, where she rolled on her side so he could wrap his arms around her.

After a short while, Jace's eyes popped open when he heard a loud vehicle from a distance sounding like it was getting closer. At first, he didn't think anything of it. They were in the cookie-cutter suburbs, after all. Ground and aero-cars went by all the time. However, the obnoxious vehicle sounded like it stopped right in front of the house, followed by the fshh of some hydraulic or air device.

Erica stirred while Jace shimmied out of bed. "What's going on?"

Jace went to the window, wondering what kind of asshole would make so much noise in the early morning and wake people up. He looked down to see a black SUV stopped in front of Brittaney's house. But not on the sidewalk as if to park, but in the middle of the street. Outside the SUV stood a large, muscular man with a rectangular piece of glass in his hand.

He leaned in a little closer, as if the two extra inches toward the window would reveal the answers he sought.

"What's going on?" Erica asked again.

Jace didn't immediately answer. He continued his observation at the strangeness before him. And though Jace didn't understand technology, the appearance of the strange man rose alarms in his mind - clean-shaven, buzz cut, tight gray shirt with light camouflage pants, and military-grade combat boots. Jace's eyes locked on the belt around his waist, noticing various tools and materials any ordinary citizen wouldn't carry.

Erica got up and stood next to Jace, then gasped. "Roberts."

That name sparked a couple of memories in Jace's mind. The most recent one being a verbal confrontation outside The Order's mountainside structure. That thought worried him. "What's The Order doing here?"

Roberts turned in a slow circle while staring at the glass.

"Looking for me," Erica replied.

"Get dressed. We don't have a lot of time."

They moved away from the window and started to get dressed.

Once Jace had on a shirt and pants, he returned to the window to see Roberts toss the glass device in the passenger side of the SUV and approach Brittaney's house. "Pack up our bags." He started to walk to the bedroom door.

"Where are you going?"

"To see what he wants."

"Are you out of your mind? That's Roberts. *The* Roberts. Don't you know who he is?"

"Don't forget who I am." Jace gave a grin and opened the door. The rest of Erica's complaint was drowned out by the barking of the dogs.

The dogs went silent just as Jace got to the second-floor landing. Brittaney, standing in her nightgown, her blonde hair a mess from her late slumber, cracked open the door. Before she could say anything, he heard Roberts say, "I know she's here."

"I don't know who you are, but—"

Brittaney's words were cut off when the front door flew off its hinges, knocking her to the ground. After kicking the door in, Roberts entered the house, stepping on the door in the process. The dogs leaped into action, attacking the intruder.

Erica came rushing out of the room, her backpack on her back and Jace's bag in her hand.

Jace couldn't hesitate any longer. "Stay here." But just as he moved to stop Roberts, Erica grabbed his arm.

"You don't know what you're doing."

Roberts swept his arm out, tossing the dogs across the room and against the couch with a yelp.

"I can't let him do this." Jace put a hand over Erica's and looked into her eyes. "Grab Brittaney and run when you can."

Before she could answer, Jace leaped over the balusters to land on the hardwood floor below.

Roberts flipped the sofa over to trap the dogs under the couch. When he turned to face Jace, he paused. "You?"

Roberts seemed larger than Jace remembered, in both height and muscle bulk. It didn't matter. Roberts was still human.

Erica called from the stairs. "What are you doing?"

Roberts looked up the stairway. "Get down here. We're leaving."

"It's okay, Erica." Jace took a single step forward and extended an arm toward the open door. "May I have a word with you?"

A sneer of anger and defiance broke Roberts' lips, then he gave a growl that drowned out Erica's reply.

Roberts' movements were much faster than most people he faced. However, his speed was still slower than his old mentor – Xin.

He sidestepped an oncoming punch, Roberts' knuckles slamming against a wall, blowing the support beam in two. With that kind of power behind his blows, Jace knew he'd have little chance of actually blocking. His defense was avoidance.

Jace dodged and ducked attack after attack, each of Robert's blows hitting air, or cleaved whatever he hit in two, regardless of how solid it seemed. He was strong. Unnaturally strong. And worst of all, he maintained his balance.

Keeping Roberts distracted, Jace made his way toward the kitchen, allowing Erica to make her way downstairs to help Brittaney from under the broken door. With the women in a relatively safe place, Jace decided to go on the offense. Or he was about to when a fist came in too fast to dodge. Jace tried to deflect it, but his block was nowhere near strong enough to stop the sledgehammer that was Roberts' fist. The impact to his shoulder had Jace launch to the side. He rolled over a small table and crashed into a dish cabinet before crumbling to the floor.

With glass all over him from broken dishes, Jace felt a sharp pain shoot through his body. He stared up at the ceiling in a daze, taking a moment to recompose himself from such a brutal hit. Very few times had Jace felt a blow like that, and none of them were human. At that moment, he wondered if Roberts was even human. Was he a demon? Would The Order even hire a demon?

He staggered to his feet and propped himself against the table, using his good arm for balance. Roberts turned and started to walk toward Erica.

Jace had to stop him, but he couldn't immediately react due to the lingering daze. "You give up, yet?"

Roberts paused and faced Jace.

Feeling like he had an opportunity, Jace kicked the table, letting it slide toward Roberts. Roberts chopped down, cleaving the table in two.

With the distraction, Jace quick-stepped forward for an attack. After ducking a punch from Roberts, Jace struck, landing a sidekick behind Roberts' knee and planting a hard blow against his kidney - a combination that had crippled almost everyone Jace had faced. Or at least dazed or stunned them a brief moment.

Roberts didn't budge.

Jace brought his arm back and punched Roberts as hard as he could into his solar plexus. It was as if Jace had just struck a brick wall, and his wrist buckled with a crack.

Before Jace could retract his crippled arm, Roberts grabbed Jace by his injured wrist and single-handedly lifted him from the ground. Jace tried to defend himself with his other arm, but the shoulder wouldn't respond to his commands. His hand, however, did make his way to Roberts' belt.

Their eyes met.

Roberts glared with squinted eyes as he brought his face a little closer to Jace's. "You're weak, just like I knew you'd be." Roberts tossed Jace through a window with apparent ease. He crashed and tumbled on the grass, his skin torn in various places from the thick pane of glass. He landed hard against a tree in a sitting position—rather fortunate for him regardless of the excruciating pains he felt in his body—feeling a strange punch in his back when he hit the trunk.

Jace did his best to keep his wits about him. He spat up blood but was able to take a deep breath. "Hey, Roberts!"

Roberts paused to face Jace.

Jace smiled, fighting through the pain in his shoulder, and lifted his hand to show Roberts the three-ring pins he had in his fingers.

Roberts glanced down and reached for his belt, but it was too late. Bright white light shot through the entire room as the taze bombs went off. Roberts jerked and spasmed as the electrical pulses coursed through his body. Electrical outlets sparked and popped, and the main breaker went off with a loud bang. A nearby car alarm went off in a deafening whine as lights popped and exploded inside the house from the electrical arcs that shot out of his limbs. Finally, he fell to a knee as the pulses stopped. He visibly smoked from every extremity, but he stayed knelt.

Jace's arm went numb and fell limp to his side.

In the moment of calmness, Jace heard sirens.

Knowing he had to leave, Jace tried to get up, but he found his body wouldn't respond. It seemed as if something stopped him from moving, like some unseen force pinned him. His body began to go numb and cold. As if his head were too heavy to hold up, his neck went limp. Along with the line of bloody drool that dripped down from his lips, Jace saw a dark liquid pool under him.

After coughing up more blood, Jace's head lolled back, smacking against the tree trunk. To his surprise, Roberts slowly got to his feet, slapping his hand on the broken window as if to hold his balance.

Jace wondered how that could happen. He considered the three rings around his fingers and the weaponry he triggered once he was thrown. One grenade can incapacitate anyone in that proximity for at least five minutes. For Roberts to take all three at once and stand up in a fraction of that time was impossible.

Roberts glared at Jace, growled, then kicked the wall. Like a wrecking ball, his foot smashed through the structure, blowing a hole large enough for him to exit.

In his condition, Jace knew he couldn't fight back.

He approached Jace with clenched fists, each stride bringing him closer and closer.

From out of nowhere, a black blur came from the side and smashed into Roberts, crashing into Brittaney's house. A few moments later, Erica leaped out of the driver's seat and rushed to Jace's aid, sliding on her knees as she approached.

His vision began to fade as the pain overtook his senses.

Erica looked to her side. "Brittaney, come here! Quick!"

A few moments later, Brittaney was there.

"Hold him."

When Brittaney grabbed his shoulder to stabilize him, Erica

went around him and out of his sight. His head lolled a little, feeling the urge to blackout. The pain in his back and side pulsed, slightly waking him up from his pending slumber. Erica audibly gasped from behind, then she knelt in front of him.

Erica lifted Jace's chin a little to look into his eyes. "Listen to me very carefully. A thick tree branch pierced your back just under your 12th rib."

Jace put all of his energy into reorienting himself. "We...we have to go."

"You shouldn't even move."

Jace leaned forward, grimacing in pain, and felt the branch slide out of his back. He fell limp to the ground in agony.

Erica gasped and inspected his condition. "Are you insane?"

As he laid on the grass, he saw the SUV shift and slowly get pushed back.

Jace gasped. Was Roberts still alive? "R...Roberts."

"Shouldn't we wait for the cops?" Brittaney asked.

"The law doesn't apply to people like him. Come on. Help me get him to the car."

"The car? He needs a hospital!"

"Trust me. That's not an option."

One of them picked him up from his legs and another from his shoulders. Every motion made his entire body surge with searing agony. As the two walked with him in their arms, the rocking back and forth pulsed with pain before his vision faded into blackness.

CHAPTER SIX

IN A FIELD OF WAIST-HIGH COLORFUL FLOWERS, A WOMAN STOOD with the sun at her back. Her silhouette, the hair, everything was signs of where he was at—a recurring dream.

"Hey, fuckhead." The woman gave an ever-familiar half-smile.

Though the details of her features were hidden in the blinding sun, Jace knew who he spoke to. "Jessica."

"What the hell are you doing?" Jessica approached, and the sun grew dim, which hasn't happened before. "You're not supposed to lose. Not to an asshole like that."

"I know. It's just..." The sun continued to dim, and he groaned in pain. "He's not human."

"Are you sure?"

Jace shook his head.

"Sure he is," Jessica's voice echoed in the darkness. "Everyone is. Are you with me?"

Jessica's voice morphed into Erica's as she called out. "Hey. Are you with me?"

He slowly opened his eyes, blinking away the fuzziness that overtook him. His gaze went to a red drape. No, not a drape, but a carpet. That's when he realized he was on some table with his shoulders and head hanging off the side. A chair with books and a pillow propped up his head, but his right arm, encased in a makeshift splint, dangled freely off the ledge.

Jace groaned in pain as he tried to get up. What caught his attention more than the agony in his back was the burning of his empty stomach. How long has it been since he's had something to eat?

Erica knelt next to him. "No, no. Don't move." When he relaxed, she laid on her back so they could look at one another. Very few times has Jace seen her in such a condition. Her dark circles ran deep, her eyes were red, and her hair was a mess. "You lost a lot of blood with that little stunt. What did I say about being careful?"

A sharp pain shot through his numbed body, shocking him in a way that made him tense up. The feeling was brief as something wrapped around his chest. Probably bandages.

"You dislocated your left shoulder, cracked your right wrist, fractured half a dozen ribs, and you have a hole in your back. I removed all of the wood splinters and patched you up until Brittaney gets back. She is out getting some supplies." After he gave a painful grimace, she continued, "I said stop moving. Do you want to reopen your wound? It's only wrapped up in a shirt with tape."

The pain passed a few moments later, and Jace relaxed with a deep exhale. "Are you sure he isn't a demon?"

"That's what I was trying to tell you. Roberts is the first of a new line of experimental bio-mechanically advanced soldiers for The Order." After a brief pause, she clarified, "He's a cyborg."

Jace wanted to rub his temples to soothe the splitting headache. Since he wasn't able to move, he'd have to endure.

"With the shortage of support equipment, The Order looked into a new way of recruitment. Titanium alloys were fused with his infrastr..." She cut herself off, blinked a couple of times, each one getting slower and slower, then let out a small sigh. "He's still human. A lot of his internal organs are still there. However, his muscles and limbs have either been mechanically enhanced or replaced altogether."

"That explains the steel plate."

Erica's blinks slowed with each heartbeat. Eventually, they stayed closed as she dozed off. He decided a little bit of sleep would be best as well, so he closed his eyes and let himself drift off into his own slumber.

———

Brittaney's voice woke Jace up from his sleep. "I dropped my dogs off at my parents."

Erica was no longer underneath him, but she spoke to the side. "Did you get the supplies I requested?"

"And some takeout."

He heard some shuffling, like objects clanking in a plastic box, then Erica walked by and placed a hand on his bareback. "I know you're awake."

Jace groaned. "Can I move yet?"

"Hardly."

Brittaney knelt next to Jace. "I'm relieved. I thought you'd be dead for sure."

"Nah." Erica removed the makeshift bandages on his back. "He's gone through so much worse."

After a wince, Jace said, "Yeah, but I had your goo to help."

"Not this time." Erica poured some sort of liquid on Jace's open wound. It sizzled and burned. "This time, we're doing things the old-fashioned way. Now stop moving."

Brittaney stood up and walked away. "Will he be okay?"

"He'll be fine. Maybe three or four weeks for his ribs to heal. His wrist will probably be better tomorrow, but he'll need to take it easy. This, though..." Jace felt Erica pinch the skin of his puncture wound together. "This will need to be closely monitored. Man up, Jace. Here come the stitches."

Agony. Painful agony. He did his best to keep focused on other things, but Jace still shifted with each dreadful pinch.

"So why can't we go to the police? Why does Jace have to bleed all over my office?"

"You're a DA, right?" After a final tug, Erica snipped the excess line. "Then you know about The Order."

"And?"

"And Roberts is one of them."

Brittaney didn't reply for a long moment while Erica finished tending to Jace's wound.

Erica knelt next to Jace, putting her hand on his uninjured shoulder. "All done. Get some rest. I'll take a look at it later."

"Thanks. I'll be okay." Jace winced as he sat up. Erica put a hand on his shoulder to stop him, but he fought through it and got to his feet.

"What did I just say?"

Jace put a hand up to paw the air. "I'll be fine."

Erica glared in reply, then slapped Jace on the shoulder and walked away toward a table with bags of takeout.

Brittaney leaned against her desk while Erica removed foil-wrapped burgers and bags of fries. "And what does The Order want with you?"

"I don't want to get into it, but he was there because of me." Erica bit down on a small handful of fries and handed Jace a burger. "Just know that you can't go after these guys. They're The Order. They've been around for hundreds of years. Maybe longer." She paused to take a drink and handed Brittaney a burger. "They have the law in their pockets with politicians bought and paid for."

Brittaney placed the unwrapped burger at the corner of her desk. "Then what do you think we should do?"

Erica bit down on another handful of fries. "I suppose we have to identify a goal. What do you want to do?"

"For one, if my memory is messed up, I want to get it fixed."

Jace nodded in agreement while he unwrapped his burger and began to eat, being very careful of his movements, so he didn't irritate his injuries.

"That'll take some time, but we can work on that." Erica took a bite of her burger. "In the meantime, what's next?"

Jace swallowed. "I want to find Brian."

"Let's start there. Brittaney, you're a DA." Erica used a fry as a pointer and gestured at Brittaney's computer. "Do you have access to some sort of tracking software to find people?"

Brittaney shook her head. "Nothing like you see on TV. We usually hire private investigators for detailed information. The software we use is compiled mostly from public records."

"Hmm. I suppose it's a start."

Brittaney sat in her comfortable looking chair at her desk and worked on her computer.

Jace couldn't believe he had to search for Brian again. For a moment, his heart sank as the past swarmed his memories once more.

"Okay," Brittaney said, snapping Jace out of his thoughts. " What can you tell me?"

"His name is Brian. He is about half a foot taller than me, a little heavier, but he lost a lot of weight. He wears glasses, and—"

"Wait." Brittaney leaned to the side and glared at Jace. "I need something more specific, like a last name. Brian..."

"Mmm, McGuen." Erica finished her burger with a huge bite. "G-U-E-N. This is the same guy from last year, right?"

Jace wondered how in the world she remembered that detail, then took a drink of his soda with a nod. He never was a fan of soda, but he figured beggars couldn't be choosers in this instance. To make sure Brittaney found the right person, he pushed himself off the table and slowly and painfully made his way around the desk.

Brittaney tapped at her keyboard, finishing just as he stood beside her. "Is this him?"

There he stood, thin-rimmed glasses gripping his nose slightly magnifying his brown eyes, the well-groomed short stubble of a beard, and carefully styled hair that made it look messy. "Yep. That's him."

Brittaney didn't immediately respond. She seemed to be looking at something on the screen, but it was only Brian's picture. Was there something he didn't see?

Erica grabbed a drink and moved beside Brittaney. "You're right. He is cute." She leaned in a little closer. "He is not heavier than you. Look at him." She gestured to the screen with her drink. "That man's a twig!"

Brittaney cleared her throat before pushing a button on the keyboard. Words popped up to the side, and she went through the information while mumbling to herself. "Date of birth, known associates, aero-operator's license."

"Aero-operator?" Erica shook her ice-filled cup before taking another drink. "Those things can be pretty hard to get."

"Ah, here we go." Brittaney highlighted a section of text. "Last known address." She clicked it, and another window popped up with a map.

Erica finished off her drink with a slurp from the straw. "That's on the other side of the country."

"This says he's been living there for the past four months."

"Oh, I read about that place." Erica prodded the screen. "That's a new city that's been building up out of nowhere. A huge technological hub for the western area."

Jace could only look at the screen, staring at the little dot on the map. Is that where Maya was? Even though the address was on the other side of the country, Jace knew he had to get there. "Get us plane tickets. I want to get there as soon as possible."

"That's not going to happen." Erica gestured to the bandages that wrapped around Jace's chest. "Do you think they'll let someone in your condition onboard? And since you're no longer employed by The Order, you'll need an ID chip, which is something you don't have."

That didn't make much sense to him as he's flown without the ID chip before.

"Okay, then..." Brittaney moved her chair backward a little and leaned back. "What do you propose?"

Jace knew what was about to be proposed, and he didn't like it. His stomach grumbled, and a bubble of acid lifted in his throat as soon as Erica said, "The bus."

———

Every moment on the three-day trip made Jace miss his car. He knew he wouldn't have the privileges of high-speed driving for his missions. But even at speed, it would have been a more enjoyable ride than the stuffy bus. Not only were his injuries cramping and painfully slowing him down, but his motion sickness plagued him throughout the entire journey.

All he could do was move as little as possible and eat, which was commonly barfed in a bag during bus rides. Erica put some small patches behind his ear in the middle of the trip. And though they helped with his motion sickness, he couldn't help wondering how they worked.

The voice of the older lady on his last bus ride echoed in his mind. Suddenly, her rantings and conspiracy theories didn't seem so ridiculous.

Eventually, the trio got into an aero-cab, flying from the bus station toward their final destination, with Jace sitting in the front to help prevent him from getting sick.

With looming clouds in the distance, the sun gave a full view of the landscape before them in the early afternoon. Massive mountains with lifeless, snow-capped tips stretched far into the sky. Lush, green foliage with hints of yellow that marked the beginning of Autumn covered the lower sections of the sloping terrain.

They followed a road that led to a bridge that stretched over a canyon. Jace looked down at the full and lively riverbed at the bottom, and a massive dam in the distance. Across the bridge were buildings that reached high into the sky. But one building stood out over the rest—a staggering pillar of steel and glass at least twice as high as the rest.

Once they entered the city, the aero-cab merged with the rest of the flying traffic. Immediately, illuminations and holographic billboards polluted the vision. Below them, the streets were equally as busy, with ground traffic and people walking. Around every corner were construction workers developing the bustling city. Everything looked new, like nature hadn't gotten the chance to soil the newly created structures of modern civilization.

The aero-cab took them to the opposite side of the city and dropped them off in a residential area. Jace slowly exited the vehicle with a painful groan, feeling his back and side ache with the movement. Brittaney offered to carry Jace's gear to prevent his wound from opening up. Erica paid for the cab, gathered her backpack from the trunk, and stood beside Jace.

The small tan house had an egg-white lining and a blue top-half, and a small glass-like overhang for an open garage.

After taking a moment to get their belongings, Erica and Brittaney approached the house. Jace stood motionless on the sidewalk.

When the ladies got to the front door, Brittaney glanced back to him. "What's wrong with him?"

Erica returned the gaze. "Oh, he's just scared." She approached Jace with a smile and set her backpack on the sidewalk. "He did the same thing at your place."

Brittaney chuckled and knocked on the door.

"Come on, hero." Erica looped an arm around his good arm. "Let's go."

Jace resisted her tug. "What if... What am I going to say? How could I face-"

"Yeah, yeah." Erica tugged more insistently, breaking his frozen posture with a staggering step.

As Jace and Erica approached, a black screen illuminated on the wall, and the familiar voice of Brian spoke. "Who is this?"

Brittaney leaned down to get her face closer to the strange device. "Uh, hi. My name is Brittaney Webbs. I'm an assistant district attorney looking for someone named Brian McGuen."

"That's me. Wait, did you say Brittaney Webbs?"

Brittaney glanced briefly at Jace and Erica. "Uh, yes."

"Holy smokes! I know someone who was looking for you. H-Hey, do you know a guy named Jace? He's a short guy. Dark hair. Mopy and grumpy."

Brittaney and Erica chuckled.

Jace blinked for a moment. Before he could get a word out, Erica covered his mouth.

"I'm not sure," Erica replied, attempting to sound like Brittaney. "What else can you tell me?"

Again, the women chuckled.

"Uh, he always looks super serious. Almost like he is holding in gas. And even though he is short, he's built like a horse."

Jace struggled, but finally broke free from Erica's grasp. "Damn it, Brian. I'm right here."

"You are? Holy smokes! Is that you, Jace?" An unintelligible sound came from the black screen, as if Brian dropped his microphone. "Hey, I'll be there in ten minutes. Make yourselves at home." The door clicked and slightly opened. "Holy smokes..."

Erica walked toward the sidewalk to grab her backpack, laughing to herself all the while.

"Brian?" Jace stepped up to the screen. "Brian, where's Maya?"

No answer.

Jace restrained a slammed fist just above the black glass. "Damn it." Instantly regretting his decision to take his frustration out on the wall, Jace entered with Brittaney behind him.

The house was indeed small, looking more like a 2-bedroom apartment. The kitchen, dining room, and living room shared the same space. What made the place stand out from the hotels Jace stayed in was the amount of fancy technology all over him. Lights seemed to be in areas where they shouldn't be, smooth, dark plates were on every wall, and the ceiling had recessed lighting all over.

Brittaney whistled and entered, her eyes going from one side of the room to the other. "Nice place."

"At least the chairs looked normal." Jace entered the front room, noticing a large holographic projector between a massive cushy couch and a big-screen TV mounted on the wall. The tiled floor made each step emanate a gentle echo in the otherwise quiet house. Jace felt uneasy around so much voodoo technology. Still, he plopped on the couch, hiding a grimace of uneasiness from his wounds.

Erica walked in, set her bag down, and shut the door. "Hey, this isn't too bad."

"I know, right? I didn't expect the inside to look like this." Brittaney went to the kitchen and inspected the appliances. "Hey, check this out!"

The ladies began wandering the house, looking over the nooks and crannies of the various technologies the place had to offer. Jace didn't want anything to do with it and stayed on the couch. What was he going to say? What was Brian going to say? Where is Maya? How should he explain himself?

Brittaney and Erica went to the backyard.

Not wanting to drown himself in pity and doubt, Jace awkwardly and painfully stood up and wandered the house, paying particular attention to the details surrounding him. He discovered a bathroom with automatic dimming lights, a bedroom with clean and well-made sheets, and a second bedroom with a smaller bed but equally clean and pressed sheets. Figuring the smaller bedroom would be the first place to find the clues he searched for, he cautiously entered. Not because he was scared, but because he had a flood of doubts going through his mind and heart.

The room had a personal-sized desk and chair in the corner, the small bed beside it, a smooth, polished box that he assumed to be a dresser to his left, and a dark wooden section flush with the wall to his right. On some flat surfaces were some stuffed animals, some boxes of unopened toys from some cartoons, and some books. The walls had posters with similar cartoons of action-based characters with crazy hair and ridiculously large muscles.

Jace approached the wooden section he assumed was the closet, noticing the dark square in the wall. He grumbled to himself, irritated at the sheer amount of technology all over the place. He swiped the screen. It turned white, and the wooden section slid back, then to the side.

A light automatically illuminated the clothing from above. Black, white, and gray shirts hung neatly on hangers. Below, on a separate rack, were pants.

Jace smiled, knowing that this was, in fact, Maya's clothing style. He grew ever more excited, and no less nervous.

A whirring sound outside brought Jace from his contemplation. He quickly exited the room just in time for the side door of the house to open. There stood Brian, looking as if he was in a near panic.

Brian smiled, and his eyes went wide. "It is you!"

"Brian!" Jace rushed toward the side door. "Is Maya with you?"

"No. She's with Ruth." Brian visually inspected Jace with his eyes locking on the bandage around his wrist. "What happened?" When the sliding glass door to the backyard opened, Brian's posture shifted as his eyes went from Jace's injury to Erica and Brittaney. He said nervously, "Oh. Hello."

Jace took a step to the side. "Hey. Where's Ruth?"

"Now don't be rude." Erica walked beside Jace.

Brittaney took command of the situation and stood to the opposite side of Jace. "Hello, Mr. McGuen. My name is Brittaney Webbs." Brian stared at her awkwardly as she continued, "I'm the district attorney for the..."

"You're Brittaney?" Brian asked. "From the orphanage?"

"I..." Brittaney cleared her throat, and her posture went from stern and commanding to broken and uncomfortable, and she turned away.

Erica stepped up and extended her hand. "Hi. I'm Erica."

Brian's complexion gained a tint of red, then he turned his attention to Erica. His eyes went from Erica to her extended hand. "Uh, yes. I-I'm..."

Jace smiled, remembering how awkward Brian had been around beautiful women. "Still?"

"What?" Brian cleared his throat, as if regaining his composure. Still, he spoke in a higher tone than usual. "Yes, hello. I'm Brian." He shook her hand.

Erica smiled. "Lovely to meet you. Jace has told me much about you."

Brittaney turned to the group. "How did you know about the orphanage?"

"The, uh... What?" Brian seemed to be flustered, as if unable to formulate a single sentence.

"He grew up with us," Jace answered.

That seemed to regain Brian's thought process. "Yes. That's it." He slightly leaned forward with squinted eyes toward Brittaney, who in returned leaned away. "You look familiar. Are you the same Brittaney who took first place in the Science and Art competition in our 6th-grade year?"

Brittaney's eyes went wide, and she turned away.

"Brian, her memory," Jace reminded.

"Oh. Oh yeah. Okay, okay."

Like a savior of uncomfortable conversations, Erica stepped in. "This is a wonderful place you have here. Is that the TX-1800?"

Immediately, Brian's expression and posture turn from awkward to confident. "What? Uh, no. That's the 1850. Well, it's *my* version of the 1850. See the small lips on the sides?"

Now that Brian had his mind back on track, Jace interjected to get some answers. "Brian. Ruth?"

Erica lightly slapped Jace on the shoulder, a silent yet painful reminder of his rudeness.

Brian adjusted his glasses. "Oh yeah. Don't worry. They're working on a huge project for school. They'll be here later."

Brittaney mumbled something, but her tone caught everyone's attention. She turned to face the group. "Was it a battery?"

"A battery?" Brian's eyes went wide with recognition. "Oh. Yes. Yes, it was. Actually, it was more like an emergency power supply created by the loose change in the judge's pocket. Very impressive work, if I do say so myself."

Brittaney's expression turned into confusion and pain. "I was an exchange student in my 6th-grade year. How...?"

Erica put a hand on Brittaney's shoulder. "Don't worry. We'll work on it."

Brian looked to Jace. "So she's..."

Jace nodded. "Yeah. They're working on it." With how smart Brian was, Jace had an idea. "Hey, now that we're here, maybe you can help."

"Me?" Brian gestured to himself. "I mean, I can try. It would be difficult since I don't know the exact root of the problem." He rubbed his chin, fiddling with the stubble on his face. "We would need a super genius in the medical field, like that Doctor Eric Patel I read about a few years ago. Did you know he got his medical degree before people usually finish high school? His work on cellular engineering sparked all sorts of ideas for cybernetic and bionic enhancements."

Erica turned her attention from Brittaney to Brian. "*His* work?"

Brian nodded. "Yeah. The theories of using and fusing nerve endings helped out on all sorts of projects."

"Those theories were proven, thank you very much." Erica crossed her arms.

Brian shook his head. "I don't think so. If they were proven, I would have known."

"You don't know about it because I never published it."

"Because you, what?" Slowly, Brian's face went from a shaking head and a confused expression to surprise and understanding.

"And I got my medical degree when I was nineteen, well after people got out of high school. And I am far from a man, thank you very much!"

Brian pointed to Erica. "You... You're..."

"Dr. Erica Patel, head of the Research and Development for Bio-Engineering for th..." Her voice trailed off.

Brian seemed to hardly register the last part of her reply. Finally, he was able to form a sentence. "You're Doctor Patel?" Brian turned around, and he put his hands on his head. "Holy smokes!" He excitedly turned back to face Erica once more. "You? You're *the* Doctor Patel?"

Noticing Erica's uneasy expression, Jace decided to step in. "Yes, she's who you're referring to. Now focus up." He nodded toward Brittaney.

That seemed to get Erica out of her funk. "Yes, we have other things to discuss. But first, can I get a drink? Maybe something with some kick."

"Yes, yes." Brian took two excited steps back and pulled out a chair from the circular kitchen table. "Sit. I'll make us some snacks."

CHAPTER SEVEN

A FEW HOURS LATER, JACE STARED OUT THE FRONT WINDOW, watching the storm slowly make its way in. Eventually, the sky darkened, and the pitter-patter of the sprinkling rain hitting the house gave a calming hum. He focused on that sound, ignoring Brittaney, Brian, and Erica's excited talking about bio-molecular-memory-whatever. No matter what they said, no matter the problem with Brittaney, Jace knew Brian and Erica would be able to solve it.

At some point in the conversation, Brian broke off and stood next to him. The two stared out the window as the sprinkles turned into a decent downpour.

"Hey, can I talk to you for a minute?" Brian peeked behind him toward the women at the table. "In private."

Jace, too, looked behind him for a moment, then nodded to Brian.

The two went outside and stood on the porch. Brian cleared his throat. "So, about Maya... You know about her, right?"

Jace's heart sank from pure shame. He broke eye contact with Brian and stared off in disgust. "How am I ever going to face her?"

"Evolved or not, she isn't a bad girl." When Jace didn't say anything, Brian continued, "Are you still angry with her?"

"Angry? I'm not..."

"Because the last time I saw you, the look in your eye... You pointed a gun at her, Jace."

"I know."

"No, I don't think you do. Do you know how hard it's been for her? How hard it was for her to understand what happened without telling her what really happened? Don't get me wrong. I'm happy to see you, but tell me why I shouldn't tell you to get out of here before she gets home? Why would I let you back in her life after what you've done?"

Jace had no immediate answer. Should he even see her? He considered what they had now - a house, a job, friends. She had a good, stable life. Maybe he should just leave and let her live the life he couldn't offer her. Finally, he shook his head, fighting back the moisture that built up in his eyes. He took a deep, calming breath. "I've never been mad at her. If anything, I'm mad at myself." He looked up to Brian, fighting back the pain and anguish in his heart. "I just abandoned her. What kind of asshole does that to his family? I just..." He tried to take another deep breath to regain his composure.

Brian didn't seem upset at the answer. "Do you still hate them?"

"Them?" Jace shook his head. "No."

"Are you still hunting them?"

Again, Jace shook his head. "No. The war is a lie. I'm done with them. The war. The lies. I'm done hurting innocent people."

That seemed to make Brian's expression crinkle with doubt. Jace knew Brian played no small part in his atrocious actions, which led to the unparalleled success on his otherwise impossible missions. Though Brian could never physically hurt anyone, he was just as guilty in every crime Jace committed. He was the designer for all of his tools of destruction, his support, co-planner, and business partner.

The two said nothing for what seemed like an eternity, and they watched a bolt of lightning flash in the distance.

"So," Brian finally said, "What are you going to do, then?"

"I don't know." Jace sniffed the air and turned toward the front yard, watching the water flow down the driveway toward the curbs.

Brian turned to stare out as well. "I don't know about you, but I don't want to be the bad guy."

Guilt formed in Jace's chest. "But I am."

"You're what?"

"The bad guy."

That made Brian face Jace once more, and he shook his head. "I don't think so. You're like..." He licked his lips and adjusted his glasses, probably more to buy time to think about what he was going to say rather than anything else. "You have this power to do awesome things, you know? I agreed to help you because it seemed like the right cause at the time."

Thunder briefly drowned out all the sounds, allowing Jace to consider what Brian had said.

When the booming stopped, Brian continued, "You want Maya back in your life? You have to be the good guy."

"You're right." He looked up at the sky, sniffing back the tears in his eyes. "You're right. She deserves better. Much better than I could ever give."

"Nope. You're wrong."

Jace looked at Brian.

"I'm willing to bet, deep down, she wants you back in her life, too. And if you're the good guy I know you are, you'll give her a life I could only dream of."

That made Jace crack a faint smile.

"But if you want my help, you have to tell me the good you're fighting for. Because I'm not going to be the bad guy." He gestured to the house. "That's why I'm helping Brittaney. It's the right thing to do."

What was he fighting for? What was his purpose? After Maya got home, then what? What would he say? How would she react?

Brian put a hand on Jace's shoulder. Though it was still tender from the dislocation, Jace was thankful that the sharp pain brought him out of his thoughts. "You got some amazing people surrounding you. And soon, Maya will be with you, too. They wouldn't be around you if you were truly the bad guy." He removed his hand. "I can see in your eyes that you want to do the right thing. When you decide, we got your back." He patted Jace's shoulder again, then walked inside the house.

Jace stood outside for a long while, staring at the falling rain. He considered what Brian had told him. Erica, Brian, and Brittaney all had his back. And he would have Maya again soon. Perhaps, it wasn't as bad as he had thought. He considered the experiences when he was with The Order, especially when he fought with the golem. He actually saved people's lives. He helped so many people, and he could do that again. He smiled to himself at that thought. Perhaps he had the support to turn his life around and do actual good for a change.

———

Eventually, Erica went to take a shower, and the conversation at the kitchen table whittled down to just Brian and Brittaney. Jace didn't participate in their discussion. Instead, he stared out the front window, thinking about what he would say and how Maya would react. He watched the storm that overtook the small but promising city. Strikes of lightning was always an awesome sight, even more so as the sun drew closer to the horizon.

The storm grew heavier as the thunder boomed louder.

He lightly twisted his back, trying to get the ache from his puncture wound out. Though it still hurt, he felt considerably better than before.

He was thrown out of his contemplation when a vehicle pulled up. His heart pounded furiously as someone exited through the back passenger door. Nerves took over and Jace put his back against the wall to get out of sight.

"Oh, hey. It's getting dark," Brian said. "Maya should be home any—"

At that moment, the door clicked and opened up. The sound of a giggling girl shot through Jace's ears. Was Maya talking? Was she giggling?

Two girls, soaked from the rain, walked inside. One, a tan-skinned girl with soaked wavy brown hair that hung around her shoulders, took off her coat. "Man, it's pouring out," the girl said. " Hello, Mr. McGuen."

"Hello, Ruth." Brian stood and approached. "We have some guests."

The other girl brought her head back, removing the hood that covered her head. There Maya stood, her long brown hair soaked from the rain through her wool hoodie. She grew a few inches since the last time Jace saw her but could pick her out from a crowd.

Maya paused when she noticed Brittaney. Her eyes went from Brian to Brittaney, and she gave a half-assed smile and gave a wrist-bending wave of hello, then took off her backpack.

Ruth wasn't looking at them. Instead, she spotted Jace while he stood with his back against the wall, staring at him with confusion. That's when he noticed she had two different colored eyes: one brown and one yellow. She nudged Maya. "Who is that?"

"Uh, well.." Brian paused, stopping in his tracks. "That's the thing..."

Maya turned. And just as her eyes went wide, a tremendous boom of thunder shook the windows. She dropped her backpack from the shock, and everyone knelt a little and looked around from the surprise, removing the strange tension Jace felt when she spotted him.

Jace gulped, still unsure of his next move. "Hi."

Her green eyes penetrated his soul. He could feel her surprise and pain.

Ruth stared hard at him, too. "Who is this?"

"This," Brian said as he took a few steps forward. "This is Jace. He's, umm... Her brother?"

"I guess that depends." Jace took a deep breath to steady his nerves.

Maya, too, seemed to have the same conflicting feelings he felt. Her mouth slowly opened so she could take an unsteady breath. After a couple of blinks, she appeared to have gained control of her senses because she took a stern and defensive posture, crossing her arms and putting her weight on one leg.

Ruth stepped beside Maya. "Is that a question? What does that even mean?"

Brian stepped in. "Hey Ruth, let's give these two a minute." He gestured to a room Jace hadn't explored yet. "Let's get everything ready for the project."

"Okay." Ruth whispered something in Maya's ear, then walked away with Brian.

Brittaney seemed uneasy. "I'm, uh...going to check out the backyard." And she exited the sliding glass door.

With Maya and Jace alone for the moment, Jace took a deep breath to steel his nerves. "Look, I..." He cleared his throat and ran his fingers through his hair, frantically thinking to himself at what to say. When nothing came to mind, he found himself rambling. "There's nothing I could say... Uh, what I mean is, what I did...I-I'm sorry." Though Maya hadn't moved an inch, Jace grasped on a train of thought. "I know what I did was wrong, and everything that happened wasn't your fault. You didn't do anything wrong."

Either his people-reading skills left him, or he once again found himself face-to-face with someone he couldn't read. With an impeccable poker face, Maya stood her ground, her expression giving no hint of what she was thinking or feeling. She stood defensively, withdrawn from the conversation.

At that moment, Jace again wondered if he made a mistake, and the conversation with Brian intruded on his mind. Maybe she didn't want him in her life. Doubt clouded his mind and took over. If she didn't want him around, he decided to speak his piece and be done with it. "I don't know what you've been through since I messed up. I just wanted to see you and apologize. It's okay if you don't forgive me. Hell, I don't know if I would if I were you. But no matter what, know that it wasn't your fault. And know that I regret that day and my actions."

Finally, Maya's stone visage softened ever so slightly, and a tear fell down her cheek. But before he could say anything, she leaped forward and wrapped him in a tight hug.

Though he wished the hug could last, the pain that shot through him overtook his senses. "Ouch. Not so tight."

Maya took a step back and visually inspected him. Her brow furrowed, and she pouted, apparently noticing the injuries Jace had gotten a few days before.

"It's hard to explain."

She gestured with her hand, as if saying, "Go on."

"Let's just say that someone we didn't want to see found us. And things got ugly."

Maya held out her hands and wiggled her fingers.

"No, not Evolved."

She pointed downward and twirled her finger.

"Are you sure?" After a nod, Jace turned around and lifted the back of his shirt. Over the bandages, he felt Maya's gentle and caring touch. Like his heart could beat with caring and love once more, Jace smiled, taking in the emotional sensation of released guilt. She always had that effect on him. No matter the burdens, no matter the stress or the injuries, Maya always made him feel better in his heart and mind.

The two looked back when the unexplored door opened. Ruth and Brian returned to the front room, walking slowly while staring at them. "Holy smokes, Jace. You said you got hurt earlier. I didn't know you got hurt like that."

Jace put his shirt down. "I'll be alright."

"Ruth and Maya have a big project due tomorrow. Maya was going to stay at Ruth's tonight. You okay with that?"

"Me?" Jace gestured to himself. "I don't see why not. I mean, if she wants to."

"Well, you are her big brother. Go get your things ready, Maya. You and Jace can talk more later."

Maya nodded, gave Jace another hug, this one being gentle, and she rushed toward her bedroom.

As if an opportunity arose, Ruth approached Jace. "Big brother, eh? Didn't Mr. McGuen say she was adopted?"

"Adopted brother." For a moment, Jace wondered if him just taking Maya from the orphanage was considered a legal adoption. He decided not to mention anything, though.

"And who is she?" Ruth gestured toward the sliding glass window, and the shape that stood outside.

"That's Brittaney. She's from the same orphanage that Brian and I went to."

"You grew up with Mr. McGuen?"

The bathroom door opened, and Erica stepped out. "Oh, I feel so much better. Did you hear that loud boom a few minutes ago? It shook the walls. Oh, hello." Erica gave a smile, rubbing her head with a towel, and approached. "I'm sorry, I didn't know someone else was in the room."

"Erica," Brian said as he stood beside Ruth. "This is Ruth."

"Ruth?" Erica seemed rather interested at that moment, and she paused, as if taking a moment to look her over. Finally, she extended a hand. "It's a pleasure to meet you. I'm Erica."

Ruth shook her hand. "It's nice to meet you."

"If you'll excuse me, I'm still a mess." Erica lifted the damp towel and smiled. "I'll be right back." She returned to the bathroom and shut the door.

"She's pretty. Is she from the orphanage, too?"

Jace shook his head. "No."

Maya's bedroom door opened, and she approached with a small bag in her hand, stopping in front of Jace.

Jace smiled. "I'm not going anywhere. I promise."

That had Maya smile and nod. After a strange one-armed hug, Maya and Ruth left after a brief goodbye.

Jace sat on the couch, took a deep breath, and rubbed his eyes wearily. "Holy crap."

"I think that went well," Brian said as he sat on the other side of the sofa. "But are you alright?"

"Yeah." Jace looked behind him toward the sliding glass door. "You want to tell Brittaney she can come back in before she gets sick?"

"Holy smokes!" Brian shot up and rushed toward the backyard.

Erica returned, her hair brushed and a little more put-together. "Oh, did she already leave?"

"There's a big project due tomorrow," Jace explained as Brittaney and Brian came inside from the back. "So she's at her friend's for the night."

"Oh. Too bad." Erica walked up to Jace.

Brian came in from the back with Brittaney in tow. "So, I wasn't expecting guests, and I need to go to the store tomorrow. How about we order pizza tonight?"

CHAPTER EIGHT

EIGHT SECONDS. THAT'S HOW LONG IT TOOK FOR A TINY RED LIGHT to blink for a fraction of a second. That dot is what Jace focused on as he laid in the dark after waking up in the middle of the night.

Being up while everyone around him slept didn't bother Jace. He used those times to think and reflect, consider his actions, and decide his next move. The reunion of Brian and Maya was on his mind as he stared at the blinking light. It went terrible and awkward, and he repeatedly silently chastised himself for how he acted. Things would have been so much smoother if he was able to think straight.

He looked over to the dark shape of Erica when she mumbled something in her sleep and shifted on the floor beside him. She seemed to be sleeping decently enough on the air mattress. Then a thought came to mind. Where would Erica fit as he worked to rebuild his relationship with Maya? Maybe he could meet with Maya without anyone around, and they could reconnect. He nodded to himself. Rebuilding the sense of family would be best done alone.

Jace sat up, taking extra precautions not to wake up Erica, or

Brittaney, who slept on the couch next to them. His back felt a lot better. For the first time since the fight with Roberts, he felt like he could stretch the muscle aches from his body.

Not risking another scolding from Erica, Jace got out of bed and went to the kitchen. With each step, the floor tiles gave a dim glow. Of course Brian would have some techy thing going on with the floor.

Brian's door opened, and he exited the room, fully dressed. He approached Jace in the kitchen. "What are you doing up so early?"

"Me? I hardly get any sleep." Jace gestured to Brian. "What about you? What are you doing?"

"I have to go to work."

Jace felt foolish. Of course he had a regular job.

"Hey, since you're up, let me show you something."

Brian led Jace through the kitchen toward a side door. The weathering scraped against the floor as he opened it. A moment later, the dark room illuminated a wide space with various tools and materials neatly cleaned and lining the walls. Recoiled mechanical arms and various other extremities were on the ceiling, curled up to stay out of the way. What caught Jace's eye more than anything in the room was the sleek car in the middle of the space. The midnight blue color paint reflected the overhead lights of the car, and the shining rims were spotless. It was clean and polished, with all of the damage done in past excursions repaired.

Jace could only stare helplessly for many surprising heartbeats. "My car." He walked up and placed a hand on the frame. Then he looked behind his shoulder to Brian.

"I did a bit of repair and maintenance on it." Brian adjusted his glasses. "Then I adjusted the internal dash systems to..."

Knowing Brian could go on and on, Jace stopped listening to his techno-rambling. He turned his attention back to the car, running his fingers along the body as he walked around. The dents and dings from chasing the shifter, the rocks that pummeled the windows during the golem, everything was gone. He pushed the button that opened the door. It shifted upward, allowing Jace to peek inside, revealing a clean and polished leather interior. The dashboard looked different, as Jace expected. Brian always modified the car one way or the other. Before he knew it, Jace found himself getting in, feeling the comfort of his seat and the ever-familiar feeling of the steering wheel.

Brian walked beside him, still rambling. "Then I repainted it with a special blend of mine consisting of bulletproof synthetic-"

"Why? Why did you keep working on the car like this?"

"This is my work, Jace. This car, the harness, the armor, they're the cornerstones of my innovations."

"I had all that stuff on me."

"True." Brian went to a sidewall and pushed a button. A section slid back, then split to the sides, revealing a mannequin wearing a dark but textured fabric and a familiar mechanical contraption on its back.

"How?"

"These were the prototypes I worked on last year. Remember?" Brian gestured at the mechanism on the mannequin. "I've made some improvements to the reload harness. It isn't as bulky, and I figured out a way to make the mesh weave better with the kevlar. I haven't been able to run tests, so they're still prototypes. But..." He paused as he gestured at something.

Jace followed his gaze, seeing the two highly customized chrome-plated .50 caliber handguns. They even had the engravings that formed a skull when they were put together. Surrounding the guns were various other instruments he used in his hunts.

"I thought I lost those."

"Maya convinced me to turn around to get you. When we got there, you were gone. But I found the guns."

"Maya..." Jace gave a deep sigh, feeling the regret build up in his stomach.

"I don't make weapons anymore. My work is focused on saving people's lives and making them better."

Jace couldn't help but to reach up and touch the harness. It looked so much the same, but different than the one he used.

"That right there inspired me to create a new form of light-weight mechanical instruments for disabled people."

Jace almost felt guilty for cracking a smile. "I still have the armor. It's in my backpack."

"Great! I can deconstruct and recycle the material. That stuff is expensive. But like I said, I am working on a new weave. The auto-fit function works a lot better after you snap it on."

Though Jace was impressed by the improvements, he took a step back and shook his head. "Those days are behind me."

"Likewise." Brian pushed the button, and the sliding door came together, then slid forward flush against the wall.

"Why did you show me this?"

Brian turned to Jace and gestured toward the car. "You were so happy to see the car again, I figured..."

Jace stared, speechless. Conflicting emotions took over, ranging from rage and regret to excitement and relief.

Brian closed the car door and put a hand on Jace's shoulder. "Come on. Let's go back inside. Oh, I'd like to show Erica my lab. Do you mind if she comes to work with me?"

When Jace snapped back into reality, he shrugged. "If she wants. I don't mind."

"I have so much to show her. Maybe we can figure out how to help Brittaney."

"Maybe." Jace shrugged.

"How about this..." Brian led Jace around the car to the door that went inside. "How about I take both Erica and Brittaney with me, and I'll get you directions to Maya's school. That way, you can meet her afterward, and you two can talk. Maybe go for a walk?"

Jace nodded, unable to contain a smile. A day with Maya. A

day he only dreamed would happen. There was no way he was going to skip out on that. "Yeah, that sounds good."

———

After school, Jace met up with Maya and spent a few hours together. They walked around the city and grabbed a bite to eat. During that time, Maya seemed defensive and withdrawn. She didn't engage much in his conversations, and Jace found himself quickly running out of things to talk about.

Eventually, dark clouds and shifting winds told Jace another storm approached. Not wanting Maya to get sick from being out in the rain, they took a cab back to Brian's before the sunset.

Rain began to fall before their ride pulled up to Brian's house. After exiting the cab, Maya paused and gestured at a neighbor's house.

"Oh, you still have that project with Ruth?"

Maya nodded.

"Will you be staying the night again?"

She shook her head.

"Okay. See you tonight then?"

She shrugged then went next door without even a look back.

Jace watched as she walked away. After a deep sigh, he went into the house, stood at the front window, and thought about his time with Maya. She was the same girl he knew, but something felt different. Maybe she hadn't forgiven him so easily. Maybe she needed more time.

A touch of Erica's hand on his shoulder popped him out of his long, deep thoughts. "Here. It's cold out." She held a cup of steaming tomato soup.

To Jace's astonishment, the sun had set, and rain began to fall. He blinked in confusion, taking the dish from Erica, and wondered how long he had been standing there. "Thanks." He took the soup and blew at its surface.

Erica stood beside him and stared out the window, looking more toward the sky than the rain. Perhaps she looked for lightning? "How's your back and chest?"

"I'm fine." He blew again at the soup.

"Fine?" She pressed her hands gently against his ribs to inspect his injuries. "How's the pain?"

"No pain."

She raised an eyebrow. "None?" She pressed a few more times. "Here?"

"Nope."

"Interesting." She lifted the back of his shirt and fidgeted with the bandages. "Huh..."

Jace peered behind him. "What?"

Erica planted her hands on his sides. "Stop moving. Let me know if this hurts." She pressed her hands and fingers at specific points on his back.

"No."

Her touch shifted to glide over his spine lightly. "And here?"

Jace smiled, flinching from the feeling, making a conscious effort not to spill his soup. "No. Stop it. That tickles."

After a few more presses, Jace finally felt a pulse of dull pain. He winched. When she released, he took a sip of his soup.

"Give me that." Erica took the soup from Jace mid-sip. "Bend over and touch your toes."

Curious on where she was leading to, he did as she asked, pressing his fingers against the floor.

"Any pain?"

"No."

Erica seemed surprised. "Really?"

Jace stood straight. "What's going on?"

"You've been on the mend for..." She handed Jace the soup, which he continued to sip, then counted on her fingers. "Four days? You should have been laid out for at least a month for your ribs. And maybe another four or five for your back."

Jace paused mid-sip. Was something wrong?

Erica didn't answer, but walked away, staring at the ground, mumbling to herself.

Knowing she got lost in thought often, Jace didn't press the issue. If it were anything important or serious, she'd let him know. So he turned his attention back to the rain and the steamy tomato soup.

Shadows of people rushing to get out of the rain briefly caught Jace's attention. With the sunset, he couldn't make out any details. But he wondered why people were out in this weather with no umbrella.

Brittaney came in from a back room. "Hey, Brian, I lost connection."

"Did you? Probably the storm. Hold on." Brian walked to the garage.

A minute later, Jace's ears caught the sound of a gentle hum. Perhaps Brian did something in the garage to fix whatever connection Brittaney needed. Except that the hum came from outside.

Brian came back into the room. "Hey, Brittaney—"

"Shh! Be quiet." Jace held up a hand as he focused his attention on the sound.

The hush apparently caught Erica's attention, and she walked beside Jace. "What's up?"

He barely heard her. He set the half-eaten cup of soup on the windowsill and went out the front door.

A boom of thunder.

The hum continued through the boom, getting louder and louder.

He stepped into the rain and stared at the darkness.

Lightning struck. The brief illumination was enough for Jace to catch a silhouette of a low-flying military-style aircraft.

Erica stepped on the porch with Brian beside her. "Jace?"

"No lights."

The aircraft flew by.

Jace's gut told him something was wrong. Though he hoped he was wrong, the best course would be to spring into action and explain later.

Jace rushed to the door and ushered everyone inside. "Brian, get Erica and Brittaney somewhere safe."

Erica turned and smacked Jace on the shoulder. "Don't push me. What's going on?"

The lights suddenly turned off.

That prompted Brian into action as the floor lights began to glow. "I have a power bank, so everything is on standby. But what's going on?"

"I think it's a raid."

Jace didn't wait to see anyone's reactions. He ran into the dimly lit garage and to the corner where his gear was. After pressing the button to open the compartment, he began to put on the armored shirt, which seemed far too big for his small frame.

Were they here for him? For Erica? With all of the Evolved in the area, maybe this was an execution. This seemed different. Something was off.

A moment later, Brian was by his side. "Jace, what are you doing? What's going on?"

"I don't know. I have a gut feeling that something bad is about to happen."

"That's it? A gut feeling?"

"Yeah. I don't know, Brian."

After a moment, Brian began unpacking things from the equipment closet.

"What are you doing?"

"Helping you get ready." Brian grabbed the next piece and tossed it to Jace.

"Which house is Ruth's?"

"Two down. The one with the big open yard."

Brian handed Jace a small box, which Jace opened before

giving a pause. He picked up the little earpiece next to the contact lens case and ran it between his fingers.

Brian continued to remove the armor from the mannequin. "Just like old times. Right?"

It was indeed like old times, and that was the problem. He didn't want to go back to how things were. He wanted to be something else. Something more. But if there was a raid going on, he needed to be prepared.

Coming to the conclusion that there wasn't any time for any more hesitation, Jace put in the earpiece and grabbed the last piece of armor. Brian activated something out of Jace's eye-shot. With a snap and a shake, the armor constricted around Jace's frame. He reached for the guns, but his hand froze mid-grab, then slightly shook. Even though every second mattered, he couldn't help but stare at the shine of the polished handguns. They were meant to kill and destroy. The guns were the tools used for countless deaths of men and women, young and old. Feeling the anxiety build inside himself, Jace clenched his hand and brought it to his chest.

"What's wrong?" Brian asked while he grabbed the reload harness.

"I can't..." Jace took a breath. "I can't take the guns."

Brian put the harness down. "So what are you going to do?"

He rubbed the back of his hand, feeling the tremor leaving his limb. Loud pops sounded from nearby. Gunshots. Jace sighed. "I guess I'll have to do this the old-fashioned way."

"Are you well enough for that?"

Jace dipped his finger into the contact lenses and leaned his head back. "I guess we will find out."

Brian whispered, "Holy smokes." He shook his head and gave a resigned sigh. "Okay, but you better be careful."

"You know me," Jace replied after putting in the second. He blinked forcefully a few times and rolled his eyes.

A loud ping hit the garage door. Brian and Jace crouched in

alarm.

"Get to a safe place."

Brian nodded. "At least take the backpack. I'll get things ready. Be careful."

Jace put on the backpack before going out a side door and charged into the rainy night, staying low and in the shadows as he made his way across the neighbor's yard. Since the contact lenses weren't activated, he could barely see, so he did his best to navigate through the darkness.

A flash of light caught Jace's eye in a house across the street. After incoherent shouts, gunshots sounded.

Jace felt the urge to charge in and save the civilians, but Maya came first. He had to find her and get her to safety.

Brian spoke over the earpiece. "I'm online."

Jace knew he didn't have to speak very loudly, and a whisper was more than enough for his voice to be clearly heard. "Brian, are Erica and Brittaney safe?"

"They're both with me. Activating lenses."

The pitch-black faded into gray hues as the contact lenses did their job. And to Jace's surprise, some color. Did Brian upgrade or adjust the contact lenses?

Erica's voice came from the earpiece, "That's pretty neat. Is that what he sees?"

"Yes," Brian replied. "Keep it down. Okay, Jace, you want to go to the next house over. Like I said, big, open property. You can't miss it."

"Got it." Jace scanned the area, seeing more than a few suspicious shapes around the neighborhood. And though he intended to be cautious and stealthy, the pop-pop of gunfire from the neighbor's house had Jace recklessly leap over the oversized fence and rush through the massive yard. He paused at the busted double-door and cautiously peeked inside. Two figures with assault rifles blocked his way, but their backs were turned, and they walked through the house.

Before Jace made his move, a shorter, glowing figure ran through the hall. The soldiers fired off a few rounds.

Jace couldn't wait any longer. He made his move, sneaking behind the rear guard and taking him out with deft actions. Just as the second turned to investigate, Jace met him with a flurry of precise attacks, laying him low.

The loud exclamation of Erica over the earpiece startled Jace. "Holy shit, what happened?"

Brittaney added, "That was amazing. I've never seen anything like it."

"I know. That's what he does," Brian said. "But be quiet. He can't hear anything with you talking."

A sound from Jace's right caught his attention. Two more armed intruders came in and fired their rifles. Jace rolled to the side, grabbing a flash grenade from the fallen soldier, and took cover behind the wall. Their bullets pierced the drywall. He pulled the pin and tossed it. A momentary burst of light and a sound of thunder briefly emanated from the room.

Jace made his final move. He charged in the room, pushing one soldier over a small coffee table with a bull rush, then jumped on his stomach for the finishing blow. The second fired his gun blindly in Jace's direction. Jace ducked, feeling a punch in his arm, then moved in. He swatted away the weapon and finished the fourth soldier with a few well-placed blows before flipping him on top of the third soldier. As he walked by, Jace kicked the guy across the jaw to silence the stirring.

Jace took a moment to listen to his surroundings and inspected his arm. The bullet tore his shirt near his arm but didn't get through the armor—a bruise, nothing more.

Brian gasped. "Jace, they're here."

Jace's heart pumped furiously, and fear and worry started to set in. "How many?"

"Just one."

"Just one?"

Erica said from a distance, "I have an idea. Stay here."

"Hey!" Brian exclaimed in a whisper. "Where are you going?"

Having her put herself in danger wasn't an option Jace wanted to consider. "Brian, stop her!"

He had to stop his search and save Erica. Jace was about to run back to Brian's when he turned to see the shorter glowing figure standing before him. Then a second came from around the corner. They stared at him as he stood over the four soldiers. Jace couldn't focus. His breath was blown from his lungs as the blood flowed from his face. Next to Ruth, who was out of the line of fire, stood Maya, glowing blue from the Fenrir Effect.

She, too, didn't move. Instead, she observed him, as if wondering what he would do next.

He tried to take a breath but found himself unable to breathe. Finally, once his body ran low on oxygen, his survival instincts kicked in, and he forced a gasp, allowing him to talk once more. "Are you okay?"

Maya slowly nodded.

Ruth asked, "Hey, what happened to these guys? Where's my dad?"

Maya pointed at Jace while he hesitated a moment longer to get his emotions under control. "Don't, uh... Don't worry about them." He cleared his throat. "It's dangerous here. We have to go."

Ruth didn't seem too thrilled at that notion. "I have to find my dad."

Maya crossed her arms in defiance.

He didn't have time for this. Erica was off doing some stupid plan, and now Maya wants him to find Ruth's father. Jace sighed and ran his fingers through his hair. "Fucking hell. Alright, let's hurry. Stay close and stay quiet."

Jace stayed low, shifting from shadow to shadow through the dark halls of the house.

Another soldier roamed the halls.

Jace signaled for the girls to stop. As soon as the soldier got close enough, Jace swatted away the rifle, flipped the soldier over his shoulder, then rolled on top of him to take him out with precise attacks.

When the coast was clear, Jace led the girls further into the house.

Finally, he made his way into the kitchen. Two bodies lay on the ground.

"Daddy!" Ruth ran over to the one in a dark suit and wrapped her arms around him. Maya followed a few steps from behind.

Jace approached, noticing the holes in the man's back, and the subtle glow that remained. After only a slight hesitation, he took the man's pulse. "He's still alive. Listen, I need you to find some things."

Maya smacked Ruth on the shoulder, snapping her out of her state of shock.

"Get me towels or whatever to stop the bleeding. Stay low and quiet."

Ruth seemed to be in a near-panic, but she nodded. Maya touched the gunshots with trembling hands.

"Maya," Jace urgently whispered.

She looked up.

"Did you hear what I said?"

Maya nodded.

"Go."

After a moment of hesitation from Maya, the girls left the kitchen.

Jace went over to the white-coated chef. He had no pulse. "Brian, are you there?"

A moment later, Brian replied, "Sorry, Jace. She went out of the room. I couldn't get her." He gasped. "Holy smokes, that's Nick!"

"Yes, I know. I need Erica. If you stopped her from whatever her stupid plan was... Never mind. Just get her on the com." Jace took out a boot knife and cut away the fabric of the suit.

"Oh, here she comes."

After a moment of shuffling, Erica said, "I'm here."

"I got someone with two gunshot wounds in the back."

"The one in the shoulder doesn't look fatal, but the one near the spine looks bad. According to the splatter patterns, I don't think the bullets went through. We need to stop the bleeding until we can get him to a hospital."

"I'm working on that, but I don't know how."

"You don't know how?" Erica mumbled something under her breath. "How on earth did you do what you did and survive without knowing how to mend a gunshot wound?"

Brian mumbled something in the background.

"Hold on. Brian said something about having some sort of cauterizing agent in your backpack."

Jace took off his backpack and started to sift through it. "What the hell did you do? You can't be going off on your own like that."

"Don't order me around, soldier boy."

"I'm not a soldier anymore."

Brian spoke from a distance. "That's it." Rushing footsteps and a clatter from the mic. "Put the needle in the wound and push the button."

Jace did as instructed and shot some white foam into the wounds.

"Jace, that guy is still here."

Before Jace could reply, Erica said, "Stay here."

"Damn it, Erica." Jace huffed and angrily squeezed the strange device Brian showed him. He couldn't waste any more time helping this guy. Not when Erica was bravely stupid like that.

The girls returned to the kitchen with a blanket and some towels, just as Jace put on his backpack.

"Ruth, prop his head up with some towels. Maya, cover him with a blanket. Keep him warm and stay out of sight until help arrives. I have to go."

Maya stood up and grabbed his shirt to stop him.

"Look, I can't stay here. Erica is in trouble, and I need to help her."

After a moment of hesitation, Maya nodded and released Jace's shirt.

"You two stay here and stay quiet. If anyone comes in, hide and don't make a sound." He put a comforting hand on Ruth's shoulder. "Take care of your dad. I'll come back when I can."

After a tearful sniffle, Ruth nodded.

Sirens sounded in the distance.

Jace couldn't linger any longer. He rushed out of the house and through the shadows toward Brian's house. Dark shapes of soldiers came from various hiding places and moved in a cover-retreat fashion.

The sirens from the law enforcement probably scared them off. Then he caught sight of something that made him gasp and hide behind some bushes.

The bulky shape of Roberts exited Brian's house.

Jace cursed to himself. How on earth did he find them?

Roberts stopped at the sidewalk and turned to look at Brian's.

For a moment, Jace considered engaging Roberts to draw him away. But he had no idea how to face an ironclad cyborg. All of his vital spots were protected by some armor or padding. He even withstood multiple shock grenades. There was no way he could face Roberts. Not without a weapon. That's when Jace considered going back and retrieving some armaments from the fallen soldiers. His fist couldn't punch through Roberts' armor, but maybe the rounds from an automatic rifle could.

A couple of heartbeats later, Roberts turned and hopped into his oversized SUV, and drove off.

Jace gave a deep sigh of relief and eyed the vehicle as it turned a corner. The siege was over. Or was this a retrieval mission? Perhaps an execution?

Flashing lights came from over neighboring houses as aero-vehicles sped into the action. Like always, a little too late.

CHAPTER NINE

ERICA TALKED WITH A GROUP OF LAW ENFORCEMENT OFFICERS AND medical personnel while Jace stood on the porch with everyone else—Brian, Brittaney, Ruth, and Maya. He hadn't gotten a chance to talk with her about the stupid actions that put her in grave danger, even if it may have played a part in The Order's retreat.

Brian had his arm on Ruth's shoulder to comfort her during her time of need. She cried as paramedics lifted her father into the back of an aero-ambulance. Like the amazing sister she was, Maya hugged Ruth so she could cry on her shoulder.

Brittaney didn't seem too pleased with the situation. "How on earth can these people get away with murder?"

Knowing any discussion would be in ear-shot of Ruth, Jace motioned for Brittaney to pause before leading her to the side. "It's hard to explain."

"No, it's impossible." Brittaney groaned before leaning against the porch railing. "I mean, look at this. They came in with guns blazing."

Though Jace wanted to reply, all he could think about were his previous missions, where he stormed towns and villages with guns blazing. Still, this seemed different. Now that The Order knew he was alive, were they after him again?

"First, it's my house. Now it's this neighborhood." Brittaney slapped the baluster. "There has to be something we can do." She nodded. "You know what? That's what I'm going to do."

"What do you mean?"

"I'm going to start building a case against The Order." She turned to face Jace. "Will you help me?"

Jace gestured to himself. "Me? What can I do?"

"I need evidence. You know all about them. Right?"

"I..." Jace sighed, then he looked back to the ambulance as it lifted from the ground. Once again, The Order's hunt for him put others in harm's way. They'll stop at nothing to get what they want, and apparently, they want him dead. Or arrested. Or what? What do they want?

Jace decided Brittaney was right. The Order must be stopped. If he was a few seconds later, Maya might have gotten shot, all because of her glow. Resolve burned in his chest once more, a feeling Jace thought had died long ago. "Yeah, I'll help." He turned to Brian to get his attention. "Hey, you got a minute?"

Brian nodded. "Sure." He knelt and talked with Maya and Ruth for a moment before approaching.

Brittaney put a hand on Jace's shoulder and whispered, "What are you doing?"

"Trust me." Jace patted her hand.

Brian adjusted his glasses and gave a weak smile. Though he tried to hide it, Brian's eyes and the quivering voice told Jace he was on the brink of crying. "What's up?"

"I need your help." Jace gazed at the body bags in the middle of the road. "To stop this from happening again."

Brian followed Jace's gaze. He took a deep breath, as if to steel his nerves.

"Brittaney wants me to get evidence against The Order so she can build a case, and we need your help with this fight."

Brian shook his head and sighed. "I don't know, Jace."

"This can't go on," Brittaney said as she gestured toward the sorrow in front of them. "I know they have police and politicians in their pocket, but if we can get the public on our side, we can stand up to them."

Brian didn't reply.

Jace said, "You told me I have to be the good guy to get Maya back." He turned to look at Brian, who continued to stare at the street. "And if I wanted your help, I needed to tell you the good I'm fighting for. Well, this is it."

Brittaney stepped between them and put a hand on Brian's shoulder. "And he needs your help. *I* need your help."

After a moment, Brian nodded. He licked his lips with an angry frown and sniffed. "Okay. Let's get these suckers." He turned to face Jace and Brittaney and adjusted his glasses. "What do you need?"

"Well..." Jace peeked behind Brian's shoulder to make sure the girls were out of hearing range. "I'm not killing anymore."

Brittaney quickly turned around. "Wait, you've killed people before?"

Jace gave a solemn nod, and he looked away in shame. "Yeah. Yeah, I have." He watched as Erica seemed to have finished her conversation with the emergency officials and began to approach.

Brian nodded. "Okay, I have some ideas. Same hardware?"

"The guns?" Jace turned to face Brian. He rubbed his fingers together, wondering if he could mentally carry his chrome-plated instruments of death.

"I could come up with some different types of ammo."

"That could work." Jace gestured to the neighbor's house. "And Brittaney, we have those soldiers. That's a start."

"Nope," Erica said once she got close. "They're gone."

Brittaney shot her a glare. "What do you mean gone?"

"They're not there." Erica looked everyone over for a moment. "Mr. York is in critical condition." She looked at Brian. "But that formula you made may have saved his life."

That made Brian give a slight smile.

"It's too soon to know, though." Erica turned to face Jace. "What's going on?"

Now that he had her attention, it was time to get some answers. "First, what were you thinking back there? I had everything handled."

"Hold your shit, soldier boy." Erica crossed her arms in a defensive pose. "Now isn't the time for your selfish antics."

"*My* selfish antics?"

"Yeah. I'm the one that authorized the police to move in."

Brittaney seemed to find that reply as odd as Jace did. "What do you mean?"

"I used my credentials to authorize their deployment. So yeah, I saved everyone." Erica glared at Jace. "So next time, maybe be thankful instead of spiteful. You never know who will do your job for you." She turned and stormed off.

Brittaney, Jace, and Brian stood in awkward silence for a long moment before Ruth and Maya walked up.

"Hey, Ruth..." Brian cleared his throat. "Uh, when is your mother due back in the country?"

"Next month."

"Alright." He gestured toward the aero-car parked beside his house. "Come on. Let's go to the hospital to see your dad."

Ruth grabbed Maya's hand. "Can she come with me?"

"I don't see why not." Brian turned to Jace. "What do you think?"

"Me? Uh..." Jace ran his fingers through his hair. "I guess?"

Brian faced the girls. "Okay, you two go get your things, and we'll head out."

Ruth nodded, and the girls ran off.

"Hey, Brian," Brittaney said as she watched the girls speed away. "Do you think it's okay to leave them alone right now?"

"I think so." Brian turned to watch the girls. "Why not?"

"I'm going to go with them to make sure they're alright. Also, I'm going to stay behind to start building my case."

Before she took a step, Jace stopped her. "Hold on. I want to make a couple of things clear." When he had their attention, Jace continued, "If we're going to pick a fight with The Order, know that they're very, very dangerous. This could easily get us all killed." He glanced at Brittaney and Brian to see if they objected. Though their expressions showed concern at that revelation, they didn't speak up. "And if we do start a fight with The Order, it's just us three. I don't want Maya or Erica or anyone else to know about it or get involved. It's too dangerous. Agreed?"

After a moment of hesitation, Brian nodded. "You got it, buddy."

"Same here." Brittaney put a hand on both Jace and Brian's shoulder.

Like a triangle of trust, everyone put a hand on each other's shoulder and stared at each other for a long moment, reflecting in contemplative silence. Then Brian and Brittaney split up, leaving Jace on the porch alone to watch the flashing lights of a dozen emergency vehicles in the street.

———

Many hours went by while everyone sat in the hospital waiting room. Maya leaned against Jace while Ruth slept on her shoulder. Erica was with some doctors while Brian sat in a chair scribbling on a notepad.

Jace adjusted his shoulder when Erica approached with a doctor beside her. Maya stirred and woke up Ruth. She pointed to

Brian, who then stood and walked over to them. When Jace moved to stand, Erica held out a hand to stop him. They talked for a moment, then took Brian with them.

A half an hour later, Brian and Erica entered the waiting room. Brian knelt in front of Ruth and put a hand on her shoulder. "Your dad will be okay."

Ruth gave an exhilarated exhale, and she hugged him.

Brian looked at Jace. "He's critical, but stable, and he wants to see you."

"Me?" Jace pointed to himself.

Brian nodded. "Erica will show you the way."

Jace's eyes went from Brian to his glaring and angry girlfriend. He followed as she led in gloomy silence.

A nurse in a white gown and mask stood next to Nick York, who laid in a bed with tubes and wires attached to various parts of his body. When the sliding glass door slid open, machines beeped in unsynchronized rhythm, and a subtle scent of bleach intruded his nostrils.

As soon as Nick's eyes opened, a machine's beeping sped up.

The healthcare worker held his hand. "Take a deep breath, Mr. York. I can't let you see him unless you get your heart rate down."

Nick gave a weak nod. Slowly, the beeping returned to normal.

"Good. I'll be monitoring your vitals from outside." The nurse approached Jace. "We normally don't allow non-relatives to visit in the ICU, but Mr. York insisted he sees you. I'll give you a few minutes, then you'll have to go."

Jace nodded.

The nurse walked out of the room, closing the sliding glass door behind her.

Jace looked around, searching for any clues on what was going on. "You wanted to see me?"

Nick's voice, coupled with his smooth and foreign accent, sounded hoarse and weak, but the emotion behind his words spoke of venomous resolve. "I heard about you. Ghost. Vengeful Spirit." Nick winced in pain as the machines beeped faster. Jace took a half-step forward with an outreached hand, wondering what he should do. A few moments later, the sounds stabilized, with Nick visibly relaxing. "You are Death, leaving nothing in your wake but destruction and despair."

"Don't assume to know me."

"Oh, but I do. I do know you." Nick pushed a button on his bed. The mattress bent with a whir, allowing him to sit up. "I do know you. You have killed many innocent people, some of whom were good friends of mine. I spent a lot of money trying to find you. And when you show up, death followed."

Xin was right. Evolved did hunt him.

Jace shook his head. "No. This wasn't my fault."

"Wasn't it?" The monitor beeps sped up. "Because of you, my daughter could have been killed."

If The Order was after him, then Nick wasn't wrong. After considering that thought, Jace looked away in shame and nodded. "Maybe it was my fault. But I'm done with them. I'm done with that life and that war."

That answer seemed to slow the beeping. "And what of your crimes?"

"My crimes..." Memories flashed in Jace's mind. Cries of mercy echoed in his ears, and screams of sorrow shot through his skull. And the mental image of a child came to mind. A child that glowed blue. A child that he executed in his mother's arms.

Jace took a quivering breath and fought back the tears of misery and guilt. Maybe he should stop running. Instead of fighting The Order, he should give himself up to the Evolved. Perhaps that would be the best. If they executed him for his crimes, at least his friends would be safe, instead of putting them in danger with their upcoming fight.

He steeled his resolve with that decision. "If you want me to stand trial, I'll stand trial. But know this..." Jace walked up next to

Nick. "I may be done with their war, but *my* war against them is far from over. In fact, it's just getting started."

"*Your* war?"

Jace nodded. "They used me. Lied to me. They're lying to the world, and I'm going to put a stop to it."

Nick gave a brief, raspy laugh. "You're fighting against them?"

"You're damn right I am."

"Why? Why would the Spirit of Sorrow want to help us? Why now?"

"Because it's the right thing to do. Because I don't want another night like tonight to happen ever again. And because if I don't, then The Order will continue their slaughter of innocent people."

Nick gave another raspy laugh. "And what could one person do? How could you fight back?"

"We're working on it. Maybe get evidence against them or something."

A knock came from the sliding glass window. Jace looked back to see the nurse tap her watch and indicated "one minute" with a point of a finger.

Jace nodded in reply and turned back to Nick. "So what'll it be, Mr. York? Stand trial and be executed, or fight back and probably die trying to help?"

Nick didn't reply for many heartbeats. Instead, he stared hard at Jace, as if visually assessing and judging him. "Mr. McGuen told me about you. And Maya trusts you. If Maya trusts you, I'll trust you...for now."

The sliding glass door opened. "Time's up."

Jace stared at Nick for a moment longer, nodded, then turned to leave. Everyone chose war. That was fine with him.

As he turned the final corner back to the waiting room, Jace paused and stared at Maya. For a moment, his resolve faltered. After all this time looking for her, he was going to leave her again. He was going to break another promise and put himself in harm's way. He hadn't changed. And now she was in more danger than before. For that moment, he felt selfish and stupid.

He shook his head as another train of thought came boring through. This wasn't about him. It was about Maya and her safety. It was about Brian and Erica. It was about Brittaney. This war wasn't about him. It was about humanity, and he was going to fight to save it.

CHAPTER TEN

THE NEXT COUPLE OF WEEKS WERE BUSY FOR EVERYONE. ERICA GOT A job at a hospital, a different one from where Nick York stayed, and spent most of her time working. In between rebuilding the neighborhood, Brian repaired and reinforced the house after being assaulted. Ruth, never leaving Maya's side, stayed with her father while he recovered from his injuries. Brian also worked on non-lethal armaments and developed a system to track The Order's movements, which has greatly increased since the initial assault. From there, it was Jace's job to disrupt their activities, foil missions, and gather evidence for Brittaney, who took some test to practice law in the new region and rented out a small office in the city so she could conduct her work in private. In addition, it allowed her to research The Order apart from everyone as not to draw any unwanted attention to Brian's house.

The jobs Jace did were relatively small - stop a delivery, acquire key components, perform reconnaissance or stop assassination of targets, and intercepting and incapacitating squads for questioning. Even though members were put in jail by some vigilante vagrant, they would soon be released on the authority of some high government official, or some ranking law enforcement officer.

That meant getting information from members on the spot.

After interrogating a scout, Jace learned some disturbing information—The Order was taking kids.

At first, the news of missing children was a sad but common occurrence. Maybe they were kidnapped for human trafficking or a couple who separated and took their kid for love or revenge, or whatever. But this was different. This was The Order. Because of that simple fact, Jace began to worry.

He couldn't interrogate the scout any further due to reinforcements arriving, but the news put him on edge, and he fled the area.

Jace walked into Brian's house emotionally down and concerned. Brittaney would be back soon. Then he, Brittaney, and Brian could finally talk, and figure out their next step.

He really wanted to take a shower to kill time and relax, but it sounded like Ruth occupied the bathroom.

The house was too damn small.

Frustrated, Jace grabbed a bottle of water and an apple and sat on the couch. Since Erica was at work for a few more hours, assuming she didn't stay to work overtime, Jace considered saying hello to Maya.

That's when Brian walked up after entering from the garage. "Hey, Jace. Guess what?"

At first, Jace thought Brian had another job, or some information pertaining to The Order. Which was good because Jace wanted to discuss his findings. However, the lack of urgency and a strange look in his eye dashed his hopes. That grim discussion would have to wait.

He sighed. "What?"

"The dam just got the approval for the hydropower design." Brian sat excitedly across from Jace. "Not only will it be ready to go soon, but they're also going to use some of my designs for the machines that—"

Another one of his techno-babble rants. Jace stopped paying attention and leaned his head back to stare at the ceiling, taking a bite from the apple. He focused on the discovery. Why would The Order be taking kids? He never saw a mission on the job board that involved kidnapping. He wondered if he should ask Erica if she knew but decided against it. She couldn't be involved. So he decided he needed to talk to Brian and Brittaney first.

"...and was bought by a private company. I had a meeting with their CEOs and—"

"Okay, I get it." Jace raised a hand. "Listen, there's something I need to talk to you about." Jace sat forward. "It's something I learned on the job."

That seemed to get Brian's attention away from his ramble as his expression went from passion and excitement to stern and serious. "Sure, Jace. What's up?"

"So I took out the small surveillance crew last night. After you hung up or whatever, I had a talk with one of the soldiers." Jace shuffled forward a little. "He said The Order was behind the kidnappings."

Brian's eyes went wide. "Holy smokes. Really?"

"Well, not all of them. But they're taking kids. Teens. I don't know why."

"That is strange." Brian put his chin in his hand and stroked his stubble of a beard. "That reminds me of that gang from SOC."

"What?"

"That gang. The SOC-G."

Jace hadn't thought about that in a long time. "What about it?"

"Do you think... What if that gang was a part of The Order?"

"That's ridiculous." Jace shook his head. Then he took a moment to seriously consider it. The Order summoned monsters to kill innocent people to cause fear. "Or is it?"

Brian said precisely what Jace thought. "What if The Order

was the gang, and they were collecting people back then? What if you stopped them, not the gang? I mean, when I looked you up a while back, I found your story about how you saved those girls, but nothing else about the gang."

"Would that stuff even be made to the public?"

Brian nodded. "There was nothing. Not even arrest records."

Jace shook his head. "Figures. So how are the guns coming along?"

Brian didn't reply. Instead, his eyes were fixed behind Jace's shoulder.

Jace turned to see what Brian looked at. Maya stood near the hallway, staring. Sweat soaked her hair, as if she got back from a run...from her bedroom? "Oh. Hey." Jace had to change the subject. "How is school going?"

Maya rolled her eyes and went back to her room.

"Damn." Jace turned to Brian. "How much do you think she heard?"

"I don't know."

Jace sighed, then peeked over his shoulder towards the hall. "I'm going to go talk to her." He went to her room and cracked open the door. She sat on the floor, doing sit-ups, taking gasping breaths between each rep. Jace blinked for a minute, wondering how long she had been doing this. He decided to talk to her another time and quietly shut the door behind him.

———

A couple of days later, Jace sat at the kitchen table when Maya and Ruth came out of her bedroom. Perhaps this was a good time to talk with Maya.

"Hey, I'm going for a run in a bit. You want to join me?"

Maya glanced at Ruth, who shrugged in reply. Then her gaze returned to Jace, and she nodded.

Finally getting a chance to talk with Maya alone, Jace smiled and stood up. "Great. I'll drive us to the park, and we can take the trail. How does fifteen minutes sound?"

She nodded and returned to her room.

"A run?" Ruth smirked and shook her head.

Jace returned the smirk. "We went for walks all the time. Why not a run?"

"It's cool." Ruth shrugged.

Jace went to the garage and prepared the car. He hadn't planned on going for a run, but he wasn't going to pass up the opportunity. He got some bottles of water ready and opened the garage door.

Ruth came into the garage. "Hey, Mr. J., why would Mr. McGuen let you drive his car? Even he doesn't drive it."

"Well..." Jace ran his fingers through his hair, wondering how he could explain his situation. "It's actually my car."

"But you don't work."

"No. I did, though. And I made some decent cash, too."

"You mind if I tag along?"

Though Jace wanted to curse, he kept it inside his mind. "I didn't know you jogged."

Ruth shook her head. "Oh, no. I hate running. Hurts my feet. But I figured I could hang out at the park while you two went for your jog."

"Well, I don't see why not."

Erica pulled up to the sidewalk with her own vehicle. She approached and gave Jace a little hug and a kiss on the cheek.

"Hey, we're going for a run. You want to come with?" Though he and Erica hardly had any time together ever since they arrived at Brian's, he regretted asking her to join them. He needed this alone-time with Maya. Next time, he promised himself. Next time he'd try to do something with her.

"I'm too tired." She went to the door. "You two have fun, though."

After a moment alone with Ruth, Jace leaned against the blue sports car. "I heard your father will be released from the hospital soon."

Ruth nodded. "Monday, just in time to meet my mother at the airport. The construction in the house is almost done, so we'll be able to move back in."

"The whole neighborhood is doing a lot. What are the plans for your place?"

"I don't know." She shrugged. "I haven't been able to see my dad, and I haven't been allowed back into the house since." She leaned heavily against the car, putting her arms on the hood with crossed wrists. "You think Maya will be able to come over?"

"To your place?"

"I think it would be safer."

Jace eyed her for a moment. "What do you mean? She's safe here."

Yeah, but..." Ruth shuffled nervously.

That's when he figured it out. It wasn't about Maya's safety, but her herself feeling safe. "Tell you what, if Maya wants, she can stay with you as long as you'd like."

That made Ruth smile. "Thanks, Mr. J.."

The door opened, and Maya came out in her hoodie, sweatpants, and sneakers. Jace smiled and shook his head. Even when going for a run, she wore her hoodie. "You girls ready?"

———

The day finally came when the hospital released Nick York. Jace didn't join Brian, Ruth, and Maya to pick him up. Not after the tense conversation they had in the hospital after he was shot. He instead decided to focus on Erica.

She looked sexy in her slacks and blouse. The tight clothes made her curves stand out, which made Jace a bit excited.

As she went into the garage, Jace followed, wrapping her in a hug, and kissed her neck while she waited for the garage door to open. "Hey, we haven't had much time together for weeks. Why don't you call out today? You and me, a nice evening on the beach."

"I can't." Erica half-pulled away, but Jace held firm.

"Sure you can. Just pick up the phone and—"

"I said I can't." She tugged, breaking from Jace's hold.

Jace stared hard at her, doing his best to hold back his sudden burst of frustration.

"Look, I..." Erica sighed. "I have been so busy with work that..." She didn't finish her train of thought. Instead, she went inside, leaving Jace in the garage.

Jace huffed and leaned against his car. After a moment to control his anger, he stared at the morning sun. The only time he saw her was when she got home from work. Even then, all she would do is go to sleep. They never had time together.

A minute later, Erica returned to the garage. She wasn't dressed in her slacks and blouse, but something a little more casual—a sundress and a tight top. "Tell you what..." She grinned and walked over to him with swaying hips and a hand behind her back. "I'll take the day off if you give me some blood." She lifted her hand to show a syringe.

Jace stared at the needle but was immediately distracted with Erica getting close. His heart pumped furiously as her vanilla scent overtook his rational senses. He didn't ask what the blood was for. At that moment, he didn't care. He kissed her passionately, their lips locking and tongues intertwining in each other's mouths. He picked her up and put her on the car hood.

At that moment, he would have done anything for Erica. What was a vial of blood? It didn't matter. All that mattered was that moment, of their passion growing heavier on the car hood, of her teeth biting down on his shoulder while she took off his jacket. All that mattered was her.

CHAPTER ELEVEN

WHITE STEAM PLUMES ESCAPED JACE'S LIPS AS HE LAID PRONE ON A rooftop in the cold rain. Under cover of night, he knew he was nearly invisible. Still, he kept his eyes open, scanning the scene below while he cautiously peeked his head over the side of the building.

Unlike his previous jobs in the past weeks, this would be the first time Jace would face off against an officer from The Order. If anyone had answers on why The Order was taking children, it would be an officer.

Finally, Brian spoke over the earpiece, indicating he was online and ready. "You there?"

"Yeah." Jace rubbed his eye. "I can't see anything in this damn rain."

"Hang in there. It's almost midnight. According to my findings, he should be there soon."

Jace brought the binoculars up with one hand and reached back to scratch a pinch in his back from the reload harness with the other. He slightly adjusted his posture to make the guns a little more comfortable. For a moment, he grew concerned about the prototype ammo Brian had supplied him. Though he remained unsure about using guns in non-lethal combat, Brian assured him that the ammo would prove vital for restraint and utility. For a moment, he considered the reload harness and the thumb toggle for the ammo types. "Remind me..." He wiped more rain from his face. "One for regular, two for rubber, three for sticky?"

"One for rubber bearings," Brian corrected. "Two for sticky, three for explosive."

"Explosive?" He lowered the binoculars while the hand that itched his back reflexively shifted away from the guns. "I thought you said non-lethal."

"I figured you could use them for utility over combat. What if you needed to open a locked door? Or found yourself trapped in a room with no exit?"

Brian had a point. "Maybe some grenade rather than a high-powered explosive device?"

"I'm already planning on some disposable throwing devices, but you're already going over your budget. I'm mostly working off of supplies we already have."

Jace cursed to himself. Getting back into the fight sucked a lot out of his savings. And unlike when he worked for The Order, everything he did was done out of his pocket. If he ran out of money, how long could he keep up the fight?

"Is that him?" Brian asked, breaking Jace out of his contemplation.

"Where?" Jace brought the binoculars up.

"Long coat and umbrella."

"That describes a bunch of them." Jace scanned the area, going from person to person.

"There. Stop. The one holding the briefcase."

Jace's magnified gaze settled on the target figure. Because of the rain and the umbrella, he couldn't be sure if it was indeed his target. "It's tough to say. I can't make out any details."

"I'm sure."

That was enough for Jace. Seeing the figure enter a multi-story building across the street, he scooted back to get out of sight, then ran toward the alleyway while putting his gear away. Once he put on his backpack, he leaped off the side, letting himself freefall a bit before grabbing a ledge a story below. Then he released, allowing himself to once again freefall for a moment before kicking himself away from the wall. He grinded his boots against the opposite wall before leaping once more to slow his descent. He tucked in his shoulder and rolled on the ground on impact, returning to his feet just at the building's corner.

Jace peeked down the street toward where he last saw his target. Not seeing the man with the briefcase, Jace started his way across the street. "Did you find out where he was heading?"

"Three-story building to the left."

He went to the aforementioned structure and reached for the door. "Electronic lock." Jace took a step back to kick the door open when Brian stopped him over the earpiece.

"Wait! Grab the card I showed you."

Jace rolled his eyes and took out the small card from his bag.

"Put it against the sensor unit." Keyboard tapping sounds came from the earpiece. "And... there."

The sensor beeped, and the door clicked. Jace entered the building, closing the door behind him while putting his gear away. "Not bad. I thought I'd have to break the thing down."

"Not while I'm around."

Once inside the building, Jace looked to the ground to find signs of pooled water where the umbrella was shaken dry. His eyes followed the trail that led across the lobby toward a door that led to some stairs.

Seeing the trail of his target, Jace took a deep breath to calm his nerves. It was time to get serious. "Go-time."

"Got it."

Jace went toward the door and entered the stairwell. Then he listened, hearing the faint echoes of footsteps and sloshing clothes over the tapping of the rain. Jace turned the corner and quietly made his way up the stairs, two steps at a time.

When Jace got to the first-floor landing, he caught sight of his target. Or at least it was the figure he saw on the street.

Before Jace made another step, the figure stopped and slightly turned toward him, as if to peer stealthily from over his shoulder. Jace paused, knowing the tapping of the rain helped hide his breaths. When he moved toward the railing to look down, Jace shifted to the wall to stay out of sight. He knelt, looking close enough to the ledge to see the figure's lower body.

The figure stood there, as if looking down the stairwell. No one moved.

For a moment, Jace thought he was caught. Perhaps he wasn't as quiet as he used to be, or he was spotted at some point. All he could do was be patient and hope his dripping clothes didn't give away his position. Like many of his missions, the element of surprise was always his biggest advantage.

The figure shifted a little, then turned to continue up the stairs.

Jace had to suppress his relieved sigh. After a couple of seconds, he continued his pursuit, moving quickly and quietly to catch up to his target.

When he got to the third floor, the figure was gone. Either he hid, or he exited the stairwell.

Just as Jace went to the door, a blur of an object swung out wide toward his head. He ducked and grabbed the swinging briefcase and stepped back from a follow-up kick before sidestepping a thrust from the folded umbrella.

While Jace held firm, the figure struggled to regain control of the briefcase. When Jace had ample footing, he pulled on the briefcase, and the figure came from the shadows as the two collided chest-to-chest against the briefcase.

Jace grinned when he recognized the figure's greased, brushed-back hair and short, groomed beard. "Hey, Freddy."

Freddy's brown eyes stared as his face crumpled in confusion. "Is that you, Jace?"

"So you do remember me."

Freddy tried to rip the briefcase from Jace's hands. Jace kicked Freddy in the gut as he let go of the briefcase. Freddy took a couple of steps back but remained in balance.

"I never expected to see you again." Freddy took a threatening step forward. "And it's Sir Fredrick."

"Sir?" Jace shrugged. "They're promoting anyone these days."

Freddy lunged forward with his umbrella. Jace took a step back. Something shiny suddenly extruded from the tip. Seeing the bladed object for what it was, Jace leaped back, pressing his hip against the handrail.

A couple of more thrusts, high and low, had Jace press his back harder against the rail. Though his planted hands allowed him to lift his legs to avoid swings and jabs, one wrong move could send him tumbling over the side.

When Jace found an opening to counter-attack, the umbrella flopped open, stopping any of his attacks from getting through. He kicked at the umbrella, hoping to bend the frame to make a side fold in. Instead of hitting a soft structure, his boot collided with a seemingly solid object, like a brick wall.

Jace was on the defensive. The umbrella stopped him from effectively moving, but he had to dodge the oncoming slashes and jabs from the blade that protruded from the umbrella. All while making sure he didn't fall off the ledge.

After a particularly close lunge that tore his coat, going off the ledge wasn't a bad idea.

Jace used the umbrella as a springboard and kicked himself up and over the handrail. Instead of plummeting three stories down, Jace gripped the railing and swung himself under it, kicking through the balusters and under the umbrella shield. Seeing an opportunity to strike, Jace brought his foot up and kicked Freddy's hand, smashing his fingers. Jace kicked again, this time low, but Freddy lifted his leg and took a step back.

With a click, the umbrella closed in on itself, and Freddy lunged down with the spear-like object. Jace rolled to the side, barely dodging the tip as it plunged into the floor.

Jace swung around and kicked the umbrella before Freddy could get it free. The blade snapped on the impact, and Freddy took a few steps back to regain his balance.

With the reprieve, Jace stood, and the two stared at each other only a few paces away.

Jace scanned Freddy, looking for an opening he could use to get an advantage. But that damn umbrella kept getting in the way. "Where's your emblem, Freddy? Are you so green, you haven't gotten one yet?"

Freddy stood in a balanced combative stance, continuing to use the umbrella as his primary weapon. "I've heard stories about your missions. I always wondered if they were exaggerated, or even made up."

"Funny, I—" A loud explosion and a hard hit in Jace's chest. He let out a grunt, took a staggering step back, then tumbled down the stairs. Finally, he crashed against a wall on the landing below.

His chest pulsed a dull pain. He looked down at his torn shirt, assessing the damage from the sudden hit. That's when he recognized the patterns. A sense of relief washed over him when he realized Brian's armor held up against such a blast.

Jace sat up and coughed. "A shotgun in the umbrella? That's kind of cheap." As he got to his feet, Jace looked up to see Fredrick approach the stairway with the umbrella pointed forward. Jace leaped to the side after another deafening blast. The handrail blew apart. "Smart." Another blast from above. A hole formed on the floor. "Now the police will be called."

Being at a disadvantage, Jace reached back and grabbed his guns, but he hesitated. He couldn't draw them, though. Not yet. A sense of anxiety brewed in Jace's chest as his fingers gripped his tools of death. Though he trusted Brian, Jace had to be sure. "Brian, non-lethal. Right?"

"Non-lethal."

Feeling assured, Jace punched through his anxiety and drew his guns.

Freddy blew another hole in the floor.

Jace took a step and aimed. He had a clear shot, but he found himself instinctively hesitating. That was enough for Freddy to open the umbrella.

Brian's words echoed in his mind. "Non-lethal."

Jace took a breath and squeezed the trigger. As soon as the explosion in his hand sounded, memories of bloodshed and mayhem swam in his mind. The bullet hit the umbrella and seemed to have ricocheted to hit the ceiling. Along with the drywall from a small hole, Jace heard the metal bearings hit the floor.

Jace took cover and breathed in deep. Non-lethal, just like Brian had promised.

"I heard you used two handguns." Freddy fired his umbrella. Missed.

Jace stepped out of his cover and squeezed off a few rounds from his other gun. The bullets impacted the umbrella surface, exploding into a strange white foam.

"Too bad your bullets can't get through." Freddy fired again before Jace could return to his cover, blowing the handrail apart. Splinters shot out, a few sticking into Jace's cheek.

"Jace," Brian said over the com. "Police are on their way. Hurry it up."

With Jace's confidence growing, he stepped out of his cover and began to walk around the stairway while the two exchanged fire. Though he felt a couple of punches on his side and leg, Jace covered the baluster and umbrella with the white foam while hitting the wall and ceiling with the ball bearings.

After firing off a few rounds from each gun, Jace put them in the harness, hearing the spring click of them being reloaded. He calmly went up the stairs as Freddy tugged and pulled at the umbrella, which was stuck against the handrail.

Freddy let out a sigh of frustration. "Brilliant!" He turned to face Jace when he stopped four paces away. "Where are your guns?"

Jace half-shrugged. "Don't need them."

Freddy grinned. "Fine. The old-fashioned way." He leaped toward Jace, arm back to give a hefty punch, but his feet slipped upon landing, and he tumbled to the ground. Jace sidestepped and watched Freddy tumble down the stairs, eventually landing where Jace did when he was shot in the chest. Unlike Jace's fall, Freddy didn't seem nearly as graceful, and a couple of limbs looked a little out-of-place.

Jace picked up the briefcase and walked down the stairs, gently kicked Freddy so he lay on his back, set the briefcase on his chest, then sat on it. "Freddy, Freddy, Freddy. I have a couple of questions for you. What does The Order want with a bunch of kids?"

Freddy struggled, even so far as throwing a weak and ineffective punch toward Jace. Jace slapped aside the pathetic attack. "Let's try this again." He stomped hard on a crippled hand.

After a struggled groan, Freddy grimaced and spat at Jace. "Just you wait til I get my support gear."

"I'll keep that in mind." Jace ground his foot against the crippled hand, hearing popping and cracking from the bones. "The Order. The kids. Talk."

"Jace," Brian said over the com. "Time's up. Police are outside."

"Shit." Jace looked down the stairway just as he heard the door open. He searched Freddy, ripping off his emblem around his neck, stood up, and kicked Freddy across the jaw to knock him out. Then he quietly made his way upstairs with the briefcase.

When Jace got to the highest floor, he peered down the stairwell toward Freddy while the police surrounded him, putting him in handcuffs. Another police officer continued, but visibly lost his footing from the ball bearings, and used the umbrella as a handhold. It shot off another round, blowing a hole into the wall.

Not wanting anyone to get hurt, Jace called out, "Watch your step. And that concealed shotgun is his."

"Who said that?" a police officer called from below. "Stay where you are."

But Jace already made his way to the roof, where he would climb down to make his way to his car. Though Freddy wasn't able to answer any questions, hopefully important information was locked in the briefcase.

CHAPTER TWELVE

BRIAN WAITED FOR JACE IN THE GARAGE WHEN HE PULLED UP IN HIS exotic blue car. When he got out, Brian couldn't help but gasp.

"Holy smokes, Jace." He inspected the torn-up clothes and the armor underneath. "I'm glad this worked."

"So am I." Jace reached into the car and grabbed the briefcase he took from Freddy. "Here. See what this is all about." He handed it to Brian, then went to the trunk of the car.

Brian tried to open it. "It's locked."

"A puzzle I'm sure you can handle." Jace gathered his bags. "The ammo seems to work nicely. That white, sticky stuff, what is it?"

"Without going into detail?"

Jace closed the trunk and nodded.

"I got the inspiration from insulation caulk and spider webs. Be careful because it's water-soluble."

"It's what?"

"Dissolves in water."

"Oh. Good to know. You could have just said that." Jace set his gear down on the workbench and began unpacking, putting stuff away in the cubby. "I want to know what Freddy was transporting. How long do you think it'll take to figure out what's in there?"

"I have to open it first." Brian set the briefcase next to Jace's bag on the workbench. "This is a nice briefcase. It could take a couple of hours to get it open."

Jace didn't want to wait a couple of hours. After taking off the armored shirt, Jace grabbed a hammer and smashed the lock. Brian flinched and leaped back as Jace hit it again and again. Eventually, the lock popped open. "Done."

"Holy smokes, Jace. You didn't need to do that."

"Nah." He put the hammer back. "But it worked. Didn't it?"

"You could have damaged something inside it. And what if it was trapped?"

Jace briefly paused. He hadn't thought about the trap part.

Brian scoffed and shook his head. When he opened the briefcase, his eyes lit up. "A computer!"

"Great." Jace finished putting his stuff away and slung his backpack over a shoulder. "Then you're the right person to look into it." He walked by and patted Brian on the back. "Let me know and see if Brittaney could use any of that stuff."

Brian adjusted his glasses while he continued to stare at the computer. " Sure thing."

―――――

After Jace's workout the next morning, he got out of the shower and saw Erica sitting on the couch reading a book. He snuck up behind her and hopped over the back of the sofa.

Erica flinched in surprise.

"Hey." Jace smiled, drying his hair with a towel.

After a particularly nasty glare, Erica slapped him, then a few more times after a brief pause. "What the hell, Jace?"

Jace lifted an arm in a pathetic defense. "Okay, I get it. I'm sorry." When she finally stopped, Jace lowered his arm and smiled. "Do you work tonight?"

"Not tonight." Erica returned to her book. "I have a couple of days off."

"Do you want to do something?"

Erica rolled her eyes, only replying absently. "Like what?"

"Well…" He considered that question for a moment. "Maybe a date. We haven't really had much time together lately."

"What do you have in mind?"

After a brief pause, Jace said, "How about we go dancing?"

That seemed to catch Erica's attention, and she looked back to Jace. "Dancing?"

"Yeah. I know you like to go dancing."

She shook her head. "I don't have anything to wear."

"Then how about we go shopping? I'll get you a dress or whatever, I'll take you to dinner, and we will go dancing after."

"Dinner and dancing?"

Jace nodded.

"Hmm." Erica's face twisted a little as she thought to herself. "That doesn't sound too bad."

Jace hopped to his feet. "Alright, I'll get ready to go shopping." He went to the backroom, excited at the day to come.

———

Jace had a love/hate relationship with his car. Eyes were drawn to it at almost every corner, and that drew some unwanted attention. However, it also gave a sense of status. So when he pulled his dark blue exotic car to the curb, valets leaped into action, as if fighting amongst themselves on who would take the keys first.

He got out of the car, buttoned up his dark gray suit coat and adjusted his matching white fitted tie underneath. After giving the keys over to the valet victor, he met with Erica on the curb. He paused when he looked at her, staring at the green dress with a thin laced back, showing her smooth skin. His eyes followed her curves down her body, seeing the slit that ran down from the middle of her thigh. Her makeup and lipstick were a matching green, giving her naturally dark complexion an alien, yet alluring, appearance.

She looked up at the building as Jace stood next to her. "The Timely Lounge?"

"A nice dinner and some dancing. As promised." Jace reached out an arm, which she took so he could lead her inside.

After the dinner, Jace and Erica danced lazily in the dim light. The music, slow and calm, had them swaying back and forth on the dance floor. They held each other, him taking in that intoxicating scent of vanilla she always wore.

When the song ended, Erica stepped back.

"What's wrong?"

"Nothing. It's just..." Erica looked around at the lounge. "This wasn't what I had in mind."

"Oh? Then tell me." Jace grabbed Erica and dipped her low to the ground.

She gasped and glared, but she couldn't hold back her smile. "How about I show you instead?"

———

If there was a polar opposite to the night Jace had planned, it was precisely what they walked into. The music thumped loudly as laser lights beamed and flashed, making them clearly visible from the fog machines all around the nightclub. Illuminated 3-dimensional visuals were everywhere, giving a strange depth to the environment. Erica, moving to the bar as soon as they got in, had a certain energy flowing through her from the atmosphere. This was her relaxation. This was her scene. She turned around with her regular order—a margarita—in her hand and looked directly at Jace.

He leaned against the bar. "Just an orange juice." When he looked over to Erica, she stared at him as if disappointed. For a moment, he thought about the last time he had a drink. But his life was different. He had Maya and Erica, Brian and Brittaney. Things were going right for him, and he figured it was time to celebrate. "Uh, with vodka." When Erica wasn't looking, Jace gestured to the bartender, bringing his fingers together as if saying, "Only a little bit."

Erica seemed like a different person in the club. She seemed wild. Sporadic. She hovered the margarita over her smiling lips. "Can you keep up?" She licked the salt from the rim of her glass and chugged her entire drink.

Jace's eyes popped open when she put the empty glass on the counter. Margaritas seemed more like a sipping and savoring drink more than a chugging one. His gaze followed her hand as she took the olive and stuck it in her mouth. She didn't chew it, but more like sucked on it.

Though he thought he would have a nice, relaxing time, Erica's display had Jace call her on the challenge. He tilted the glass back, fighting the burn in his throat as he finished his drink in a couple of gulps.

The fucking bartender didn't listen when he asked for only a little vodka.

Finally, he put the empty glass beside hers, and he gasped. "Holy shit!"

"That's my soldier boy!" Erica put an arm over his shoulder and ate her olive as she motioned for two more from the bartender. She was promptly served the drinks. "One more, then let's go!"

"One more?" He hesitantly took the offered drink.

Her answer was a lick of the salt and a chug of her drink and sucked on her olive.

Not wanting to be showed up, he followed suit, quickly

finishing his drink and setting it down on the bar. This time, Jace couldn't hold back a cough.

Before he could recover, Erica grabbed his arm and dragged him to the dancefloor. They swerved in and around the crowd, making their way to the middle of the room, where she lifted her hands and bounced with the beat, shifting and swaying with the masses around her.

This was her scene. Her outlet for the stress and anxiety. And Jace had no idea what to do. So he tried to go with the flow, bobbing his head, and attempted to compliment her movements.

She made exotic, sexy, and seductive moves that made Jace's heart skip beats. She'd bring her lips up to his so he could feel her breath, but she wouldn't kiss him. She'd rub her body against his and ran her hands all over him. Everything she did—expressions, movements, everything—turned him on.

Then the main lights turned off, making only black lights illuminate the area. And that's when Erica's look really popped. All over her skin were patterns that glowed in the blacklight, with an intricate feather design wrapping over her eyes. Jace then understood her choice in dress, and why it took her so long to get ready.

Time blurred by. Whenever the two were not on the dance floor, she had a drink in her hand. That meant Jace had to have a glass of booze as well. Early in the night, he could get his message across to the bartender, explaining that he'd have to drive so he couldn't get drunk. He still put vodka in his drink, but at least not a lot.

Jace had his coat and tie slung over a chair, and the top buttons of his shirt were unbuttoned to help him cool off.

Erica, her damp hair loosely hanging around her face and her makeup blurred from the sweat, finished another drink. Then she leaned in to whisper in his ear, "I'm not wearing any panties."

Jace almost dropped his drink at that proclamation. He watched as she walked away, not toward the dance floor, but toward the corner. Jace went to set down his drink, but found the glass broken on the floor. Did he drop it? He made a mental note to pay the bartender an extra tip for the mess, and he began to follow Erica, noting a stumble in his step.

He watched her go through a door near the corner. After what seemed like an eternity, Jace finally navigated through the crowd and followed.

When the door closed, the loud thumps were muffled, and he realized how disorientated he was. The door led to a thin and dimly lit hallway with stairs on either side. But before Jace could do anything, Erica took control, aggressively kissing him. She slammed him against the wall, and she bit his lip, her hands gripping his hair.

Before Jace could suggest they go somewhere private, Erica ripped his fitted shirt and ran her hands over his exposed chest. He couldn't tell if it was the alcohol in his system or the sexual nature that takes over human sensibility, but after hours of teasing and grinding, Jace stopped caring. He kissed her passionately, their breaths heavy and wild. He didn't care about where they were at, if someone walked in, nothing. All that mattered was his lust for her.

———

Jace and Erica snuck back onto the main room of the club. They made their way to the bar, where he paid his bill, added a nice tip for the broken glass and the mess, and left.

They stood at the sidewalk while they waited for the valet to pull up with his car. He looked at Erica for the first time in hours in something other than a blacklight. She was a mess. Her hair was soaked in sweat and in a crazed frizzle. The makeup, especially her lipstick, was smudged all over her face, and her nice green dress stuck to her skin. She held her heels in her hand, and she drank a bottle of water. At least she took care of herself post-dance and post-sex, and it seemed as if she worked to sober herself up.

Jace fixed his shirt as best as possible, but it was trashed. Even funnier to him, Erica's makeup was smeared all over his clothes.

Their time in the stairwell got a little crazy.

Finally, Jace's car pulled up. Money and keys exchanged hands, and he helped Erica into the passenger seat, then climbed into the driver's seat. But before Jace could start the car, police vehicles surrounded him, trapping him in.

Jace and Erica looked at each other for a moment, confused at what was going on. Finally, a voice on a loudspeaker called out, "Driver, come out with your hands up."

Keeping his hands visible as best as possible, Jace opened the door and got out of the car.

Erica leaned over from her seat. "Jace, what's going on?"

"I don't know. Maybe they think I'm too drunk to drive?"

She scoffed and sat straight in her seat while four officers approached, two heading to him, the other two going to the passenger side of the car.

"Good evening, officer. What seems to be—"

They grabbed his raised hands and brought them behind his back. One said, "You're under arrest."

"What for?" Erica called out as the police officers opened her door.

The officer went through a series of charges, ranging from reckless driving to felony murder. Out of all the things he thought he'd be arrested for, none of them were on the list.

Erica, too, was put in handcuffs. More because she shouted with drunken rage than her doing anything wrong.

Jace called to her over the car just before she got into trouble. "Erica. Hey. Look at me."

She turned to face him with flushed cheeks and shot a glare.

"Listen, everything will be fine."

"Bullshit, asshole! You're not an officer anymore."

Jace's eyes went wide. Did this have to do with his previous jobs? Was this The Order's doing? If so, he was screwed.

While they read him his rights, they began to arrest Erica, citing disorderly conduct, and saying she would be put in the drunk tank.

At least she would be okay.

After they were searched, Jace and Erica were put into separate squad cars and eventually hauled off to jail.

———

The next morning, Jace sat in a cell with a couple of others. Thankfully, none of them tried to start any trouble. They just stayed quiet and kept to themselves, which suited Jace fine.

A police officer walked up to the cell and unlocked it. "You're free to go."

Jace pointed to himself. "Me?"

"Yeah." He unlocked and opened the door. "You posted bail."

"What about Erica?"

"I wouldn't know. Come on."

The officer led Jace through the process of getting discharged, where he signed some paperwork, gathered his belongings, and was eventually escorted out of the building. On the sidewalk stood Brittaney, with Erica sitting against a three-brick high wall holding her head.

Brittaney approached, as Jace took a step toward Erica. "She's fine. Just a hangover. We have some serious problems."

"So I heard."

"Good news. You're out on bail, and I got your car out of the impound. They wanted to use it as evidence, saying it was the key to linking you as the owner. But I argued that it was only material, and not an item directly linked to the accused crimes. You're lucky you didn't have any of your gear on you, or you'd be put away for a long time."

"Music to my ringing ears."

"I even convinced the judge not to have you chipped, citing your freedoms. I don't know how long that'll last, though." She peeked over her shoulder toward Erica, then returned her gaze to him. "Bad news is you can't leave the city. And you can't get into trouble. Like, at all."

Jace shrugged. "Shouldn't be a problem."

"What I mean is, so long as you have this much attention on you, we're out of business."

"Well..." Jace ran his fingers through his hair, feeling the sweat and grease that built up throughout the night. "We can keep doing jobs. I just can't get caught." His eyes locked onto his car parked across the street.

"If you want to risk it, and if you think you can. And..." She followed his gaze to the car. "You can't drive that car anymore."

"Why not?"

"Are you kidding? Look at that thing. That car is a magnet for attention! Every law enforcement officer will probably recognize it and pull you over for the smallest thing. And if that happens, your bail is revoked, and you go back to jail."

Jace sighed. "Shit."

"Don't worry. I'm sure I can get you out of this. From the sounds of it, they don't have much evidence, and a lot of it is circumstantial."

After a moment, Jace nodded. "Thanks. You're saving my ass."

Brittaney smiled. "Don't mention it." She gestured to Erica. "Now go take care of your girl. I have some more paperwork to fill out before we can safely go."

Jace returned the smile, and the two parted ways. He sat next to Erica and put an arm over her shoulder. "You alright?"

"Yeah." Erica scoffed. "I half-expected to wake up in some strange hotel room with some water and headache medicine on the nightstand."

"Not this time."

Erica closed her eyes and took a deep breath. When she exhaled, she took a drink of water. "So, do you know what's going on?"

"Kind of. It sounds like they're trying to get me for jobs I did when I was with The Order."

That seemed to have surprised Erica as she opened her eyes and stared at Jace.

"Brittaney is handling it, though. She seems pretty confident that she can get me out of this mess."

"Good. Because you don't have legal immunity anymore. Your past may come back to haunt you more than you know."

"Yeah, I'm figuring that out now." Jace rubbed her back. After a few moments, he looked her over. "You're a mess."

She smacked his leg. "You look no better."

He smiled, kissed her on the head, then hugged her.

"So what about your sister? Aside from Brian introducing us some two weeks ago, I haven't seen her much to get to know her."

"You've been working a lot. And she has school. Ever since the attack, her friend has stuck by her like glue. I think it's kind of a comfort thing. And since her parents are back home, they've been staying at their house for a while."

"So, when did you adopt her? I mean, she's obviously an Evolved."

That took Jace by surprise. "How did you—"

"Come on." She looked up at Jace and shrugged. "Isn't it obvious?"

Jace stammered for a moment, trying to figure out what to say. Was Maya being Evolved so obvious? Maybe they were too close for him to see it before the incident at the hotel. "We've been together for a long time."

"How long?"

"I don't know." Jace shrugged. "We spent years together at the orphanage. I think I adopted her shortly after I joined The Order."

"That long?"

Jace nodded. "Yeah. She's been in my life for years, only being apart from one another when I took a job."

"Interesting." Erica looked lost in thought as she absent-mindedly nodded.

They didn't say much after that. Even so, Jace's thoughts returned to his current situation. What was his next move? Every action, every step, every breath would be under tight scrutiny. He had to be on his best behavior. He was thankful he had Brittaney in his corner. This was her fight. Her time to shine. All he could do was wait until she said otherwise.

CHAPTER THIRTEEN

AFTER SEEING MAYA DOING SIT-UPS IN HER ROOM THAT ONE TIME, Jace asked her if she wanted to start exercising with him. Of course he wouldn't do his heavily physical activities, especially the specialized actions centered around combat. Regardless of his censorship, she seemed to like the idea, and they began jogging together. He slowed his pace for her, often stopping to let her catch her breath. And as to not get bored, Jace looked for new places to explore during their runs. And even though Maya joining him lessened his cardio workout, he was happy she was with him.

A couple of days after getting out of jail, Jace pulled up to the hiking trail with Maya. He and Maya got out of the car he borrowed from Brittaney and started to stretch in the early morning.

Explaining why he couldn't drive his usual car was difficult. Luckily, Brittaney stepped in with a solid reason, even though it threw him under the bus. But not to look like they were hiding something, Jace accepted the "He didn't have a job, so he can't pay for it" reason.

The sun had already risen, which was later than his usual runs. Though he typically enjoyed watching the sunrise from some scenic view, he didn't mind. His time with Maya was worth it.

They walked on the path toward the mountain trail before their run.

"So, will you be going back to Brian's any time soon?"

Maya gestured the number "two" with her fingers.

"Two weeks?"

She nodded.

"That's a long time."

After a few footsteps, she brought her hands up and gestured, as if she fired a gun.

"That's something I wanted to talk to you about. How are you doing after that? I mean, that's a pretty stressful situation."

She gave a thumbs up.

"Really? Because you've been rather distant. I haven't seen you around lately, and Erica said she only met you when Brian introduced you two."

She shook her head and shrugged.

They reached the entrance to the nature trail. Jace stared down the different paths for a moment, then pointed to each while he looked at a sign. "So, an easy run, moderate run, and difficult run. What do you want to do?"

Maya pointed to the moderate path.

"This is kind of a long run. Are you sure?"

She patted her water bottle around her side and nodded.

"Alright, let's go."

They jogged down the semi-gravel path. After a short distance, the gravel turned into natural ground, the way only visible from the constant pounding of pedestrians as they strolled by. Grassy hills flanked them while the trail curved with a gradual incline.

"Do you want to stay at Ruth's?"

Maya shook her head with a shrug, then she patted her chest near her heart.

"So you're staying there because of her?"

She nodded.

That answered some questions he had. She seemed fine after the attack, but Ruth was the one that was psychologically impacted. She was the one that needed support, and Maya, being the amazing young woman she was growing up to be, was there for her. Jace felt a great deal of pride at that moment. He couldn't ask for a better sister.

After a short while, Maya slowed her stride and put her arms over her head. Sweat glistened from her brow, but her hoodie remained up to cover her head.

Jace met her pace. "You doing alright?"

She nodded after an exhale.

He turned to face her while she caught her breath. How did Erica peg her as an Evolved based solely on her appearance? He inspected her once more, taking in the details of her face. Brown hair, green eyes. Nothing seemed out of the ordinary. Then how?

That's when his thoughts were side-tracked by how much she had matured. She grew up so much in the last year. How much had he missed? What memories was he not there for? His eyes went down the hill toward the park's parking lot. Should he tell her the truth? After all, hiding his life from her is what got him into trouble in the first place. It was that kind of deception that made him miss those memories.

After another deep exhale, Maya looked into Jace's eyes and gave him an affirming nod.

"Okay, let's go."

She continued their jog up the trail where it took a steep climb up into some trees. Maya slowed.

"You want to walk it?"

She didn't answer. Instead, she rushed the hill, charging up it like a soldier attacking a bunker, leaving him behind. She took long strides, using stones and roots to help her foothold.

Jace could only smile at her strength and determination. After a few moments of watching, he followed in her footsteps, climbing up the steep hill with equal speed.

When they were on a more even path, Maya slowed for a breather and some water. She looked down the hill toward the street, and the ant-sized cars that drove by.

Jace decided this would be a good time to tell her the truth. "Hey, I want to talk to you about something."

She glanced in his direction, lips pursed to help regulate her breathing.

"I... My old job..." His heart beat faster than if he would be jogging. His palms clammed up, and he felt his throat dry. To buy him a moment, he took a drink of water. That moment made him doubt his decision to tell her the truth. After all, she was still a kid, and she needed to be protected from the dangerous world. Sure, she was an Evolved, but did she have any power to control? Did she even care about that?

Doubt overrode his confidence. And though he picked a fight with The Order that may bring the battle to her doorstep, the words that came to mind weren't of the truth, but of more coverups. He sighed. "My old job kept me away for so long. I won't let that happen again." He looked at Maya. "I'll get a job in the area so we can stay in one place. Give you the life and stability you deserve."

She simply nodded and turned her gaze back to the scenery.

Jace cursed to himself, swallowing the guilt that stuck in his throat. She was too young to know the truth. At least, that's what he kept telling himself.

———

A couple of days later, Jace got an invitation to have dinner at the Yorks. He and Erica dressed in semi-formal attire, him wearing a suit and tie and her in a dark red cocktail dress and a light coat to cover her shoulders.

They approached the newly developed guard post in between the high fenced property. When the security guard let them through, they walked up the driveway toward the recently fortified house: reinforced foundations, thicker windows, and even a fresh coat of tan and light blue paint. Being a prime target for The Order, Jace figured it was a good start to keep themselves safe.

Jace rang a doorbell when they arrived at the front door.

A tan-skinned woman with dark hair with red tips answered the door. What caught Jace off guard was more than her seemingly casual dress wear—an unbuttoned light cardigan, white undershirt, and blue slacks—was her smile and her immediately hugging Jace before introductions. "You must be Jace. I can't thank you enough for saving my husband's life."

Erica extended a greeting hand. "It's nice to meet you, Mrs. York. I'm Erica."

"Please, call me Wanda." She skipped the handshake and hugged her, too.

Erica's eyes went wide, and she looked at Jace.

He could only shrug in reply.

"Please, come in." She took their coats and led them into the house, which looked to be heavily remodeled. As they made their way through the halls, Jace's eyes subconsciously locked toward the kitchen, where he found the dead chef and the dying Mr. York.

"My husband will be down in a minute. Dinner is almost ready, so you're just in time."

They made their way into the dining room. Though simple, the lit fireplace and cozy environment deeply contrasted the dark shades of death that Jace witnessed not long ago.

Wanda showed them to their seats before sitting across from Erica. They started with idle chatter, talking about how lovely each of them looked, the house and the remodeling, and how thankful she was for watching her daughter during their time of need.

The conversation shifted when a man who leaned on a cane entered the room. Regardless of his other arm being bandaged and in a sling, he looked slick in a casual dark-grey suit, with his thin mustache and copper-toned skin. "Thank you for coming." As soon as he sat down, a waiter served some appetizers.

Jace looked around, noticing only four dishes. "What about—"

"It's just us four." Nick grabbed a glass of wine. "No need for the girls to partake in this event."

Wanda and Erica continued idle conversation during the meal. They giggled and smiled, always talking lightly about whatever conversation was brought up. But Jace wondered what was really going on. Mr. York hardly said anything after sitting down. After the conversation they had when Nick first went to the hospital, Jace couldn't imagine what he had in mind.

Finally, after the main course was completed, Nick dabbed his mouth and leaned back into his chair. "Now, on to why I brought you here. As I'm sure you're aware, there has been a lot of activity in the area from The Order."

Erica's eyes glanced between Nick and Jace. "Why would he know something like that?"

"Because of who he was, and who he is." Nick sipped at his wine.

"Mr. York," Jace said after setting down his napkin. "As I said at the hospital, I'm no longer affiliated with The Order."

"So you said. Still, I can't help but wonder if your past has come to haunt you. And I can't help but wonder if your recent actions have something to do with their increased activity, or if it's all just a coincidence. I'd wager the former. After all, what you've been up to as of late has been far from subtle."

Erica glanced at Jace. "What's he talking about?"

"Uh, well, I uh..." Jace ran his fingers through his hair, struggling to come up with an answer.

"Swatting at the hornet's nest." Nick set down his glass of wine. "And the hornets are biting."

"Jaaace..." Erica glared at Jace. "What did you do?"

"Well, I..." He cleared his throat. "I've been interfering with The Order."

She narrowed her eyes. "Interfering how?"

"Well..." He gazed at Nick and Wanda for a moment, who both sat straight and quiet as if waiting politely for an answer, before returning to Erica. "I've been screwing with their missions. Intercepting deliveries, stopping patrols and such."

"I see. Mr. and Mrs. York, do you have a place where we may have a private discussion?"

"But of course." Nick stood and extended an arm. "This way, please." He grabbed his cane and escorted them to a room in the back with a bay window, a desk, walls lined with books, another lit fireplace, and a few comfortable-looking chairs. "We will be in the dining room when you're ready." He closed the door behind him, leaving Jace and Erica alone.

After a couple of seconds, Erica's rage exploded. She smacked him hard on the arm. "What the hell are you doing?" She hit his arm a couple more times, and she growled through gritted teeth. "Are you fucking stupid? Are you trying to get yourself killed?" She glanced at him with wide eyes. "Is that why you were arrested? You didn't kill someone. Did you?"

He shook his head. "No. I don't kill anymore."

Before Jace could say anything else, she smacked him once more. "Then why? Are you fucking stupid?"

"Okay, that's enough."

She stomped her foot and stared hard at him. "Why didn't you tell me?"

"Because it isn't your fight."

That resulted in another smack. Though each hit didn't hurt, she had a knack for hitting the same spot, which began to get painful. "Bullshit, it's not my fight."

"Okay, stop. I get it. You're upset."

"Upset doesn't come close." She turned and walked a few paces, then faced Jace once more. "So why didn't you tell me? I want a better answer."

"Well... I guess it's because I didn't want you to worry."

She crossed her arms. "Didn't want me to worry?"

"Yeah. Well, I didn't want you to worry, and I didn't want to put you in danger."

"You know how stupid that sounds?"

Jace half-shrugged. "Now I do."

She took a step forward and lifted a hand to smack him again, but she stopped, crumpled her face, then began to pace once more. "Do you know why I'm angry?"

"Because I'm putting myself in danger?"

"No, you moron." She whipped around and stomped her foot. "Because you didn't tell me! How the fuck do you do something so stupid without telling me first?"

Jace had enough. It was time to push back. "You already have some half-robot asshole chasing after you with some sort of cyborg hard-on. Why on earth would I put you in harm's way?"

"He already knows where I am."

"How?"

She gave an exaggerated shrug before throwing up her hands and pacing once more.

Jace turned and leaned against the mantle of the fireplace to stare at the flames.

The two said nothing for what seemed like an eternity.

Finally, Erica said, "Alright, I'll help."

That was out of the question. Jace turned to face her, shaking his head. "I can't let you—"

"I'm not asking." She approached and stared at him sternly, her tone going slow and steady. "I'm in."

He looked hard at her, but she held firm. There was nothing that could be done. Jace sighed and shook his head in defeat. "Okay. Fine."

"Good." She went to the door. "Come on. We can't keep our host waiting."

They returned to the dining room where Wanda and Nick sat patiently. Upon arrival, Nick stood and remained standing until Erica sat down.

"I suspect you had much to talk about." Nick lifted his hand. Servers came out with trays. "I hope our dessert didn't get too cold."

The server placed a cookie-brownie concoction with half-melted ice cream in front of Jace. "I never thanked you for having us for dinner."

Nick lifted a hand. "Please. It's the least I could do for what you've done."

Not much was spoken while they ate their desserts.

When everyone finished, Nick again dabbed his lips with his napkin and leaned in his chair. "So, are you still going to swat at the proverbial hornet's nest?"

Jace glanced at Erica, who returned with an affirming stare. He nodded. "Yeah."

"And what have you learned from this endeavor?"

For a moment, he wondered if he should even be talking about the details of the jobs with Mr. York. Then again, he already seemed to know all about his operation. So maybe whatever he said wouldn't be news. "First off, their assault wasn't because I swatted the hornet's nest. I started my fight against them after their assault."

"Interesting." Nick put his fingers in a temple, which looked odd considering his bandaged arm, and leaned forward with interest. "Go on."

"It was actually the assault that made me decide to fight back. After seeing what they did, I wanted to do what I could to prevent something like that from happening again."

"And what reassurance is there that they won't retaliate?"

Jace shook his head. "None."

"None." Nick leaned back against his chair and put his chin in his hand while he stared hard at Jace. "And where do these 'jobs' take place?"

"I used to do jobs all over the region. But with some recent problems with the law, I can't leave the city."

"Have you caused any problems in my city?"

"Nothing too bad, really."

"Indulge me."

Jace cleared his throat, and he once again looked at Erica. She seemed to stare at him with equal interest. "Small stuff, mostly. Nothing like I used to do."

Nick didn't seem entertained by that answer. "Go on."

"Well... Okay. A, uh... A few weeks ago, I intercepted a scout near the lake."

Nick raised an eyebrow. "Go on."

Jace grew nervous. He swallowed, wondering if he should talk about the disturbing news they recently discovered. Again, he looked to Erica for support. She stared back, seemingly with the same intrigue as Nick. He was stuck. "Okay. Uh, I questioned the scout before his reinforcements arrived. And I heard some rather disturbing news. Apparently, The Order is taking kids."

Nick leaned forward. "Kids?"

"That's what the guy said."

Erica scoffed. "That's stupid. What would they want with children?"

"As I said, it's what I heard."

She shook her head. "I think he told you a lie. I've never heard of The Order doing something like that."

"Maybe," Nick said, and he grabbed his wine glass. "Maybe not."

A servant entered the dining room. "Pardon me, Mr. York. The Senator is on line two. He says it's urgent."

Nick nodded, and the servant left. "You have an interesting tactic to carry out this war of yours. And though I can't say I approve of your methods, you did save my daughter's life. For that, I am thankful, and I shall remain silent to your actions. Because of that, any debt you feel I owe is repaid." He put down his wine glass and stood. "Now, if you'll excuse me, I have an important phone call." He looked at Wanda. "My dear, please show them out."

Wanda smiled and gave a gentle nod, then stood. "It was a lovely evening. I'm so happy to have finally gotten to meet you."

Erica returned the smile. "Yes, I had a wonderful time. Everything was delicious, and your company was delightful."

Wanda escorted them to the door. "Do come again some time. I'd love to hear more about your work. Both of you."

"I'll try." Erica took her light coat, and the two left the house.

They exited the property and walked down the sidewalk.

Erica put her arm around Jace's. "You know he probably lied, right?"

That caught Jace off guard. "Who? Nick?"

"No. That scout."

He shrugged. "I don't know. It seems possible."

"But not probable. Where's the motive?"

Jace couldn't argue that point, but maybe Brian had some answers. After all, he had Freddy's briefcase. So he decided to change the subject. "They have a nice house."

"Oh, it's beautiful. Did you see how many fireplaces they had?" She laid her head on his shoulder.

CHAPTER FOURTEEN

It took three weeks for Erica to not seem angry at Jace. It didn't help that she exploded in anger when she realized both Brian and Brittaney were in the fight, too. Regardless of the mood she brought, Jace still had work to do.

With The Order's vast resources, Jace chose his jobs with great caution. He carefully planned his actions with Brian and Brittaney to avoid any trouble with the law, which allowed him to take a couple of jobs out of the city. Often, he'd return to Erica to be mended from the injuries he sustained.

Brian didn't get much from the computer in the briefcase, but he found some detailed movements from The Order to find someone who could give some answers about the kidnapping claim. Brian discovered a problem. The target was a highly trained assassin, and they were scheduled to evaluate someone for The Order in a neighboring region soon.

It didn't matter to Jace. A job was a job, and they needed answers. So they planned his trip, renting a car in Brian's name to avoid any suspicion, and discussed his alibi in case the police asked.

The last time Jace stood in an illegal fighting arena, he evaluated Zoey Forest for The Order. Their recruitment techniques churned acidic bile in his gut. He wondered if she was able to escape The Order's recruitment. Then again, it had only been about a year and a half, so she was probably still at her orphanage. For a moment, he considered checking on her. That was before the lights dimmed, and the match he had been waiting for was about to begin.

A tall, bald teen got on the stage as the announcer spoke. "Bets are closed for Y3-1. Gladiators, fight until knockout or tap out. Get ready!" The kid punched his hand and flexed, showing an impressive muscle tone for his pre-adult age.

When his opponent came in from the other side, Jace leaned forward with extreme interest. Every fight before, the contenders had little clothes to avoid being grabbed and grant unrestricted mobility. But as soon as he saw the kid's opponent, he knew he had found his target.

The woman hardly had any skin showing. A thin veil covered her nose and mouth, and loose crimson fabric hung from her neck down to her feet. Her dark hair was in a tight bun and was held in place by two long sticks.

"There she is." Jace grabbed the rail with anticipation.

"Jace," Erica said over the com. "I know her. She's extremely dangerous."

"Yeah, I know."

Brian asked, "So what are you going to do?"

"Say hello." He leaped over the railing to land on the arena floor.

Cheers and jeers erupted from the patrons as the announcer said, "What's this? I think someone fell from the stands."

Jace stood straight, brushing the dust from his clothes, and he approached the oval-shaped stage as the audience's vocal eruption quieted down a little. "Hey, kid."

"What the hell you doing, Smalls?"

Jace couldn't help but chuckle. First, it was Backpack from Zoey. Now it's Smalls from this kid. He hopped on the stage. "You're from Caring Hands, right?"

The teen glared at him. "The hell you know?"

"That you're going to lose." He glanced to the strange, red-dressed woman, who stood with a calm he would expect from the officer of The Order. Still, with Brian's warnings scratching the back of his mind about her being an assassin, he'd have to keep an eye on her, even when he wasn't looking her way.

"I ain't lost yet. And I ain't going to lose now."

"You sure about that?" Jace smiled, seeing the determined and incredulous look he got from him. Then he got an idea. "Okay, how about this? I'll give you two minutes." He turned and started to walk to the edge of the stage, eager to see his upcoming opponent's movements and style.

"Psh, she ain't going to last that long."

"Two minutes," Jace called over his shoulder. "Then I'm stepping in."

"The hell you are!" The teen whipped his hand out. "This is my money. You get in my way, I'll beat your ass, too!"

Jace stood at the edge of the arena and pawed the air. "Calm down, kid. I'm not here for you. I'm here for her." He pointed to the woman, then to the teen. "Who is here for you. Now go on. Your time's ticking. And a gentleman doesn't keep a lady waiting." When the kid didn't move, Jace shooed him away. "Go on, now. I have things to do, and you're wasting my time."

The stupid kid threw a punch at Jace. Though quick and balanced, Jace had ample time to grab his wrist and throw him over his shoulders onto the stage. Not quite the reaction he wanted. Now the assassin had the opportunity to watch him instead.

The bald teen got to his feet.

Jace rolled his eyes, keeping the assassin in the corner of his gaze. "Do you really want to do this? You're not even getting paid."

"I'm going to kick your ass for free." The teen charged, throwing one punch after another.

Jace ducked and weaved the punches. "Can we just meet outside after?"

The bald teen's answer was a "nope" in the form of another punch.

Jace sighed, grabbed the teen's wrist, kicked out his leg, and used his momentum and weakened balance to toss him off the stage. With that out of the way, Jace took a few steps toward the woman in red. "Now, let's talk. Shall we?"

The assassin's eyes narrowed, but the veil around her nose and mouth hid any other expression. She had an accent, speaking in slow, clear sentences, so their natural accent didn't get in the way. "Who are you to—"

"Wait!" Came the shout of the bald teen.

Jace sighed and glanced over his shoulder to see the teen hop back on the stage. He looked back to the woman. "Just wait a minute. This won't take long." He turned and backed up a few paces to keep an eye on the two on the stage. "You lost, kid."

"Getting knocked off isn't losing."

"No but getting knocked off so easily should be a sign."

The teen didn't listen. Instead, he came in with reckless attacks. Maybe it was the rage the kid had in him, or perhaps the determination, but the kid's speed improved. Not enough, though.

Jace kept on the defensive, blocking and bobbing. "Come on, kid. Give it up."

Brian spoke over the com. "Jace, I think she's leaving."

Reflexively, Jace turned his head to look at the woman. Brian was right. She walked away. And before he could do anything, a sharp pain struck his jaw. Jace stumbled a step, feeling some moisture trickle down from the corner of his lip.

Jace wiped the blood with his thumb, feeling his rage build up from the hit. "Okay, kid. I'm done with you." Jace ducked a right cross, landing one of his own in the kid's side. He bobbed to avoid a jab, planting a boot on the kid's knee. Every single attack the kid did touched nothing but air but gained a counter-blow in return.

The kid lunged forward. Jace leaped back, grabbing the kid and rolling backward, kicking him high into the air. Jace went with the roll, deftly getting to his feet, and turned just as the kid plunged face down into the dirt below. He jumped off the stage and landed near the kid's head. "You should have listened." When the kid tried to look up, Jace punched him across the jaw, laying him low.

He ignored the audience and announcer as he stood and wiped his lip again with a sneer. "Fucking kid." When he looked around to find the woman, he couldn't find her. She was gone. "Brian, where did she go?"

"Try the door. There."

Jace sprinted when he saw the double doors. His hands slapped the wall as he took the corner toward the exit. He kicked the exiting door, almost knocking it from the hinges, and stepped outside into the biting cold rain. Each breath let out a white plume, and each drop of water that dripped under his jacket sent a chill through Jace's spine.

Though his eyes should have been locked onto the woman in red as she walked under a bamboo umbrella toward an aero-vehicle, he couldn't help but notice the trunk of his rented car that was parked next to the woman's vehicle cracked open. Did he accidentally open it when he got out? Or maybe someone broke into the car while he was inside? No matter. That would be a puzzle for another time.

Jace regained his focus and put his attention on the matter at hand. If the woman got into the aero-car, she'd be gone, and he'd have no way of catching her. That meant he wouldn't get the answers to the troubling question. He had to get her attention. "Leaving so soon?"

The woman paused for a moment before turning to face Jace. "My business here is done, and you are not a part of my business."

"Ah, but you're a part of mine." He smiled and took a couple of steps closer, his boots sloshing through the soaked grass and drops of water from his wet hair dripping down his face. "The boy didn't pass. I get it."

That seemed to get the woman's attention as her gaze went from casual to focused. "You know nothing."

"I do, actually." He stopped a half dozen paces away, getting a closer look at the dangerous woman. He noticed a bracelet around her wrist under the loose fabric—especially the gems set into the metal. "I'm curious. What do they call women in a knightly clan, or whatever? A madam? Woman?" He gave a playful smirk. "Sir?"

She visibly inspected Jace. "I know you. I have seen you before." She took a single step toward Jace, which was a relief to him as it was a step away from the aero-vehicle. "You are the Fallen. Are you not?"

Jace smiled. She even talked like Xin. After an exaggerated shrug, he said, "You still haven't answered my question."

"Dame Moon, Knight of Grace, Third Class."

Third class. A decently high rank in The Order. Again, Brian's warning scratched his mind. "Damn Moon. Kind of a strange name, but okay."

"We have been warned of your treachery."

"See, there you go again." Jace began pacing to the side, increasing the distance from the two by a pace. "They all think I'm the traitor, but they're the ones who lied to me." He stopped and faced Dame Moon. "You know they're lying to you too. Right?"

When she didn't reply, Jace continued his pacing. "See, I know you have been with The Order for a relatively long time. You've received commendations for Gallantry, Service, and Combat, to say the least." He paused and faced her once more. "So I'm sure you know the truth. The *real* truth. The truth about the pain and death The Order causes to humans. Non-Evolved. Just so they can cast fear on the populace."

"You know nothing."

"Didn't you say that already?" Like Jace had hoped, the tapping of Brian's keyboard came from the earpiece. Then Brian began to read off a list about her, which Jace repeated as he paced once more. "Four years ago, you assassinated an ambassador in the consulate. I wonder if you consider that a success, since the international war you wanted didn't happen." Jace pursed his lips, holding back a wince from the gash the kid left on him. "I bet you used poison on that job."

Though subtle, Jace noticed Dame Moon's muscles tense.

"Then there was the job of wiping out an entire line of a royal family. Even the children had their throats slit while they slept." He paused and turned toward the assassin. "The housekeeper found their bloody corpses all around the house." Seeing her hand wring the handle of her umbrella, Jace knew he had her. He decided to ask his question. "So, why is The Order taking kids?"

Her eyes narrowed in a deadly glare. "You should not have come." She casually closed the bamboo umbrella and leaned it against her aero-vehicle. Her tightly woven hair began to fall apart from the press of the rain, and her clothes started to lose their baggy shape. She spun her arms in tight circles, wrapping the loose cloth in her hands, and she took a fighting stance very reminiscent of Xin's.

Jace patted the air. "A gentleman doesn't harm a lady. But if you do something stupid, I will lay you low."

Commotion and a loud thump came from behind Jace that made him reflexively grab his guns from the back holsters. With one gun pointed toward the noise and the other at the assassin, Jace saw two men pause in shock, staring at the door that fell off the hinges, and at the gun pointed at them. They turned and fled.

"Shit." He turned his attention to the assassin, who had retrieved her bamboo umbrella and reached for the aero-vehicle door. "Don't move."

"I do not fear you, Fallen."

Jace shot the umbrella, blowing it into pieces. He had to hand it to the assassin. She didn't flinch, even at the fragments that hit her cheek.

She turned to face Jace, her head held high and her hands behind her back. "Does a gentleman shoot an unarmed woman?"

Jace grinned. "We both know you're not unarmed." While swapping the gun pointed at her, he approached the woman, keeping a few paces between him and the assassin, reloading the first gun with different ammo. He didn't want to shoot her with anything fatal, after all. "I'll ask again. Why would The Order take kids? Tell me, and I'll let you go."

After a brief pause, she replied, "Tests."

Well, that was easy.

Jace scoffed. "Tests? What kind of tests?"

"I do not know."

He stared hard at her. For a long moment, he could hear only the falling rain. And with each passing moment, the cold bit more and more through his clothes.

Moon's bun collapsed from the weight of the rain. For a moment, Jace noticed the rain stop hitting her, like she had some invisible bubble an inch away from her body. Then, with seemingly impossible quickness that took Jace off guard, she caught and threw one of the sticks that fell from her bun. He returned fire, white blobs exploding onto the aero-car, as he barely dodged the stick, seeing the shimmer of steel from the tip. The first two shots missed as she went to the side, but the third caught her arm. The web-like material gripped her arm and stuck it to the vehicle.

Jace bobbed to the side, dodging the second stick as it flew by. He fired again, shooting her other arm and securely sticking it to the car frame. Just to be safe, he fired another round on each limb to firmly entangle her hands.

Now he knew why she gave in so easily. She was trying to get him to drop his guard.

Brian spoke over the com, "Jace, remember those rounds dissolve in water."

He nodded in reply, breathed deeply, and stared in total amazement at the speed of the dangerous woman. He had seen fast movements before, but that quickness rivaled even Xin. Maybe quicker than him? Or maybe he was just too rusty, and he was the slow one?

The woman said something to Jace he couldn't understand. He figured it was a curse or some swear in her native language. Then, she said, "I shall find you, Fallen. I shall find you and destroy everything you hold dear. Everyone and everything you love, I shall enjoy watching them being ripped from your life."

A commotion from the arena sounded in Jace's ears. Security, probably. And they'd be armed. Or they would have called the police. Would they call the police? After all, they were running an illegal fighting arena. Regardless, he was out of time.

Jace swapped his gun with the one in the holster, which was armed with some experimental rounds, and he approached Dame Moon, pointing the gun at her. "You should have taken my deal." Just as the white foam dissolved from the rain, Jace fired. The taser round hit squarely in her chest as flashes of white and blue tendrils encased the assassin. She lightly convulsed, then slid to the floor in a groan. To his surprise, she wasn't unconscious. Dazed, but not unconscious. Was she a cyborg, too?

To be safe, he shot her two more times. Finally, he got the result he had expected. She violently shook, and she went limp.

He knelt and felt the first impact point, feeling some sort of girdle or armor on. He ripped some of the cloth, just to be sure. He gazed at the leather vest that covered her torso. It looked highly decorative, with writing etched all over the dark surface. For a moment, he figured it was her native language. But some of the symbols caught his eye—symbols he had seen before.

"Brian, are you seeing this?"

"Yeah."

Jace ran his fingers over the symbols. They gave a faint green glow, and Jace could swear he felt a slight breeze that wasn't from the cold wind that gnawed at his skin. "What is this?"

"I don't know. Do you think we should bring her back?"

Erica stepped in. "Are you serious? She's dangerous. Don't bring her back here."

Brian agreed. "Maybe she's right. Where would we keep her?"

His eyes locked onto the vest and at the writing. "I know I've seen this before."

"Jace, people are coming. You have to get out of there."

He turned toward the sticks that held Moon's bun in place, noticing they were buried deep into the building. "Pretty sneaky."

Erica said, "Jace, I have to go to work. Are you okay? Do you need me for anything?"

"No, I'm good. Have a good day."

After putting the gun away, Jace knelt and took her bracelet, knowing she'd get off scot-free with that identifying mark on her. At least with it gone, she'd be out of commission for a short while.

"Brian, get me directions. I'm on my way back." Jace ran to the rental car and opened the trunk. The shock at the sight almost had him fall flat on his ass. Why the hell was his little sister hiding in the trunk? "Maya, what the hell are you doing here?"

He didn't have time to get an answer. The commotion from the arena arrived, and a crowd shouted at Jace.

"Come on." He pulled Maya out and closed the trunk. "We have to go."

She went to the passenger side while Jace got into the driver's side. The tires screeched as the mob rushed them. A bang and a bullet hit the back window. Jace and Maya ducked down to avoid getting shot as more bullets hit the rental car.

After a corner, Jace looked into the rearview mirror, assuring himself that they weren't giving chase.

Another turn and Jace felt they were enough in the clear. He glanced at Maya, who stared out the side window. "What the hell are you doing here?"

She crossed her arms.

"Brian?"

"I thought she was with Ruth."

Jace's hands angrily gripped the steering wheel, and he glanced at Maya once more. What was she doing there in the first place? How much did she see? Having a conversation with her was difficult enough since she refused to talk, learn sign language, or even write a note to him. Now he'd have to interpret her simple gestures for the answers to his questions. That would be later when he could sit and watch her movements for her replies.

After a calming breath, Jace focused on his driving. "Brian, you're going to have to fix the car before we return it."

CHAPTER FIFTEEN

AFTER JACE DISCOVERED MAYA IN THE RENTAL CAR'S TRUNK WHILE on the job, he sat her down to have a serious conversation. With how dangerous his jobs could be, he knew having her around would cause endless complications. And throughout his questioning, she hardly looked at him. Instead, she sat defiantly, arms crossed, and a scowl on her face.

When they pulled up to the house, Maya didn't hesitate to head over to the Yorks, not looking back as Jace called out to her. Frustrated, he went inside to discuss his displeasure about the lack of supervision for his younger sister.

His confidence faltered when he saw Brian in the garage working tirelessly on some device he used around the house. He rubbed the bridge of his nose and sighed before looking back into the magnification device to continue his precision work.

Jace paused, taking a deep breath of his own, waiting for Brian to finish his work.

When Brian finally leaned back, Jace approached. All across the table were parts of some device cluttered in colonies of similar-looking pieces. "Hey, we need to talk."

"Not now, Jace." Brian returned to his work.

"No, now." He stood beside Brian with his arms crossed. "It's your responsibility to watch Maya."

"No, it's supposed to be yours." A wisp of smoke emanated from the device Brian soldered.

Jace was about to protest when Brian turned his chair to face him. "You wanted back in her life. And now you are, and you're hardly doing anything to take care of her. Stop deflecting your responsibilities and be in her life."

Before Jace could argue, Brian continued, "No, Jace. I'm working two jobs here." He gestured to the device on the workbench. "I have to fix this device so I can continue to monitor The Order's movements."

Jace eyed the contraption and at the seemingly hundreds of small parts strewn all over the surface.

"Yeah. This broke while you were out. And after this, I have to finish a project for work for tomorrow morning." Brian turned back to the bench.

"One small thing—those taser rounds need some adjustments."

"Sure, Jace. I'll get to them when I can. I don't think I'll be getting any sleep tonight."

Brian always stayed up late working in the garage. And more times than not, he was awake around the same time Jace woke up. Then it occurred to him—Brian ran off less sleep than he did. Immediately after that insight, Jace's anger and frustration washed away. Perhaps he asked too much from Brian.

Jace put a hand on Brian's shoulder. "Tell you what. Brittaney is back home to work on some case, and Erica is going to some convention for her hospital. So how about I take Maya, and we go out of town for a bit and give you some time off."

That gave Brian pause.

"How does a week and a half sound?"

Brian reached for a part on the table without even looking. "What about school? And what about the police?"

"Don't worry about the police. You'll just need to rent another car for me. Make it a truck. I know a good place where we can go camping." That prompted a sigh from Brian as Jace continued, "As for Maya, she's done home learning before. She'll be fine."

"Hmm..." Brian lightly smacked his lips. "Okay, Jace. Have it your way." He glanced at his wristwatch. "You have to be back by next Sunday. And no more bullet holes. Deal?"

"Deal." Jace half-smiled and patted Brian's shoulder and left him to his work.

———

After a couple of days away from the city, Jace and Maya went on a hike up a mountainside. He and Erica discovered a spot where they could sit and stargaze while camping under the open sky. He figured that would be a nice place to talk to her about his recent activities. More importantly, to try to figure out why she was in the trunk of the rental car in the first place.

When they reached a plateau that overlooked a hillside, Jace took off his backpack. "We're here." He grabbed a drink and sat on a fallen tree trunk.

Maya plopped beside him and drank from her own bottle.

Jace gestured over his shoulder. "There's a small river a quarter-mile up where we can get water. We can fish there, too."

Maya glanced at him and shrugged.

"I don't know. Erica told me why the fish are up this high, but I don't remember what she said."

She rolled her eyes and shook her head before taking another drink.

"Do you know how to fish? How about I teach you tomorrow morning."

She shrugged.

They set up their camp as nighttime rolled around. Jace started a campfire and warmed the stew he brought with them. After dinner, Jace sat her down so they could see the clear night sky and the countless stars that twinkled above them.

After a short while, Jace decided it was time for him to tell her what was on his mind. But instead of questioning her, he decided to just talk to try to explain. He figured if he took the initiative, she'd open up to her reasons.

"So, hey. I wanted to talk to you about something."

Maya sighed and began to stand up.

"No, no." Jace held out a hand. "I'm not going to argue or whatever. I'm just going to talk."

She paused, eyeing him suspiciously. Then she adjusted her hood and sat back down.

Jace choked. How much should he tell her? He glanced at his little sister from the corner of his eye. He had to say something. Otherwise, she'd continue to be upset at him, and in a time where he wanted to rebuild their relationship. He decided to be honest for a moment to see her reaction and adjust his topics from there.

"So, there's this organization in the world that hurts innocent people."

Maya didn't react. Not blunt enough?

"This organization is called The Order, and they have this unofficial war against the Evolved."

She glanced in his direction.

"I don't know why or how, but the governments have little to no power over The Order. And I guess this war has been going on for years. I heard hundreds of years. Anyways, these are the guys who attacked the neighborhood."

He had her attention as she stared at him.

"So Brian, Brittaney, Erica, and I are working to stop them." He gazed at her from the corner of his eye. Maya went back to staring at the stars. Did she lose interest? He decided to stop being so subtle. "But since the government hardly does anything, we decided to act. We are fighting back. To protect people, we are fighting back."

That seemed to catch Maya's attention once more. Perhaps brutal honesty was what she wanted to hear. But if he told her the truth, would she become afraid of the world around her? But if he didn't tell her, she'd go out to learn everything independently, which meant her possibly sneaking around and following him on his jobs. He sighed, deciding the truth would be the best to keep her out of harm's way.

"What we do is extremely dangerous. The jobs I take put me in the line of fire, which is why I come back home with bruises and such all the time. But if I don't do it, people will get hurt, or even die."

Maya looked at Jace. She covered her mouth with one hand and spun a spiral over her head with the other.

"That woman in red?"

She nodded.

"She's one of them." Again, he considered holding back the details. "She's a trained assassin that will kill anyone that The Order told her to kill. Men, women, children. It's all the same to her."

Maya clenched her fists and punched the air, then covered her head with her hand. Did she mean the bald teen in the arena? She saw that? He decided to confirm his suspicion.

"You mean that kid on the stage?"

She nodded.

Jace sighed. She did see. "No. He's just an orphaned kid, much like us. But his life was being molded into a different life than what you had." His mind spiraled into the past, remembering his life turning into hatred and violence when he arrived at the Sanctuary of Orphaned Children. He smiled, remembering the foul-mouthed woman that took him under her care. "He didn't have a Jessica."

Maya stared and blinked.

"Let's lie down and stargaze and let me tell you about Jessica."

She went to her back and stared at the stars.

"Do you remember how the showers at SOC were laid out? With the tiled floors and the showers in the back?"

Maya nodded.

"Okay, so..." Jace couldn't help but smile as he lightly chuckled. "I remember a couple of days after I arrived at SOC, I was running from something. I don't remember what or who, though. So I ran into the one place I felt I could - the women's bathroom."

Maya glared at him.

"No, no. It's nothing like that. Just let me tell you the story."

She relaxed and turned her attention back to the stars.

"So I ran into the bathroom and hid. When I saw someone walk into the bathroom, I ran further back, not knowing that's where the showers were. So I ran blindly through a shower curtain and smacked into someone. I remember the sting from the soap getting into my eyes, and her screaming as I slipped while being entangled from that shower curtain. It was a total mess."

Jace glanced toward Maya. She stared at him, giving him the attention he used to have a year before. "What? I didn't know there were showers in the bathrooms. Like I said, I had only just arrived, and it's not like that."

She nodded unconvincingly.

"Anyways, when, uh... Mrs. Stevens finally got a hold of me and was able to show me around, I discovered that there were the boy's and the girl's wings in the orphanage, and everything was symmetrical. I obviously didn't know at the time. The next day, I was in the cafeteria when some older girl started yelling at me, saying she would beat me up and I was some pervert. Behind her was some other girl who looked red from embarrassment but no less as angry. I had no idea what was going on, but it turns out that my face went between her, uh...chest, and that's why both eyes were blinded."

Maya sat up and smacked his arm.

"What?" Jace sat up and rubbed the impact point with a smile. "That's what happened."

She glared at him with crossed arms.

"Relax." Jace laid back down, which Maya followed suit shortly after. "Gah, what happened after that? Something happened sometime later that landed us both on nighttime dish duty. Jessica, the girl I ran into in the shower, not the one who threatened me. So Jessica sees me, and she raises a huge fuss, cursing and swearing like she always did. But no one was around to hear her complaints. After a while, she gave in, and she split the duties between us. She washed the dishes, and I dried them."

Jace paused to reflect on those times, all while smiling at the ridiculousness of his stupidity. "The first two nights were awkward. She didn't talk to me. I couldn't talk to her. But the third day, I was in a bad mood."

Again, Jace paused and chuckled. "Brittaney, actually, was in my literature class. And the teacher called on me to do something. It turned out I was the only kid in class who didn't know their ABCs. And though I got ridiculed by my classmates, Brittaney took pity on me and asked if I wanted her help. Being a stubborn kid, I said no."

"So I went into dish duty that night just angry. Jessica sees me and says something like, 'what's your problem, ass-hat?'" Jace chuckled. "She always swore. Like every sentence she said had at least one curse in it. But I tell her. I don't know why, but I tell her about my day. Then she proceeds to sing the ABCs, telling me to follow along. And throughout the night shift, we sang the ABCs."

Jace had to pause while he smiled and shook his head. He stayed silent for a long moment, basking in the memory of his distant past. "But we became friends. Her and her overly-protective friend. Until running into her, I was lost and alone. She grounded me when I spiraled out of control and comforted me when I got into some fight or felt angry. Truth be told, she probably saved my life."

Maya clenched Jace's hand.

Jace could only smile in reply. "Those were some of the best days I had in the orphanage. It was a night like this when..." He paused, thinking about how he discovered Jessica's internal pain and torture. He decided to keep those details out of the conversation. "Claire, the over-protective friend, got adopted. And it was a night like this when I last saw Jessica. She wasn't adopted, nor did she run away. The reason I got from the staff of SOC was, 'she was transferred for her own safety.' I never saw her again."

Maya gripped Jace's hand again.

He looked over at her and smiled. "Yeah, I don't talk about that much." His eyes returned to the stars. "I spent years looking for her to figure out what had happened. It's like she vanished, dropping off the face of the planet. But I have always wanted to find her and tell her what she did for me. If nothing else, to thank her for how she saved me. Because without her, I'd either be dead or worse, like that assassin in red."

A gentle gust of wind gave Jace a slight chill. He sat up. "I'll be right back. Going to grab the sleeping bags so we can keep staring up at the stars."

———

Jace couldn't have asked for a better vacation. After the many hikes and camping trips, he and Maya drove back to make sure she returned by Brian's requested day. And at the pace they went, they'd make it just in time for lunch. And though he didn't get all of the answers to every question he had, he felt she wouldn't follow him anymore, now that she knew what was going on.

They pulled onto the last stretch of highway and made it to the bridge only to see a dead-stop traffic jam that stretched for miles. After a while of hardly any movement, Jace exited the rental truck and stood on a tire to get a better look. That's when he realized the entire city looked to be without power.

Jace leaped down and grabbed his backpack from behind the driver's seat. "Looks like a massive blackout." He took out the earpiece from the carrier and put it in his ear. When he tapped it to call Brian, it made a strange continuous "beep-beep" sound. "Huh." He got up on the bed of the truck. Maya got out and mimicked Jace, climbing on the back of the truck, and they both looked down the endless line of vehicles.

It would be a long time before they could get into the city.

Jace sighed. "Well, while we're back here, how about some sandwiches?"

———

Late in the evening, Jace was finally able to pull up to Brian's house. Not long after he got out to stretch, the figure of Nick York stormed over toward Jace. No cane. He must be making good progress on his recovery. He seemed stressed, though.

Jace still waved. "Hello, Mr. York."

"You son of a bitch!" Nick aggressively grabbed Jace by the shirt. Jace had to make a conscious effort to restrain his reflexes from fighting back. "This is your fault!"

"Whoa, whoa. Hold on." Jace raised his arms wide in a non-threatening manner. "What's my fault? What's going on?"

Mrs. York ran from the house and shouted for Nick to stop.

"She's gone."

"What are you talking about?"

"They took her!" Nick punched Jace on the cheek.

When he went in for a second punch, Jace wrapped the attack under his arm and held it in place. "Calm down. What are you talking about?"

Wanda caught up to Nick and grabbed him.

Jace released Nick. "Will someone tell me what's going on?"

"The Order," Nick spat.

Already, Jace had a bad feeling about what had happened.

"The Order took Ruth."

Just then, a cold breeze bit through his clothes, chilling him to the bone. Even though he tried to prepare himself for the news, Jace still recoiled in shock. "What? When? How?"

Nick seemed to have had enough, and he walked away in a rage.

"Mrs. York, tell me what happened."

"Earlier today, we lost power. Shortly after, some goon squad came in, took our daughter, and left before we could react."

His mind wandered toward Maya. If they didn't go on their little vacation, could she have been taken, too? His heart sank at the idea. "Just her?"

"I don't know. We can't get a hold of anybody."

"Anyone hurt?"

She shook her head. "No. At least nothing serious."

A drop of rain splashed Jace's freshly punched cheek while his eyes went from Wanda to Nick. "Please believe me. I had nothing to do with this."

"I know. It's just..." Wanda sighed and turned toward her husband, who paced in a circle while mumbling to himself.

"What about the police?"

"They can't do anything. Especially with the blackout going on."

Jace whispered, "What the hell is going on?" He sighed and turned to look toward Brian's house. However, his gaze was diverted to Maya, who sat in the grass with her head buried in her hands. Was his interference with The Order putting her in danger again? He would have to spend more time around her, just in case.

He sat next to her and hugged her. She leaned heavily against him as her tears soaked through his shirt. He looked up at the sky just as a boom of thunder struck. It was going to be a long, cold night.

CHAPTER SIXTEEN

ERICA RETURNED THE FOLLOWING MORNING BUT CAUGHT SOME strange flu from the convention. She went straight to the bathroom without saying a word before occupying Brian's bedroom to rest. And with the storm in the middle of a blacked-out city, it's no wonder she got sick.

Late in the morning, Jace answered a knock at the front door. There, in the pouring rain, Nick and Wanda York stood, well dressed and pampered under an umbrella.

Mr. York cleared his throat. "Hello, Jace. May we speak for a minute?"

Jace turned to look at Maya, who continued to cry on the couch. "Yeah, sure." He took a step outside and held the door open at a slight crack. He didn't want to get his socks too wet.

"Firstly, accept my apology for attacking you last night."

Jace shrugged. It was hardly a hit. Nick's hands are for pencil-pushing, not to induce punishment. "It's fine."

"Very well. Secondly, I have come to ask for your assistance."

"Me?" Jace prodded his chest with his thumb. "What do you need me for?"

"You are fighting The Order. Yes?"

"You already know that answer."

"Then allow me to assist."

Jace eyed Nick with suspicion. Then his eyes briefly went to Wanda, who seemed genuine in this conversation. "How?"

"I wish to join in your crusade."

"It's hardly a crusade."

"But it is a conflict, and they have just made a grievous error."

"Is that so?"

Nick nodded. "They took our daughter."

"What about the police?"

"They can't do anything. That's why I'm asking for your assistance."

Wanda stepped forward. "Please, help us. Help us get our daughter back."

Jace got a sour amusement at how reversed the Yorks attitudes were this time around. Nick seemed more put-together while Wanda was on the verge of losing it.

Nick put a hand on his wife's arm. She took a breath and stepped back.

Jace's gaze went from Wanda to Nick. "What do you have in mind?"

"I believe I have a method of battling The Order. They are powerful and rooted deep into the world governments."

Jace nodded, signaling he understood what was said so far.

"So I have an idea on how to uproot this evil that has plagued our world for so long. You said at the hospital you were gathering evidence. We can use that evidence to attack their reputation."

That took Jace by surprise. "Their reputation?"

"Yes. Though your efforts in quelling their designs are admirable, it is ultimately for naught. However, if the world learned the truth of their presence, the people would rise up and spark the governments into action."

"That's a little beyond me."

"Ah, but you do not see the big picture." Nick brought his hands out in a grandiose gesture. "We will be but the first step in a revolution that shall shake the very foundations of civilization."

"And how do you think that'll go down?"

Nick clenched his fists and brought them to his chest. "In flames."

"Wow. Not a very good reason to do this then."

"But within the flames, we, like the phoenix, shall rise from the ash."

Jace rolled his eyes.

Nick sighed to recompose himself. "Jace, let me reiterate my request. I want you to do what you're already doing, but I will pull my strings to give you your much-needed leeway."

That caught Jace's attention.

"And I shall fund your enterprise."

"So, you want to pay us for doing what we're doing anyways?"

Nick nodded. "And I shall use whatever resources I have to provide you with relevant information and jobs that I'd like done."

"We can manage that on our own."

"Ah, but can you get the influence of local governments to assist you in your duties?"

Jace scoffed. "You can't even get the police to help you now."

"I didn't say they won't help. I only said they can't. And I can develop personnel of my own."

After a moment, Jace gave a deep sigh. "Let me talk with my friends. They're in this as much as I am."

Nick nodded. "Very well. We shall await word." He extended a hand, which Jace shook after only a brief hesitation. "Good day." He and Wanda turned to walk through the rain, which seemed to have slowed down a bit.

Jace went back inside. Maya sat on the couch and stared at him, but not in the same spot she was before. "Hey, how are you doing?" He sat next to Maya and put an arm over her shoulder.

Maya's eyes were red and puffy. She shrugged after a sniff.

"You want something to eat? How about some soup?"

She nodded.

Just as he stood to go toward the kitchen, Erica exited the bathroom and paused as she looked at Jace. She gave a single cough and cleared her throat. "What's going on?"

"Not much. Just about to make some soup for Maya." He approached Erica. "How are you feeling? Would you like some soup, too?"

Her eyes darted between him and Maya before pointing to her.

"I think she'll be fine. Her friend was taken by The Order last night."

She seemed shocked at the news. "Wait, her friend?"

"Yeah." Jace put a hand on Erica's shoulder. "Come on. Let's get you back to bed. I'll bring you some soup when it's ready."

Erica went to Brian's room and laid in bed. Jace tucked her in, kissed her on the forehead, and shut the door behind him.

So much was going on. For a moment, Jace wondered if he could keep track of it all. First things first, the soup.

———

Later in the evening, Jace stared out the front window when Brian got home from work. He mumbled something as he walked in, and he seemed frustrated and stressed.

Brian took off his coat and hung it in the closet to let it dry. "Damn power plant. I think the new owners really screwed things up. I couldn't get ample power to run my tests at work."

That seemed to catch Jace's attention. "Is that what caused the blackout?"

"No." Brian shook his head and adjusted his glasses. "The power outage was something external. I have no idea what happened." He went to the living room and sat in the recliner. "Hey, Maya. How are you doing?"

Maya shrugged.

She seemed to be doing much better than earlier. She stopped crying and had regained her focus. Perhaps she wanted to stay busy so she didn't think about her friend.

"Hey, Brian. You got a minute?" Jace gestured to the garage just as Erica clambered out of the back room.

Brian greeted Erica. "Oh, you're back. You don't look well."

Jace shook his head as he moved to assist Erica. "She caught the flu while at her convention."

Erica lifted a hand to stop Jace. "I'll be fine on my own." Keeping herself propped against the wall, she made it to the bathroom and shut the door behind her.

"Geez." Brian picked up the dishes from the coffee table and went to the kitchen before going to the garage.

After they entered the garage, Jace shut the door behind him.

Brian went to his workbench and sat down. "When is Brittaney due back?"

"Wednesday." Jace approached.

"Any updates on Ruth?"

"Kind of? Nick and Wanda visited me this morning."

"He's not still mad, is he?"

Jace shook his head, and he leaned against his car. "In fact, he kind of asked to join our crew."

"He did?" Brian rubbed the stubble on his chin as he looked away in thought. "Holy smokes, that's some interesting news."

"Yeah. He wants to finance our operation and use the information we got to attack The Order's reputation."

"He does?" Brian couldn't contain a smile. "That's awesome news! What did you say?"

"I said I'd talk to everyone."

Brian stood up. "Well, he's got my vote."

"We still have to talk to Erica and Brittaney."

"Erica doesn't look well, and I know Brittaney will be on board." Brian put a hand on Jace's shoulder. "And if either of them protest, I'll take the blame."

"That's noble of you. But I don't think it'll fly."

"Why not?" Brian went back to his workbench. "After all, someone with as deep of pockets as Mr. York will help us greatly." He picked up some flat green piece from the bench. "This stuff isn't cheap, and we are quickly running out of money." He tossed it back nonchalantly.

Jace's face crumpled in confusion as he looked from the discarded item to Brian.

"It's shot. I have to get a new one, anyway. But listen..." Brian approached Jace again. "If Mr. York is on board, it will open a lot of doors in this fight."

"You think so?"

Brian nodded.

Jace always trusted Brian's judgment. And with how eager he was about the prospect of bringing Nick in, he knew it would work out somehow. He nodded. "Okay, let's go over there now and get some more details."

"Awesome!" Brian smiled and raised a clenched fist. "This will work out. You'll see." He brought his hands forward, as if to make a calming point. "And let me do the talking. I have some questions I'd like answered."

———

After the front security check allowed them to pass, Jace noticed additional personnel roamed the property. He also observed thin lines in the windows as they approached the tan and light blue entryway. More security? Structural reinforcement? Regardless, the house continuously seemed to be updated. He figured, at this rate, it would be more secured than most military bases.

After knocking, a butler answered and led the two to the study where Nick York waited. He sat at his desk with a computer off to the side while he held a glass of booze.

"Greetings, gentlemen." Nick gestured at the chairs opposite of the desk. "Please, have a seat."

When the two sat down, Brian said, "Hello, Mr. York. Jace told me about your proposition."

"Yes." Nick drank the contents of his drink and set the glass on a coaster on his desk. "As I have told Jace, I am willing to fund your enterprise and grant you permissions to exit the city once more. With some stipulations, of course."

"Okay." Brian adjusted his glasses. "And what are those?"

"That any information you retrieve on your operations will be delivered to me. That way, I can figure the best way to benefit from said information."

Jace leaned to Brian. "Everything is already being funneled to Brittaney."

"True, but maybe Brittaney and Mr. York could work together."

That sounded fair to Jace, and he returned fully to his chair.

Brian nodded to Nick's request. "Anything else?"

"Yes. None of this can be traced back to me or my family."

"For your reputation?"

"That, but more for my daughter's safety. Who knows what The Order will do if they discover my hand in their downfall."

Jace shook his head. "That'll be pretty tough. Especially if you'll be giving us cash, they'll find out."

Nick poured himself another drink. "Then find a way to make it happen." He took a sip.

Brian leaned forward in his chair. "I have my own stipulations, Mr. York."

Nick eyed Brian from behind his booze glass. "Do you now?"

"Yes. If you want to do this full-time, the entire crew will need to be on a payroll. And I want to set up shop in a new location." When Nick didn't reply, Brian continued. "The shop will need to be in a secure location and be able to contain my work."

The lights flickered for a moment.

Brian began to fume. "That includes ample power! And we will need privacy and safety if something happens."

"What about your current position?"

"Not a part of the discussion."

Nick stared at Brian before taking another sip of his drink. "And how big will this shop be?"

That gave Brian pause. He looked away in thought. "I don't know. Maybe the size of the 4th street warehouse?"

Nick set down his drink and started to type on his computer. "Is that all?"

"Well..." Brian adjusted his glasses. "I guess the warehouse will need some sort of backup power supply just in case another blackout happens. Like I have on my house, where the solar panels charge a—"

"Done." Nick pushed a final button on the keyboard, leaned back, and grabbed his drink.

Jace and Brian blinked in confusion.

Brian asked, "Done?"

"Yes." He chugged the rest of his drink and poured himself another.

"What do you mean 'done'?"

"I purchased the 4th street warehouse and all of the property surrounding it."

Brian and Jace looked at each other for a moment, then they went back to Nick. Jace shook his head. "Won't that leave a paper trail back to you?"

"Not if you find a way to purchase it from me."

"I don't know. This seems suspiciously dangerous."

"Don't worry. I have a plan."

Again, Brian and Jace sat silently for a long moment.

"Anything else?"

Jace tried to swim through the bewilderment that clouded his mind to think logically once more. However, before he could get an answer, Brian stood up and extended his hand. "Mr. York, we have a deal."

Nick stood and shook his hand. "Superb. Send me your salary requirements as well as any contracts you wish to secure. Good day, gentlemen."

Jace shook Nick's hand, and he and Brian exited the house, not saying a word until they stood dumbfounded on the street.

"Brian, did we win?"

Brian smiled. "Jace, this is a huge step for us!" He turned excitedly. "Do you know what this means?"

"I think so." Jace ran his fingers through his hair. "So... what now?"

"We need to figure out how to get those funds from Mr. York. Maybe someone who can handle the massive transactions."

"Like an accountant? Someone who knows about economics and such?"

Brian nodded. "Yeah, like an accountant."

"Brian..." Jace patted Brian's shoulder. "I think I have someone in mind."

———

Due to Maya's schooling, Jace asked Nick and Wanda York to watch her while everyone went to get their business started. And after the Yorks increased the security of their home, Jace, Brian, Brittaney, and Erica set off to the 'someone' he had in mind.

The group of four exited the oversized taxi at the large house on a small hill of grass. It had a fresh yellow coat of paint, a newly dug trench near the end of the patio, and a pile of bricks on a pallet at the far corner of the driveway.

As Jace crawled out, he coughed into a handkerchief, then stumbled as he slowly got to his feet. He leaned back and took a deep breath while the other three grabbed some bags from the trunk.

"You could have warned me about the car sickness," Brittaney said as she reached up and closed the trunk.

Erica scoffed. "Who would have thought the Terror of the Evolved could be brought down from a simple car ride?"

The girls chuckled at Jace's expense as he slowly made his way around the car, keeping his hand on the vehicle for support.

Brian walked up next to Jace with both of their bags on his shoulders. "You going to live?"

Jace coughed once more into the cloth, then nodded. "Yeah. I'll live. I gave the driver a nice tip for barfing in his car."

When Jace regained enough of his balance to be without support, he stood up straight and patted the car to signal the driver they were done.

Brian turned to look at the yellow house. "So, this is the same Claire you had me search for?"

Jace nodded. "After I found out Maya was an Evolved, I somehow ended up laid out on her lawn."

"You must have subconsciously made your way here."

Again, Jace nodded. "She saved my life, and reminded me of..." A burp escaped his lips, and a sudden burning in his throat made him cough into the handkerchief.

Brian put the bags down and grabbed Jace to hold him steady.

Erica quickly flanked him, grabbing his right side. "Why don't you lie down a moment?" Erica led him toward the grass. "Give your equilibrium time to sync with your eyes."

Jace didn't object. With help, he made his way to the grass and nearly collapsed. Brian and Erica caught him, then slowly brought him down. They knelt beside Jace, making sure he didn't hit too hard as he made his way down. Jace looked up at the sky, focusing his gaze on the distant clouds. "We can't waste any time," he said in a weakened voice. He noticed Brian looking up as Erica turned her head toward the house.

"Oh, hello," Brittaney said aloud.

"Is that...?" Jace heard a familiar voice say. "I swear. Why is it every time we meet again, you're lying helpless on my lawn?"

Jace shifted his head to look upon Claire standing just above his head. With a grin, she rubbed her hands with a towel, then crossed her arms at her chest. Under a sizeable tan sun hat, her shoulder-length hair was a bright blue with purple tips, with the color turning darker as it made its way to her bangs that hung loosely over her right eye. She wore overalls and a white shirt covered with dirt.

Jace gave a single cough. "Just motion sickness this time."

"Motion sickness?" Claire shook her head. "I didn't know you even got motion sickness."

He can get pretty bad." Erica stood up and extended her hand. "I'm Erica."

"You're the woman he talked about?" Claire gave a beaming smile. She stepped in place a couple of paces, then reached and shook her hand. "You're even more beautiful than Jace described."

That gave Erica a pause, then she blushed.

Brittaney extended her hand for an introduction. "Brittaney Webbs."

"The girl with the memory. My, you're a cute one too."

Brittaney's eyes widened, and she, too, blushed.

"Uh, I... Um..."

Claire examined Brian, scanning his look for a long moment. "Smart looking, handsome, but awkward. You must be Brian." She extended her hand in a greeting.

"H-Handsome?" Brian stammered, and his eyes went to his left at Brittaney, then to his right to Erica, as if searching for answers. After the long moment of awkwardness from Brian, he finally noticed the extended hand. "Oh, uh... Y-yes. I'm Brian."

"I heard you were the one that tracked me down after I got adopted." Claire gestured to Brittaney. "And you tracked her down, too."

"I, yes. Wait, did I?" Brian looked to Jace.

"Don't give his strangeness a second thought." Jace reached his arm up to cover his eyes. "He's always like that around girls he doesn't know."

"So, you're super nervous?"

"I, wait. Me?"

That seemed to have answered Claire's question. She hopped over Jace and hugged Brian. Then, before Brian could even register what was going on, she grabbed him by the cheeks, and gave him a quick kiss on the lips. "There. Now you know me."

Brian took a step back, totally lost at what had just happened. His cheeks were flush, and he just stared at Claire blankly.

"So, what brings you ass-hats to my house?"

Erica laughed before turning to Jace. "First, let's get this 'ass-hat' inside and hydrated."

———

Jace sat on the couch next to Erica, listening to the women as they got to know each other. Brian sat in the side chair, speechless, apparently still in shock.

Feeling a little better, Jace stood and began to walk around. He got to the entryway that had the side room with the many musical instruments. Though he never heard them used, they weren't where he remembered them. He continued to walk around, staring at the many pictures and paintings, before stopping to examine some framed pieces of paper. After skipping some lines in fancy writing, his eyes focused on a couple of lines. "The faculty and the Board of Trustees hereby grant the Degree of Masters of Science in Business and Economics." He smiled, then saw another below it. The framed page looked the same, but it read, "Masters of Sociology" instead. They were dated just a couple of weeks ago.

Claire's voice broke Jace out of his contemplation. "So where is this angel you spoke of before beating up my ex and running from the cops?"

Brittaney looked over at Jace with a seemingly angry glare. "Problems with the law again?"

"She's at a trusted friend's house," Erica answered, dismissing Brittaney's stare.

"Oh?"

Jace turned around. "Something came up, and we need your help."

Claire's expression went from her usual playful look to serious and concerned. "What happened?"

Jace walked up and sat in a vacant space next to Erica. "Remember me telling you about The Order?"

Claire nodded.

"Well, long story short, they're kidnapping kids for some reason."

Claire gasped and put a hand over her mouth. "That's awful. Why would they do that?"

"We don't know."

"Can't the police or something help?"

"The Order isn't a part of the government," Erica explained. "In fact, they're above it, in most cases. We have a benefactor who is willing to financially support us against The Order."

"Why would he do that?" Claire asked.

"Because his daughter was one of the kidnapped children," Erica answered.

Claire gasped again. "Oh, no."

Brittaney leaned forward. "The benefactor we spoke of is a public figure and cannot be traced to this operation. Therefore, we need you to take his place and find a way to legally yet covertly allocate the funds from him to us."

Claire's eyes widened, and her head recoiled in shock. "Me?"

Jace nodded. "Yes. I saw that you got your economist degree, or something like that. You know business and how to handle money."

Claire raised a correcting finger. "Economics and business, actually. And yes, I do. But—"

"We have great talent and brilliant minds," Erica said. "Brittaney can help with the legal matters, but we still need someone who can handle large quantities of cash. We're offering you a job because you can fill the role we need. And most importantly, Jace trusts you, so *we* trust you."

That made the room silent for many heartbeats.

Claire slowly started to scan her guests, eventually locking her eyes on Jace.

Jace's heart started to sink as Claire sighed and shook her head. "What would you do without me?" Claire grinned. "Okay, if you think I can help, I'll help."

CHAPTER SEVENTEEN

EACH BREATH CREATED A WHITE PLUME OF STEAM AS JACE AND MAYA jogged around the city park. When she signaled that she was too exhausted to continue running, the two paced a bit to regain their breath, then started to walk into the city. After a couple of blocks, Jace noticed Maya's clothes getting a little tight on her. She's growing.

Jace dug into his backpack for some cash to put in his pocket. "Let's get you some new clothes while we're out."

After a nod, they approached the business district and at the newly constructed buildings that surrounded them. Jace looked through the aero-vehicle traffic above to the architecture, seeing that modern-day structure designs were going for a smooth look. That meant fewer handholds.

As they arrived at a crosswalk, Jace paused and stared up at the rooftops. Something he couldn't explain gnawed at his consciousness that kept his attention focused on that building.

Maya tugged on his sleeve, breaking his gaze from the roof. The light was green, indicating they could cross.

"Oh, sorry." Jace gave Maya a nod, and they began to cross the street. He looked at the shops—a sweets shop with a golden illuminated sign, a red sign of a clothing shop with mannequins dressed in various clothes in the windows, and a multi-level hotel under construction with reflective windows.

Again, Jace paused, looking at the rooftops. "How about we try here?" He indicated the clothing store, then looked down at Maya.

Her gaze went from the store to him, and her expression seemed to be one of incredulity.

"Hey, they may have something you like." Jace pointed at the sweets shop next door. "And we'll get a little snack after. Okay?"

That seemed to buy her approval. She smiled and nodded, and the two went into the clothing store.

Though the place seemed like an upscale store, with polos and slacks and preppy-looking mannequins, Jace's attention was on the building itself. What was it about this place that bothered him so much?

A greeter in a red coat and slacks smiled and approached. "Welcome."

"Do you have a restroom?"

"Yes, down the aisle and turn right at the back wall."

Even though he spotted the bathroom sign on the back wall before asking the employee where they were, Jace's eyes locked onto the double doors that led to the rear.

Jace put a hand on Maya's shoulder. "Have a look around. I'll be right back."

After she nodded, he left her on her own to investigate his gut feeling. When he reached the back wall, he went left before going through the doors—storage and overflow, and what looked like an office or a break room. But the stairs that led to a ladder to the roof were what Jace looked for.

As he climbed the stairs, a voice called out to him. "Hey, you're not supposed to be back here."

Jace didn't listen to the protesting employee from behind and continued toward the ladder.

The protesting voice called out, "Bob, call security. We got some guy in the back going to the roof."

Jace reached the small platform and quietly opened the door that led to the roof. There he saw a man in dark clothes and a beanie placing small objects on the far side of the rooftop in a pattern Jace knew all too well.

Jace looked up at the late morning sky. Was tonight a full moon? And why this building? The hotel was much taller, and it wasn't populated. People would be able to see the device from there. On top of that, if he understood the mechanics of the devices, they needed to be unobstructed from the night sky, and the hotel would definitely block whatever it does. Was he on the wrong rooftop?

Jace suppressed a chuckle. It didn't matter. He quietly closed the door behind him so he could confront the stranger. "It's a nice day. Wouldn't you say?"

Beanie stood and turned to face Jace. He wore a mask to cover almost every feature of his face except his brown eyes. "This isn't a concern of yours. Get lost before you get hurt."

Jace took a couple of steps closer to get a better look at the stranger. As the man in the mask shifted, Jace noticed several throwing knives strapped all around his clothes. An interesting weapon of choice. Limited, but silent and effective. "You can't be very high up in the ranks. In fact..." Jace scrutinized the placement of the nodes. "I'd say Sergeant. You're too ignorant to be of use."

Beanie stood in a threatening pose. "Who are you?"

"Doesn't matter. What does matter is you need to pick up your..." Jace made quote marks in the air. "'Sensor' units and leave."

Beanie quickly extended an arm. A knife lethally flew toward Jace.

Jace barely reacted fast enough and pivoted to dodge the attack. Luckily, he had good balance beforehand. Otherwise, he doubted the dodge would have been so graceful.

He'd have to play it calm and cool. Not only because Beanie tried to kill him, but a massive factor in a fight is morale.

Jace stood casually and did his best to remain unphased. "Last chance to pack up and go."

Beanie brought back an arm.

Jace smirked, energized, and ready to go. Then he realized he didn't have any gear on him. All he had was a short-sleeved shirt, polyester pants, his boots, and his backpack. So if he didn't dodge that knife, he'd probably be dead on the floor. At that moment, he regretted picking a fight with Beanie, silently scolding himself for not ambushing the guy when he had the chance.

The door behind him opened, and the protesting voice called out, "There he is."

Beanie launched some more knives. Not at him, but at the store employee and the security.

Jace spun around, using his backpack as a shield for the civilians, and kicked the employee in the gut. When the employee stumbled a step, Jace slammed the door shut, and he rolled to the side, the thunk of two knives burying themselves hilt-deep in the door.

He hoped the employees wouldn't interfere, and the presence of knives piercing their door would hopefully be enough to scare them off. They would be in grave danger, and their presence would only hinder his efforts.

When Jace looked at Beanie, some more knives were thrown at him. Jace leaped over one while the second naturally missed. Jace took off his backpack and held it like a shield, deflecting another bladed blow.

Being a few paces away, Jace couldn't get in close enough to counterattack. So he used the only weapon he could think of—his backpack.

After Jace dodged another knife and blocked a second, he threw his backpack at Beanie, who sidestepped it. But the step was enough of a pause for Jace to charge, leaping headlong in a forward roll.

Now in melee range, Jace bobbed a swing and pivoted a thrust, then gave a couple of punches in return.

Beanie slashed at Jace, a thin line sliced in his shirt, then step back to get some distance.

Jace eyed Beanie while silently scolding himself for letting him get some distance.

They stood off for a long moment as a chill breeze hit his skin, and an uncomfortable sting pulsed on his chest. The slash actually cut his skin, but it was only a sting. Nothing too deep.

"You're good, deadman." Beanie played with a knife in one hand, finally ending up in a reverse grip.

"Luck doesn't hold up in the end." Jace took off his shirt and held it at its end. That's when he realized the rooftop door was cracked open. Those fools from the store had better not get in the way.

Just as Beanie went to throw a knife, Jace snapped his shirt forward, hitting his hand. Beanie's hand reflexively opened, and the knife was flung aside. He quickstepped forward and ducked a slash from the reverse-gripped blade, then swatted aside a stab. Jace snapped his shirt once more, entangling the arm with the reversed grip. With the arm locked, Jace made his move, using the momentum to assist in his pivot as he threw Beanie over his hip and to the rooftop.

Jace stomped as Beanie rolled away, barely missing his hand to hinder his weapon use. But before Beanie could get to his feet, Jace landed a boot square in Beanie's jaw. He fell to his back and rolled away.

Apparently out of throwing weapons, Beanie, blood soaking through his dark mask, reached back and took out two wicked-looking knives with curved blades. As if spurn to life, the metal flared in a red glow.

Before Jace could react, Beanie lunged forward and gave a

backhand slash. Jace blocked. Or he tried to. Jace found himself launched back half a dozen feet before painfully skidding on his side across the rooftop.

Jace rolled to his hands and knees as Beanie stood confident a few paces away. There was no way Beanie had that kind of strength. Not with his noodle-like frame. Could this guy be a demon? Or maybe another stupid cyborg?

Beanie began to play with his weapons, spinning them around his fingers like it mattered. "You should have left when I gave you the chance."

That's when Jace's eyes caught the red trail of light from the knives.

Beanie charged, stabbing downward from a reverse grip. Jace went low and kicked out a leg. Beanie began to crash down, one blade falling to the ground while the other, the one Beanie attacked with, came stabbing straight toward Jace's chest. Jace let go of his shirt and caught Beanie mid-fall, barely stopping the blade from plunging into his torso, feeling a strange heat against his skin. Jace and Beanie struggled with the blade, neither of them making any progress for many heartbeats.

Jace was in trouble. His strength was quickly draining while holding up Beanie.

Feeling his skin sear made Jace sneer in pain. He shifted his foot outward, hoping to use his leg for leverage.

The tip touched his flesh and it sizzled.

Beanie sat up a split second, then pressed down with his body weight. That gave Jace the opportunity he needed, and he pressed his foot against the ground, and he twisted his body. The blade went between his chest and his arm.

Jace elbowed Beanie across the face, and he fell to the side. Jace rolled in the opposite direction to his hands and knees. He clenched his chest to feel the burn mark before his eyes gazed at the strange dagger that stuck hilt-deep into the roof.

Beanie and Jace stood, Beanie holding the second curved

blade in his hand. They stared at each other for a few seconds, eyeing one another while only a few paces away from each other.

That gave Jace a moment to think about the situation. Beanie was obviously from The Order. Throwing knives were his weapon of choice, but with his seemingly superhuman strength, Jace was baffled. He couldn't have been a cyborg. Or at least not in the same category as Roberts. And The Order used demons, not employed them.

His time to think ended after Beanie attacked. Knowing Beanie had some strange, unnatural strength, Jace kept dodging and weaving, only swatting when he had to misdirect an attack. After ducking a slash, Jace counterattacked, jabbing at Beanie's abdomen. The hit gave Beanie pause, and the two stepped back.

Beanie held his stomach with his free hand.

No, this wasn't a demon. The strength came from somewhere else.

He adjusted his mindset, thinking about how he always fought opponents stronger than him. They were usually bigger and slower, and not swinging red-hot knives.

Jace smiled after a deep breath. A nice, cool breeze brushed his skin. "You feel that? That's the sign of your luck changing."

Deciding to wing it, Jace took a calm step forward, ready for whatever attack came. He ducked a slash and countered with a quick gut punch. He sidestepped a lunge and Jace snap-kicked Beanie's knee. Every time Beanie attacked, Jace defended and countered as quickly as possible. Whether this guy was a cyborg or a demon, Jace knew that each blow alone wouldn't be enough to stop a lumbering giant. But one after another, hitting the same few points again and again, would eventually take its toll.

And so it was when Beanie gave a slow slash. Instead of dodging, Jace quick-stepped forward and used his momentum to shoulder-throw Beanie to the rooftop. As Beanie's face crashed against the ground, Jace brought the knife arm behind his back and used joint locks to hold the limb in place. Beanie growled and struggled, but eventually Jace was able to get the knife from Beanie's hand.

Being on top, Jace took a moment to inspect the blade. It was indeed red hot, but strange patterns etched into the metal caught his eye. "What is that?" Jace leaned a little closer to the blade. "Is this...writing?"

While distracted, Beanie lurched back and tossed Jace off. Jace rolled from his back to his feet as Beanie stood. Blood clearly soaked his clothes, and his posture showed he favored his left side.

Beanie lifted the bottom of his mask to spit blood on the rooftop. "Who are you?"

"Where is your insignia?"

"My what?"

Jace looked incredulously at Beanie. He went to his backpack, took out the four knives stuck in the front, and dug through it until he found the golden jewel-adorned bracelet. He lifted it up to show Beanie.

"That's Dame Moon's!"

"Ah, so you do know what this is." He put the bracelet back in his backpack and approached Beanie. "So, where is it?"

Beanie's eyes went to the blade in Jace's hand.

"Oh, this?" Jace lifted the dagger, waved it from side to side, watching Beanie's eyes lock on it. "I don't need this." Then he tossed it to the side. Seeing Beanie's eyes follow the discarded dagger, Jace lunged forward, landing a few hard-hitting blows across his face and body. Beanie fell on the roof.

Jace knelt on Beanie's chest and leaned in a little. "Your insignia."

With shaky hands, Beanie reached under his shirt.

"Slowly," Jace warned.

Beanie grabbed a piece of folded leather and presented it. Jace took the item and opened it up. Inside, Jace saw the unadorned symbol that marked a soldier of The Order. "See? Barely a sergeant." He finished Beanie off with a hard cross to the jaw. Beanie went limp.

Jace stood and took a moment to catch his breath. That's when he heard sirens in the distance. He was running out of time.

After putting the folded leather in his backpack, Jace turned his attention to the strange daggers, and he knelt to pick up the one he tossed aside.

It no longer glowed.

Was there a switch or something?

Not knowing if there was some sort of electronic trap in the strange weapon, Jace ripped his tattered shirt in half and wrapped the tossed dagger. As he approached the one embedded in the rooftop, Jace wondered if he was going to be able to retrieve the blade or if it would be stuck in the rooftop. After covering the hilt with the rest of his shirt, he pulled hard. It came out with ease, and Jace almost fell on his ass.

Again, he looked at the strange blade, and the writing etched on it. He had seen something like this before, but he couldn't remember where.

It would be a riddle for another time.

Jace put the wrapped-up daggers in his backpack and looked at the door. What was he supposed to do now? With the sirens getting closer, Maya would indeed be caught up in all of this if he went inside. But he couldn't just leave her behind.

A gust of wind blew his hair to the side as a police aero-vehicle hovered near the rooftop. Did Nick York tell the police to leave him alone? Would they listen? He couldn't delay any longer, nor could he risk it.

Jace ran to the aero-vehicle and leaped off the side of the roof, gripping what Jace figured was a landing gear with no small amount of pain shooting through his chest, and swung over to the hotel, landing in a roll from an uninstalled window.

Jace glanced over his shoulder at the police vehicle spinning around as he ran down a flight of stairs. He raced toward a window and peeked outside. The clothing store was being evacuated, and Maya would be in that crowd.

When the aero-vehicle moved around the building, Jace went up a floor and leaped out the window he went through, catching himself against the clothing store's outer-wall, and climbed back to the roof. When he peeked his head over the ledge, he saw two police officers putting Beanie in handcuffs.

Jace shimmied himself around the ledge furthest away, turning the corner just as the aero-vehicle returned to the alleyway. When he was far enough to the side, Jace peeked once more over the ledge. No one looked in his direction.

He lifted himself over the ledge and hid behind the door just as two more police officers got to the roof. Jace looked between the door and the doorframe. When the coast was clear, he slid inside, climbed down, and leaped to the warehouse floor, avoiding the stairs in case more law enforcement went to the roof.

On the way toward the showroom, Jace grabbed a dark shirt and hat, went toward the sales floor, and kept toward the back wall until he made it to the bathroom. Then he brushed himself off and casually walked out.

A police officer spotted him.

Jace feigned shock.

"What are you doing here?" The police officer questioned.

"Uh, just finished using the toilet. What's going on?"

The police officer briefly inspected Jace. "Come on." He ushered Jace out the front door and behind the forming barricade.

Jace stared at the scene. He'd have a warrant out for his arrest again, or maybe Nick York could clear things up. Regardless, he couldn't take the chance of being arrested.

After a few seconds, Jace made his way through the crowd until he found the familiar hooded figure. Jace put a hand on Maya's shoulder. She spun around in shock but eased when she gazed up at him.

Jace gestured with his head away from the scene. "Come on. We have to go."

Maya nodded, and the two left.

———

Maya didn't seem to care about being escorted out of the store by the police without Jace. Maybe it's because she had an idea of what was going on. Maybe it was something else, but Jace didn't bother figuring it out. Not yet, at least.

After they got back to Brian's place, Jace led Brian to the garage and put his backpack on the workbench.

Erica walked in, still looking a little pale. "Where have you been?"

"Out." Jace gestured to his backpack. "Come here. I want to show you two something."

She made her way to the bench as Jace unzipped his bag. "Do you think..." Jace took out the blades and began to unwrap them. "That The Order is cheating somehow?"

Erica stared hard at Jace. "Cheating? How?"

That's when Jace presented the daggers.

Brian adjusted his glasses. "Those are fancy looking."

"Jace," Erica said while only glancing at the blades. "Those things are common among The Order."

Jace was taken aback by that comment. "What?"

Erica nodded. "Officers are often assigned support equipment to complement their natural talents."

"You're kidding." Jace looked at the daggers. "How come I haven't heard of them?"

"I've been trying to get you assigned the proper equipment for months. You were..." She gave a muffled burp, and she turned pale. "...never around long enough for the appropriate assessments."

"Why don't you get some more rest?" Jace put a hand on Erica's shoulder and ushered her back to the door. "I'll be back to check on you."

She didn't seem too happy about that request, but she gave in and went back inside.

Jace returned to Brian's side. "Have you seen or heard of anything like this before?"

Brian moved one of his magnifying glasses to closely inspect the weapons. "No." He tapped the blade. "It's warm."

"Yeah, that's what I noticed, too."

"So what happened? Where did you find these?"

"Got into a fight with someone from The Order."

That caught Brian's attention, and he looked at Jace. "With Maya?"

Jace shook his head. "It was on the roof of some clothing store. She was inside during the whole thing."

Brian adjusted his glasses and visually inspected Jace. "Is that why you look like a retired golfer?"

Jace chuckled. "Shut up, dick."

Brian grinned, then returned his attention to the daggers. "Hey, you mind if I run some tests on these?"

"They're all yours, buddy. I want to know how The Order has been cheating this whole time."

"You got it."

Jace patted Brian's shoulder. "I'm going to go change out of these golfing clothes."

CHAPTER EIGHTEEN

LOOKING THROUGH THE STEAMY MIRROR, JACE TRACED A FINGER down the slash across his chest, finally settling on the burn mark in the middle of his torso and the small puncture wound in the center. They weren't significant injuries, and they were already in the scarring stages. However, the fight with Beanie shook him, even if he didn't want to admit it. Even when he fought demons and wound up with broken bones, he never felt so close to death. If the slash was a millimeter closer, or the tip of the blade a hair deeper, he would have been done for.

He shook off the lingering dread that clung to his heart and put on a shirt to cover his injury before exiting the bathroom.

Maya, holding a plate with a sandwich and a handful of chips, walked toward her room.

"Hey, Maya. One more week until the new place is ready. You excited?"

Maya hardly looked up at him and gave a single-shoulder shrug, and went to her room, closing the door behind her.

Claire walked into the house looking exhausted and sat on the couch. "How in the world did you get affiliated with someone like Nicolas York?"

"Is that a bad thing?" Jace sat in the seat opposite Claire.

"No, not at all." She leaned back and took a deep breath. "That guy has deep pockets. I think I have everything taken care of. The money is coming in from various resources and being funneled into separate accounts. Hopefully, it'll be enough to not draw any attention to him."

"Well, money seems to be coming in, so I think Nick thinks everything works."

She shrugged.

Brittaney entered from the garage and approached the couch. "Hey Jace, good news. Owen Stent isn't getting out of jail for a while."

"Who?"

She sat down, took off her heels, set a briefcase on the coffee table, and opened it up. "Owen Stent. The guy with the knives."

"Oh, that guy."

"Yeah. Apparently, a ton of charges are being placed on him, and the judge denied bail."

Claire propped up her head. "Awesome."

"Yeah." Brittaney dug through her briefcase. "Mr. York and I have been working on your involvement. We may have an angle but stay inside for another day or two."

Jace sighed. "I thought Nick had some sort of connections or something."

"Oh, he does." Brittaney handed Jace a piece of paper. It was a picture of him on the rooftop. "You were already on the police's radar before this happened, and this picture from an aero-cruiser got a nice photo of you."

"Oh, let me see." Claire sat up and looked at the picture. "What's that on your chest?"

Jace subconsciously put his thumb on the burn mark. "A cut I got from Beanie." When he realized they looked puzzled at him, Jace clarified, "Owen Stent."

"So, does the police know where Jace is?" Claire asked.

"Kind of." Brittaney took out a folder stuffed with paper and put it on the table. "But they know about this place."

"Does that mean Brian will get in trouble?"

Brittaney shook her head. "Thanks to Mr. York, they won't even question him."

Jace picked up the folder. "What's this?"

"Your current records." Brittaney closed the briefcase, gathered her shoes, and stood up. "They go back a few years, but apparently, you've got warrants out for your arrest everywhere."

Jace opened the folder and began to browse the file, with Claire getting up to look over his shoulder. "Wait, these were from missions when I was with The Order."

"Don't worry." Brittaney began walking toward the back room. "I'll take care of everything. You just keep a low profile for a bit."

Claire gasped. "Holy shit, Jace. Look at this stuff."

"Yeah." He snapped the folder shut and lightly tossed it on the table.

Claire returned to her spot on the couch. "That can't all be true. Right?"

"It might be."

"Holy shit, no wonder you were passed out drunk on my lawn."

Brittaney poked her head from her room. "Oh, Brian said he wants to see you."

Jace looked up at her. "Any idea why?"

"Nope." Brittaney vanished behind her closed door.

Claire grabbed the folder. "You mind if I look through this?"

"Be my guest." Jace stood and headed toward the garage. "Don't get any wrong ideas from that. Who knows what kind of lies The Order told in there."

"I won't." She leaned back on the couch and started to look through the folder.

Just as Jace opened the door, he heard Claire gasp. Maybe letting her read it wasn't such a good idea.

The garage was packed with various work projects from Brian. Much more than usual. As he walked around his covered car, Jace noticed Brian's legs stuck out from under some computer console. Brian fidgeted with wires and cables, and he mumbled to himself.

Jace leaned over to look inside where Brian worked. "Hey."

Brian flinched, smacking his head against something. "Ouch! Hey, Jace. You scared me."

"Brittaney said you wanted to see me?"

"Yeah. Hold on." Brian audibly struggled while he worked on something, then he let out a deep exhale. "Finally." He slid out from under the console with a grunt and got to his feet. "Okay, okay. You have to check this out." He sat in a high-back swivel chair and rolled it to a desk beside the console. He tapped a few times on some touchpad, then a holographic image of the warehouse popped up. "See? How awesome is that?"

Jace stared at the illusion in front of him. They seemed more detailed than the advertisements he saw all over the city, but he couldn't be sure. "That's...neat?"

"You haven't seen nothing yet." Brian grinned, and he touched some buttons near the edge of the desk. The holographic image turned into a mountainous landscape.

"I still don't-"

"Touch it."

Jace blinked for a moment. "Touch it?"

"Yeah."

"I don't want to touch it."

"Just touch it."

Jace sighed, then reached a hand out. As soon as the tips of his fingers broke through the light, it felt as if he touched a solid object, like every sensation in his brain told him what he touched was real. He wiggled his fingers. Nope. Not solid. It was a surreal sensation.

"That's my prototype!" Brian's grin grew as he beamed with pride. "Holographics that emit micro-electrical sensations to the nervous system to simulate the touch of an object emulated by the projection lasers."

Jace took out his hand and rubbed the tips of his fingers.

"Erica has been helping me with the neuro-theory, and we made a huge breakthrough! Just think of the possibilities. We could cure phantom limb from amputees, restore damaged—"

Brian continued his rant, but Jace stopped listening. He looked at Brian's many projects around the garage, the various computer or mechanical parts strewn over the surfaces, the tools that hung on the walls, and the shelves cluttered with strange pieces. "Brian..."

"And this is just a start. Just imagine if we could actually physically form—"

"Brian!" He turned toward his ranting companion. "What does this mean for us? How is this going to help?"

Brian stared blankly for a moment. "Uh, actually. Hold on. One more thing." He turned to the computer and tapped a few more buttons. Then he turned toward the door that led back into the house. "There."

Jace followed his gaze. "What?"

"You don't see it?"

"See what?"

Erica's voice called out from some unseen space. "Brian, you're a genius." Then she walked through the door without opening it.

Jace lightly leaped back in surprise, knocking some contraption over. "What the hell?"

"Pure genius." She took a swig from a bottle of water and sat in a chair next to him. "You even got the neuro-sensors to work."

The two began to chat amongst themselves, with Jace not understanding a single thing they talked about. With each passing heartbeat, he grew more frustrated. "That's nice and all, but why did you want to show me this?"

Erica and Brian turned to face Jace.

Brian adjusted his glasses. "What? No, I didn't want you to come over to show you this." He reached under his desk and took out a briefcase. "I wanted you to see *this*." He put it on the desk, knocking some strange parts aside, and opened it up. Inside were the curved blades he got from Beanie.

"You got something?"

Brian grinned. "Maybe. Check this out." He grabbed a spray bottle and shot a mist onto the blades. A moment later, the red metal glowed blue.

Erica seemed interested. "Hey, that looks like..."

"Yep." Brian grinned. "It's my personal solution to the Fenrir Effect. I had to alter the solution to work on non-organic materials." The glow began to fade. "It doesn't last long, though."

Jace stared intensely at the knives. "Wait, does that mean..."

"Yep. The Order is using magic." Brian resprayed the knives for them to glow, as if to drive home the point.

Jace grew angry at the revelation.

Erica turned and went inside the house without saying another word. Maybe she was just as angry as he was?

———

As the conversation between Jace and Brian died down, Jace thought about Maya and how she didn't get the opportunity to get warmer clothes. Figuring it would be an excellent opportunity to spend some time with her, he finished the conversation and headed inside to see her. That's when he saw Erica bandaging Maya's hand at the kitchen table.

Jace approached, seeing the bloodied cloth and other medical supplies at the table. "Hey, what happened?"

"There was some sharp edge on the corner." Erica gestured to the hallway.

"There is?"

Before Jace could investigate, Erica said, "I already took care of it."

Jace returned to Erica and Maya. "She going to be okay?"

"Yeah. She won't need stitches, but that hand needs to be kept wrapped and cleaned."

"Geez." Again, Jace looked toward the wall. "What cut her?"

"Something under the drywall. I don't know." Erica finished bandaging Maya up, stuffing the bloodied cloth in a sealed bag, then began putting the medical supplies away.

Knowing his little sister couldn't be in better hands, he left it at that. "Hey, Maya, let's get you those clothes we couldn't get last time."

Maya cradled her hand and nodded.

Jace gazed back at the garage. Not wanting to feel trapped, he decided to push back to show he wasn't afraid of The Order and the lies they've been spreading. "And how about I take my car?"

Again, Maya nodded. This time with a little more enthusiasm.

"We'll be back." Jace leaned over and kissed Erica on the head.

Erica, not looking up, continued to put away the medical supplies. "Take your time."

————

Although it was a cold and wet afternoon, Jace had more fun than he had in a long time. Since he drove his car once more, Jace sped around empty parking lots, ate ice cream and pizza like they used to, and played some of the games they used to play. Jace knew that Maya forgave him for his poor choices in the past, which took a huge weight from his shoulders.

On the way back, as Jace turned the last corner that led to Brian's neighborhood, the car suddenly shut off. Even the windshield display and all of the fancy gadgets Brian had installed in the dash went dark.

After the moment of curses and confusion passed, Jace used the car's remaining momentum to pull it to the side of the road.

"Guess Brian needs to work on the car again. Come on. We're almost at the house."

Jace and Maya got out of the car, but he paused as he looked around. No lights were on. At least in front of him. But a few houses back had electricity. Another blackout? Maybe that power company was crap. Or maybe it was something else.

"Leave the bags. We'll get them later." Jace closed the door and made his way around to the trunk of the car. He shuffled into a hidden compartment and grabbed one of his guns. Better safe than sorry.

The two walked in the pitch black with only the cloud-covered moon to guide them. Since he couldn't see anything, he listened. No gunfire. No screams. Maybe this was just a blackout.

Finally, they were two houses down from Brian's. A lifted SUV was parked awkwardly in front of Brian's driveway. At first, Jace thought they had broken down, too. But the shape of the vehicle rang alarm bells in his mind.

That's when a massive, bulky figure exited Brian's house, standing straight and tall. Beside the figure walked a shorter, petite figure, which looked a lot like Erica.

Alarmed, Jace crouched and guided Maya off the sidewalk behind a fence. "Stay here." Before he took a step, Maya grabbed his coat sleeve. "I don't have time to explain. Please, trust me on this. Stay here and keep out of sight."

Maya nodded and sank into the bushes.

Jace approached, staying low, and snuck up behind the massive figure. As he got closer, his heart sank as he confirmed their identity.

Just as they got to the SUV, Jace took out his gun and pressed it on the back of Roberts' head. "That's far enough."

Roberts stopped walking with Erica a pace ahead. "Don't meddle in my affairs."

"Erica, get away from him. I got this."

"You don't understand, runt." Roberts turned around, seemingly unnerved from Jace's hand cannon. "She willingly offered herself."

"Bullshit." Jace's finger hovered over the trigger.

"No, Jace." Erica lifted a hand. "It's true."

His heart sank, and his finger paused, resting against the trigger, and his gun lowered a little. "What? Why?"

"She doesn't have to answer to you, runt." Roberts put a hand on her shoulder.

The anger revitalized his motivation, and he brought the gun up again. "Don't touch her."

Roberts scoffed, then removed his hand from Erica's shoulder.

That single gesture told Jace a lot. A point-blank shot with a fifty caliber could hurt or kill him. At least that's what Jace figured Roberts thought.

"Jace, just trust me on this."

"Tell me why."

Even under the dissipated moonlight, Jace could see Roberts sneer. "You don't get it. It's either her or everyone."

He couldn't quite understand, and Jace's face crumpled in confusion.

Erica stood beside Roberts. "Jace, listen. Let us go."

"But you're sick. You can't go anywhere."

Roberts scoffed. "Don't worry, runt. I'll rip that baby out and cure her of her morning sickness."

Jace's heart stopped, and he struggled to take a breath. "What?" After a moment of digesting what Roberts said, Jace lowered the gun a little. "Is that true?"

"It won't matter." Roberts turned around. "Get in."

"I said don't move!" He pressed the gun on the back of his

head again. "Or I swear, I'll blow a hole through your fucking head."

"Go ahead and shoot, runt. You'll be the one responsible for killing your friends."

His eyes went wide, and he tried to look behind him, all without moving his head. Brian, Brittaney, and Claire. "What did you do?"

"Damn it, Jace. Listen." Erica peeked from around Roberts' bulky frame. "Either I go, or they die. You get it?"

His limbs tingled from fear and confusion. What should he do? Roberts was taking Erica, and she might be pregnant. But his friends were in danger. Or were they?

His eyes locked onto Erica.

"So long as I go without a fight, they're safe. Trust me."

"Why didn't you tell me?"

"Enough talking." Roberts opened the door and hoisted Erica into the seat. When he closed the door, he turned to Jace. "Run, runt. I won't be so forgiving the next time I see you."

Jace took a half a step forward and looked up at Roberts. "I was going to say the same thing."

Roberts sneered.

After a few heartbeats, Roberts turned and got into the SUV. Just then, the lights from the neighborhood turned on.

Jace watched them as the SUV started up in a roar, then drove away, taking a corner with a screech of tires. "Maya!" he shouted, then he ran into the house to check on his friends.

Brian and Brittaney were tied up and gagged on the couch. Maya ran in shortly after.

"Get Brian." Jace began to unbind Brittaney. "Are you two okay?"

Brittaney nodded, then said after the gag was removed, "That asshole! Was that the same guy who tore up my house?"

"Yeah." Jace finished unbinding Brittaney.

"Are you serious? How did he find us?" Brittaney rubbed her wrists.

"I don't know." Jace looked at Brian just as Maya finished unbinding him. " How are you doing?"

"I'm alright." Brian picked his glasses up off the cushion. "And don't worry about Claire. She's out dealing with some business."

Jace sat on the seat across from them. "What happened?"

"I was working in the garage."

"I was in the front room working," Brittaney added.

"When the power went out. At first, I thought it was the hydroelectric plant acting up again. But when my flashlights didn't work, I had a feeling it was something more."

"My laptop wasn't working. Even on battery power, it shut down."

Brian nodded. "So I came inside just as that guy kicked down my door. We were caught and brought to the front room. I thought we were done for, but Erica came out from the back room. The two talked for a moment away from us. It sounded like Erica made a deal with the guy."

"He said we were alive because of Erica," Brittaney said. "Did you see her? Is she okay?"

Jace looked over his shoulder toward the door. "Yeah. At least, I think so." He stood and walked to the busted doorframe. She saved his friend's life at the risk of her own. And his kid.

His kid. That thought echoed through his mind.

Brian walked up and stood next to him. "You alright, buddy?"

The sorrow that he held back burst through his chest and tears escaped his eyes. "Find her, Brian. Or find someone who might know where she is."

CHAPTER NINETEEN

JACE STAYED UP ALL NIGHT, STARING OUT THE FRONT ROOM WINDOW. He could only think about Erica, and the many mental excuses he made for himself on why she didn't tell him.

Brian came in from the garage. Apparently, he stayed up all night, too. "Hey, I got something you should hear."

Jace sparked into action, and he quickly turned around. "Whatcha got?"

"I'm doing what I can, but with my messed-up equipment, it's hard to make everything out." Brian didn't bother to sit down, but his eyes were dark and his skin pale. He was exhausted. "What I can gather, there has been a lot of movement going on. And we are the focus."

Concern sank in Jace's chest. He can fight a dozen people and come out victorious. Even a handful of trained soldiers would be a win. But any more than a single officer from The Order would cause problems. Now, an unknown amount converged on his location.

"And something else. Dame Moon is making her way here."

"What?"

Brian nodded. "Yep. As soon as word got out, she dropped everything and is flying in from across the country. I suspect she will be here in a couple of hours."

Jace took a moment to ponder what he had just heard. His concerns turned into a deep worry, remembering what she said after their last encounter. "Come on." Jace exited the house with Brian in tow.

"Where are we going?"

"We have to talk to Nick to tell him what's going on and see if he can increase the security around the city."

When they got to the sidewalk, Brian's breaths became quick and sporadic, as if he were beginning to panic.

"Hey." Jace stopped and put a hand on his shoulder. "Calm down. Take a breath."

Brian nodded, and he tried to control his breathing.

"How long until the warehouse is ready?"

"Maybe Monday."

"Can we move in any sooner?"

"I suppose, but there wouldn't be anything set up. No security or tracking."

Jace sighed and rubbed his eyes, feeling the exhaustion beat on him, too. "We have to keep everyone safe. What option do we have?"

"Well, I have that panic room."

"What?" Jace's eyes went wide. He wanted to smack Brian. "Why didn't you all use that when Roberts kicked down the door?"

"Because it was so sudden. We didn't have a chance to do anything, much less open a security door under the rug in Maya's room."

Jace gave a resigned sigh, and he rubbed the bridge of his nose. "Yeah, I suppose. Okay, we stay at your place until the warehouse is ready. Then we move." He patted Brian's shoulder. "Come on. Let's talk to Nick."

———

The city was on heightened alert. After Nick York reported to the federal government to call for aid, they said, "With nothing more than the word of some renegade nobody, we will not be able to provide support" under the claim that the threat was a false alarm. Being that the government was bought and paid for by The Order, the outcome was exactly how Nick predicted. That made him suspect they wanted to take the city down all along.

So it was up to the city to defend itself.

After Nick announced his findings to the public, the city locked itself down, which prevented Brittaney from re-entering after going home for some trial. When news got out, many citizens left the area while they could. Some neighborhoods created local militias, arming themselves with guns, flashlights, and radios. They'd watch out for themselves, often taking the law into their own hands as if it were some lawless land. Others didn't believe the stories and were angry at the new rules being pressed by law enforcement. Most people, however, stayed home as best as they could to avoid the often violent protests in the streets. With the riots and looting, the city was divided and in constant conflict. It was far too much for the police to handle on their own.

Out of the chaos rose Nick York. He stepped up his efforts, recruiting his private militia of Evolved to protect the city, attempt to restore order, and fight back against The Order's actions, all under the guise of the people's freedom and protection from an external force.

Over the next few days, Jace kept busy engaging in one squad of The Order after another. All the while, he kept hunting for officers, which were surprisingly nowhere to be seen. And in the back of his mind, he kept an eye out for that dangerous assassin who swore vengeance on him and his family and friends.

After following up on one of Brian's reports, Jace engaged with another unit held up in some manufacturing plant. After incapacitating multiple soldiers, he relocated to the industrial part of the complex to continue the fight.

The hum of idle machines helped disguise Jace's movements as he stealthily maneuvered through the factory. Getting the feeling he would be expecting company, he slid under a conveyor belt and waited.

After a minute, a pair of boots unknowingly walk by. Like a shadow, Jace snuck up behind the armed soldier while he grabbed one of his pistols, put a hand against the soldier's mouth, and pressed the barrel to his head.

Jace whispered, "Drop the gun."

The soldier released his rifle.

Before the rifle even hit the ground, Jace punched the soldier in the kidney, then smacked the temple with the butt of his pistol. He collapsed.

In a swift and seamless motion, Jace dismantled the rifle in two pieces, tossed the parts away from one another, and then moved through the factory to find the next soldier.

It didn't take long before a soldier turned a corner a few paces away.

Jace charged.

When the soldier turned to face Jace, he yelled, "Over here!"

Jace leaped at him, feeling a punch in his chest and leg from the fired rounds. When he hit the soldier, they struggled for a moment before Jace twisted, taking the rifle from his grasp and kicking him against some equipment. When the soldier bounced back, Jace swung the gun, breaking it against the side of his helmet. He fell to the ground, and Jace kicked him across the face.

Sparks erupted all around as some more soldiers fired at his location.

Jace took cover to catch his breath, and he rubbed his chest from the bullet hit. He groaned. "That'll leave a bruise."

"Jace," Brian said over the com. "Three more. Two high, one low."

"Got it."

He usually preferred Brian to be quiet when he was in these types of situations, but he found Brian's input useful, even in the middle of a firefight.

Jace fired some rounds at the two incapacitated soldiers. White webbed glue-like substance covered their arms and legs, securing them to the floor. Afterward, as not being in the best position to defend himself, Jace leaped over a rail as the area around him exploded in gunfire. He got another punch in his arm before he got to better cover. "Damn it." He rubbed the hit. "Those fucking things hurt."

"Hey, it's keeping you alive. Right?"

"Don't think I'm ungrateful. It's just another for the collection." Jace positioned his gun so he could use the chrome as a mirror. He grabbed his second gun with the updated experimental ammo, broke cover, and quickly fired a few rounds at an exposed target. The first two shots missed, but the third hit the guy's leg. Immediately, flashes of white and blue tendrils encased the soldier as he convulsed in pain, then he fell to the ground in a moan.

Jace returned to his cover as more soldiers shot toward his location. "Holy shit, Brian. That worked like a charm." A bullet punched through the wall. "Are they almost here?"

"Almost. Just hang tight."

Jace nodded and put his guns in the holsters to reload, then he sat on the floor. "I didn't see an officer."

"Neither did I."

"Are you sure your intel is correct?"

"Not anymore. I think they're on to my tracking methods. Okay, they're here."

Jace closed his eyes. Through his eyelids, he saw a bright flash. Temperatures fluctuated from extremely hot to frigidly cold as shouts and curses echoed through the factory. After maybe ten seconds, the shouting and the flashes of light stopped.

Jace stood up and called out, "It's about time."

A voice shouted from the factory, "I thought you were going to wait."

Jace walked out of his cover with a grin. Ice clung to various parts of the warehouse, melting from the strange and unnatural heat that the two men brought with them. "Tell Nick an officer wasn't here."

One of the men gave a nodded salute and left the factory.

"Hey," Jace said to the second as he tapped his forearm. "Looks like you're injured."

The second guy inspected himself, then stared at his blood-covered hands.

"Hold on." Jace took off his backpack and grabbed the bullet kit Brian made. "This'll hurt." He squeezed the gel into the bullet wound in his arm. "Go to a hospital."

"O-okay." The guy held his arm and walked out of the factory.

Jace approached one of the two he had subdued and knelt. The soldier grumbled and groaned, still stuck to the floor. "Hey, looks like you might be the only one left." He bluffed, but the soldier didn't have to know that. "If you want to remain alive, maybe you can answer some questions for me."

The soldier groaned as he tried to break his arm free. Jace kicked him in the side to settle him down.

"Now, tell me. Where is Roberts?"

———

Jace walked inside the house, tossed his backpack and jacket on the floor, and slowly and painfully sat on the couch. He leaned back and groaned, rubbing the spots where the bullets hit him.

He had been shot many times in the last few days. And each bullet was mostly absorbed by Brian's armor. However, each hit left welts and bruises. He figured he'd be used to getting those types of impacts by now.

213

As he agonizingly slid off the armored shirt, he inspected the chest injury. His body had more dark spots than his normal skin tone.

Maya walked in from her room. Her eyes went wide when she saw him.

Even though it was too late, he didn't want her to see his injuries. He put down his shirt and smiled. "Hey, you. How was your day?"

She pointed at his chest.

"Oh, don't worry about them. Just part of the job."

Maya sat on the couch next to him and hugged him. Almost instantly, he felt much better. Her hugs always made him feel better.

Brian walked in. "Hey, Jace. Two things. I got another group in the city. I think a squad of six."

"Can't Nick's men handle this one?"

"Yeah, they could." Brian sat across from Jace and Maya. "But you know there would be casualties if you didn't lead the charge." He reached over to pick up Jace's jacket. "Holy smokes, Jace." He poked a finger through one of the many holes. "Are these from—"

Not wanting Brian to say they were from bullets, Jace said, "Yeah."

Brian stroked his chin for a moment. "Hey Maya, can Jace and I talk alone for a minute?"

She didn't seem too pleased about being asked to leave. She crossed her arms defiantly.

"Go on," Jace said. "I'll make us some sandwiches when we're done talking."

She glared at Jace, then rolled her eyes and started toward her bedroom.

When she was out of sight, Brian put down Jace's jacket. "I didn't know things were like that."

Jace briefly wondered what Brian thought things were like.

How couldn't he know? He watches every mission through the contact lenses.

Brian continued, "Are you okay? How is the armor?"

"Nothing I can't handle. And the armor is holding up."

"One more thing. I found Moon."

That was good news indeed. He sat up, ignoring the pain in his body. "Where?"

"She's staying at the Lacie Hotel downtown."

"Maya and I have driven by there many times. That place looks nice. With everything that's been going on, I'm surprised it's still open." Jace got to his feet and stretched a little.

Brian shrugged.

"Claire still at the Yorks?"

"Yeah. She's been working on the accounts."

"So she's safe."

Brian nodded. "What's the plan?"

Jace wondered that, too. "Well, she did make all sorts of revenge promises, and she has a reputation for killing anyone without hesitation."

Brian nodded.

"So, I guess to get her before she gets me."

"Alright, I'm with you. When do you want to do this?"

"Tonight. The sooner, the better."

Brian gestured to the jacket. "Are you okay enough to meet her?"

"I have to be."

Brian nodded and picked up the backpack. "Okay, I'll get everything ready."

CHAPTER TWENTY

IN THE MIDDLE OF THE NIGHT, LONG AFTER CURFEW, JACE PULLED into a parking garage a few blocks from the Lacie Hotel. He put in the contact lenses and began going through the trunk.

Jace tapped the earpiece to call Brian. "Do you have a room number?"

"No. But it's locked, so you'll have to find another way in."

Jace put on the rest of his gear, secured the car, then started to make his way to the sidewalk. Even from his distance, the hotel was clearly visible in the awkward night, like a finger poking the night sky.

He walked by a mini-mart, seeing the broken window and the trash scattered all over the ground. "I just don't understand why people do this."

"Necessity," Brian answered.

Jace paused and kicked some broken glass on the ground. "Was it necessary to destroy a small business?"

"Supplies are scarce. People are desperate."

"Doesn't excuse this crap."

"No, but you know people do what they have to do to survive."

Jace shook his head, not agreeing with Brian's statement as he continued toward the hotel. "I bet The Order is inciting these riots."

"That's a possibility."

The more he thought about it, the more sense it made. "I wouldn't put it past them. Think about it. It's a way to cause chaos in a city they want to take over. What better way to discredit a city's reputation than to show its citizens causing anarchy?"

"Do you think I should talk with Nick?"

"Let's do it when I'm done here." Jace approached the hotel.

Protective gates surrounded the building, guarding it against any vandalism, and closing off the parking garage, stopping any intruders. He walked up to a keypad near the front entrance. "I think this is a security thing. Can you open this?"

"No. At least not very quickly. I looked into it earlier. It's all internal."

Jace shook the gate before looking up at the six-story building, searching for hand and footholds on the structure.

"I know what you're thinking," Brian said. "That's a long way to climb."

"You should have made that climbing gear." Jace began to scale the fence.

"What about security?"

"Then I'd better hurry."

Jace continued his silent climb, avoiding windows as best as possible. Even though everyone was probably asleep, and the lights were off in their rooms, Jace didn't want to risk getting spotted, which would cause more complications. About halfway up, Jace held himself up in a corner by his legs.

"Almost there," Jace whispered as he shook his hands to relax his fingers before continuing his climb. "Maybe I should have just rented a room here." After a grunting lift, Jace pushed himself up to another floor. "Or maybe I should just break a window and get in there. It would be so much easier than this shit."

His fingers finally reached the ledge to the roof. As he lifted himself up and over to reach solid ground, the power from his contact lenses went out. He didn't have time to ponder as a figure sat in the moonlight. At least he wouldn't have to go looking for her. But her just sitting on the rooftop in the middle of the night wasn't normal. It couldn't be a coincidence.

Dame Moon sat with her back toward Jace. "You finally arrived."

No, it wasn't a coincidence. She was waiting.

Jace had a gut feeling something was off. He glanced around to get an idea of his surroundings. But with the lenses not working, he couldn't see anything in the night. Figuring he didn't come all this way for nothing, he took a couple of steps forward. "I have some questions."

"Of course you do." She stood and turned to face Jace. Again, all Jace could see were her eyes. Red cloth covered every other inch of her body.

Jace stopped his advance. "Where is Roberts?"

"Did it take long to get here?"

"I'm the one asking the questions."

"No, I don't think you are." Moon calmly paced to the side, her hands behind her back. Jace met her motion, keeping an equal distance between them. "You have an interesting record, Fallen."

"You don't know shit."

"But I do. The first we met, you knew all about me. And now, I know all about you—Dr. Patel, about your comrades, about that little girl."

Jace clenched his fists and took a breath to control his mounting rage. If she knew about them, then she'd have to be stopped here and now.

Moon stopped pacing. "But perhaps you don't know as much as you think."

"You don't know what you're talking about."

"I have done my research, Fallen. And I don't think you know the whole truth."

"If you have something to say, spit it out. Because if you don't, I'll beat Roberts' location out of you."

She lightly scoffed. "I shall make a deal with you. Once I'm through with you, assuming you survive, I shall tell you about my mission and how futile your efforts have been."

"Roberts." Jace reached behind him and pulled out a gun.

She snapped into some exotic fighting stance with her arms out wide. Two fans opened in her hands.

It was Jace's turn to scoff. "Tell me where he is, and I'll let you and your silly paper fans walk away."

Moon gave a slight laugh. After a moment of pause, the fans snapped shut, and she brought one to her face to tap her chin. "Very well. If you somehow come out on top, I shall include everything I know about Roberts."

Jace aimed squarely at her chest. "Last chance."

"For you, maybe."

Jace fired. Moon snapped open a fan. The white webbed round hit her fan and exploded. Instead of it sticking to the fan, she flicked it off to the side. Jace blinked in confusion for a long moment.

"Do you wish to try again, Fallen?"

He fired another round, this time for her hip. Again, she blocked it and tossed the goo aside.

Impossible! How could she block a gunshot from a few paces away?

Jace reached behind him, grabbed his second gun and fired a beaded round. Moon opened her other fan, deflected that shot, and the tiny ball bearings flew harmlessly over her.

"Is that all you got, Fallen?"

Jace stepped to the side to try to get an advantage. She matched his movements, effortlessly blocking every shot he fired.

After a few seconds, Jace stopped to think of a new plan. As he gripped his hand cannons, he figured hand-to-hand would be his best bet. Though he didn't have much time, hand-to-hand suited him fine. He put the guns away. Moon matched his movements and she put her fans away.

That simple action struck Jace as odd. Something was going on that he couldn't figure out. "What's your game?"

Moon didn't answer.

"Fine. The hard way it is." Jace quick-stepped forward to close the distance, and he began his assault. His goal was to disable her. That way, she could tell him what he wanted to know. But his punches hit nothing but air. His kicks came in contact with a swift kick of her own. Every attack, she successfully and effortlessly defended against.

Jace stopped his attacks. Not because he couldn't hit her, but because she wasn't fighting back. Then he understood. "You're stalling."

She harmlessly gestured to herself. "Am I?"

Her feigned ignorance confirmed his suspicion. He looked around, more to other buildings than anything else. He had just fired off half a dozen shots from fifty caliber handguns. Where were the police or security? Why hadn't anyone at least turned on their lights to check what the noise was? Then it hit him. He tapped his earpiece. "Brian, are you okay? Brian?"

Dame Moon made her move. She stepped in while Jace was distracted and gave a punch. Jace went to block, but the punch was a feint. Her other arm came up and over, hitting Jace square in the chest. He felt a sharp pain, and he took a step back.

"I will admit, I can see how Sir Xin had such difficulty fighting you. You are the fastest person I have ever faced."

"I could say the same." Jace took a step back and clenched his chest as a strange cold began to sink in. That's when his eyes locked onto a slender object in Moon's hand - the hand that struck him.

"But you've lost, Fallen."

Jace's arms and legs went numb, and he fell to his hands and knees.

Moon casually approached and nudged Jace onto his back with her foot. She knelt and lightly slapped his cheek. "Don't worry. You won't die. At least not immediately. You will lie here helpless, and your limbs will rot away from the inside while slowly suffocating. All the while, thinking of your last thoughts, not knowing if the darkness is the night sky or your lost vision."

Jace could feel his chest tighten as he struggled to breathe. And even though it was a chilly night, Jace began to heat up, feeling a bead of sweat drip from his brow.

Moon leaned in close. "And your final thoughts will be of your failure to protect your friends, and the Yorks' uprising will be squashed like a bug. This city, and all of its inhabitants, will be utterly destroyed. And that little girl you call a sister, I'm going to visit her." Her voice went stern and serious. "Know that the rest of her life will be of unimaginable pain and agony, all because of you." She patted Jace's cheek again and stood up, her voice returning to a natural tone. "Farewell, Fallen. Try to enjoy your last moments before my poison gets to work on your nervous system." She walked away.

CHAPTER TWENTY-ONE

VIOLENTLY AND SUDDENLY, JACE'S EYES POPPED OPEN. A BRIGHT white-blue glow from a dark hooded shape, their features hidden by deep shadows, replaced the black night sky. Dark spotted red swirled in the white-blue, like drops of dye in water. Then, their hand lashed back, and a sudden agonizing burst of burning pain shot through his torso as a stream of liquid was ripped from his chest.

Jace grimaced, containing a scream from the pain. But as quick as the agony hit, it vanished. He coughed sickly and went limp. His blurry vision started to regain its focus. He struggled to sit up, but a petite hand held him down.

"M... Maya?" He tried to look around, but all of his limbs were numb.

The strange white-blue light faded, and Maya stood up to look around.

With each heartbeat, Jace felt his strength slowly return. The numbness was replaced with the pins and needles of sleeping limbs, and each moment went from unbearable pain and suffering to simple, tingling agony.

"Maya, what did you do? And what are you doing here?"

She pointed to herself, gave a "walk" motion with two fingers, then pointed to Jace.

Feeling his senses return and his limbs functioning once more, Jace slowly sat up. "You followed me? I told you it was dangerous."

She shrugged, then pointed repeatedly between him and her.

"What about—" He tried to stand, but his legs gave out from the pseudo-pain, and he fell to his hands and knees. Maya was by his side in a heartbeat and held him up. He groaned and winced but regained his composure. "What about us? You shouldn't be here. It's too dangerous."

Again, she shrugged, and she helped Jace get to his feet.

He wobbled a little while Maya assisted him in keeping his balance. Once he felt comfortable with the rogue limbs, he hugged Maya. "You have no idea how glad I am to see you."

After he released the hug, he looked into her face and at the tears that rolled down her cheeks. Jace wiped them away with his thumbs before kissing her forehead and gave her another hug. "Thank you. I don't know what you did, but I think you saved my life."

The hug broke, and he saw his wonderful little sister smiling.

"Come on. We have to get back. The others are in danger."

Maya nodded.

That's when Jace wondered something. "How did you get up here?"

She pointed to the door for roof access.

"Of course. Come on." He took her hand and led her to the stairs.

The corridor was pitch black, and the door closed behind him.

Jace fumbled with the door to find the handle. "Damn it. I usually have these..." He pointed to his eye, as if she could see him. "...stupid lenses that let me see in the dark. Do you have a flashlight or a—"

A small flame flickered above Maya's open palm. Then it grew, but only for a moment before it formed into a floating sphere, lighting up the hallway in a half-dozen pace radius.

Jace had to hold back a gasp as the sphere lifted from Maya's hand and hovered freely. "Where did you..." His eyes went from the floating light to Maya. She was an Evolved. Why was he so surprised?

She shrugged as if it didn't matter.

After a deep breath, Jace looked down the stairwell. "Okay then. Let's go."

They went down the stairs until they reached a fire escape. When he opened the door, Jace wasn't surprised when no alarm went off. After a few paces in the open, Maya waved a hand, and the floating light popped like a bubble and vanished in a brief wisp of smoke.

Jace turned to face the building. "A fire escape. Why didn't I think of that?" He looked around. Nothing suspicious. "I think they think I'm dead. Again." He gave a half-laugh and shook his head at the stupidity. How many times were they going to try to kill him? "Come on. The car is this way." He took Maya's hand and led her away from the hotel.

––––––––

With a screech, Jace turned the last corner that led him to Brian's neighborhood. The strobe lights of law enforcement vehicles lit the area. His heart began to sink. Was he too late?

When they got closer, they saw dead bodies all over Nick York's yard, and fire crews going over the house, which was burned to the ground. A little further up, Brian's house was destroyed. Not from a fire, but from some physical force, like a wrecking ball. Sitting on the back of an aero-ambulance, Brian gripped a blanket around his shoulders, his face a dirty mess.

Jace and Maya got out of the car and tried to approach, but the police stopped them.

"Hey, that's my friend." Jace pointed at Brian.

Brian called out, "Jace!"

The police officer let him and Maya go through the police line and meet Brian. Though he looked like a total mess with red puffy eyes and seemed panicked and pale, he appeared in relatively good health. "What happened? Are you okay?"

"I'm fine. I got to the panic room when everything happened. I messaged Brittaney once everything was over. She got an exception for the borders and is coming to the city tomorrow. My house..." He looked toward the flattened structure.

"What about the Yorks?"

Brian's reply was a total loss of composure, and he hugged Jace. He felt Brian's tears soak through his shirt. For a brief moment, he wished he had his jacket with him.

Jace had no idea what to do. He awkwardly raised a hand and patted Brian's back.

"I'm sorry, Jace. I'm sorry."

"Sorry for what? Is everyone okay?"

Brian removed his face from Jace's tear-soaked shoulder. "It's Claire."

"Claire?" Jace's heart skipped a beat, and he felt the blood from his face drain. "What about her?"

Brian turned to face the Yorks.

That's when Jace realized she was over there working on the accounts. He, too, turned to stare at the rubble of the York's estate. "You mean she... Are you sure?"

Brian could only nod.

Jace's legs gave out, and he fell to his knees.

Maya grabbed Jace's hand. And though her touch usually made Jace feel better, his sorrow was too much. Brian crouched next to Jace and put a comforting hand on his shoulder.

Jace needed to focus on something else to regain his numbed senses. After a struggling breath, Jace asked, "What about Nick and Wanda? What about their staff?"

"Five bodies have been recovered from the house so far. Claire and Wanda were among them." Brian paused to take a deep breath. "Nick has severe burns. He and two others are at the hospital."

Jace brought his gaze up to the Yorks. "What about those in the yard?"

"Security, mostly."

From a glance, Jace figured dozens of people were killed. His tenuous sense of control waned as anger began to fill his chest. He gritted his teeth. "Where is she?" Jace got to his feet. "Where is Claire?"

He approached and was met with police resistance. "Sir, you can't come in here." They held him back as everyone began shouting at one another.

"Let me go!"

Brian repeatedly called from behind, "Jace, stop!" His arms wrapped around Jace and, with strength that surprised Jace, Brian pulled him away from the police line.

Jace flailed and struggled, tears streaming freely down his cheeks. "Where is Claire? Let me go, asshole!"

"Jace, stop it!"

Maya stood in front of him, as if blocking his way.

After a moment, Jace stopped his struggles, and Brian put him down.

Maya gave him a comforting hug.

After a recomposing sniff, Jace took a deep, calming breath and held his little sister.

Brian fixed his crooked glasses and picked up the blanket that fell from his shoulders.

When Maya released the hug, she stood by Jace's side. He shook his head as his eyes returned to the destruction.

"Come on, Jace. We should go to the hospital to check on Nick."

Jace's eyes lingered over the rubble. What could he do here? How could he help? What could he do to get her back?

Nothing.

Feeling defeated, he hesitantly nodded, and the three walked to the car.

———

Jace, Brian, and Maya sat in the crowded waiting room at the hospital. With the riots, the city has been in chaos, and the hospitals were packed with people. It seemed like yesterday that they were there to see Nick after he had been shot.

After a few hours, a doctor walked down the hall. "Mr. McGuen."

Brian stood up. "Here."

The doctor gestured for Brian to walk over, and the two had a private discussion. A minute later, Brian turned to Jace and Maya. "He's awake, and he wants to see us."

Jace and Maya stood, and the three followed the doctor to the back.

Again, Jace approached Nick in a hospital bed. Again, he was attached to beeping machines and trailing tubes. This time though, most of his body and face were wrapped in bandages.

"He is heavily sedated," the nurse said. "I'll give you a couple of minutes. He needs his rest."

Brian sat in a chair next to Nick. Maya sat opposite and held the unbandaged hand. Jace stood at the foot of the bed, staring at the tears that fell down Nick's cheek.

After a minute of silence, Nick said weakly, "The Order, they took everything from me."

"We're sorry, Mr. York." Brian put a hand on Nick's arm but quickly recoiled it when Nick winced in pain. "Oh, I'm sorry. I didn't..."

Maya rubbed the top of Nick's hand.

"I don't want your apologies." Nick's heart monitor rhythm momentarily increased. "I want you to get my daughter back. She's all I have left."

"How?" Jace asked. "The city is tearing itself apart. Every soldier we arrest, they send in two more to take their place. They have cyborgs who can walk off getting hit by a truck, and stupid fucking goo that heals them after an ass-kicking." He jerked a thumb over his shoulder. "I just got into a fight with someone who could block bullets from close range and who kicked my ass without even trying."

Nick grimaced. "Get stronger."

"Really? That's your answer?" Jace snapped an arm out as his pent-up anger began to spill over. "That's a stupid answer."

Brian stood and shot a glance at him. "Jace—"

"You don't get it. We lost."

"No," said Nick. "We've only just begun to fight."

Jace rolled his eyes.

Maya, apparently through with Jace's shit, angrily stood and slapped him across the face. Jace could only stare at her in total shock. She had never raised a hand against him.

Brian got to his feet. "Maya!"

Jace rubbed his stinging cheek while she gestured between herself and Jace.

Knowing she had something to say but couldn't say it, Jace played along. "Okay. Us..."

She pointed to Brian.

"And Brian..."

Then to Nick before forming a box with her hands.

Brian seemed to know what she wanted. "The warehouse?"

She confirmed with a glance and a nod.

"That wasn't the end. I think she's right, Jace. If The Order knew about the warehouse, I think they'd have torched that as well."

Jace sighed. "I don't know."

That sparked a violent response from Maya, and she smacked his chest. After a brief pause, she glared and repeatedly hit him again and again. Normally, they wouldn't have hurt, but with all the bruises he had gotten, every punch produced deep, biting pain.

"That's enough, Maya." Jace caught a flying fist.

She huffed and yanked her arm from Jace's grasp.

Brian looked up at him. "Jace..."

"Who else will die because of me? Who else is The Order going to take because I failed?" Jace turned around and took a deep breath. He needed a moment to recompose himself.

Nick weakly said, "Do not give up. I'll fight to my last breath."

"You don't get it." Jace turned to face Nick, but he couldn't take it anymore. Feeling his emotions getting the best of him, Jace figured he needed to be alone. "You know what? Here." He tossed Brian the keys to the car. "It's over. I'm done. I'll not have anyone else get hurt because of me." Before anyone could protest, Jace left the room and made his way out of the hospital. He wandered into the night so he could be alone, sat on a bench in the darkness, took a deep breath, and began to sob uncontrollably.

———

Jace cried the night away, doing everything he could to cope with the loss of his dear friend. Memories of her chipper attitude, the fun times they had together, and how she saved his life were all he thought about for the many hours of the night.

He awoke under a blue morning sky on a park bench. But to his surprise, he had some form of blanket covering his arms and chest. With achy muscles, he painfully sat up and grabbed the cloth, only to discover it wasn't a blanket but Maya's hoodie. That's when he saw her lying on her side, curled up in a ball in the grass a few feet from him, using her arm as a make-shift pillow.

"I'm such an asshole." He ran his fingers through his tangled hair. Then he got to his feet and gently draped her hoodie over her arms. "Hey."

Maya stirred awake, and she took a deep breath before looking up at him.

"Were you here all night?"

She nodded and sat up, taking the hoodie from Jace's hands and putting it on.

"It was cold last night. You shouldn't have done that."

She glared at him and kicked his boot.

"Yeah, I know. I should have grabbed my jacket from the car."

Maya got to her feet and sat on the bench.

Jace sat next to her and put his arm over her shoulders. He decided to protect her, so he needed to tell her what was going on.

"Do you know why? Why they're coming after us?"

She gave a sleepy nod.

"It's because of me. You don't know this, but I used to be in The Order." Memories ran through his head—flames flickering from barricaded houses, the countless bodies, and the painful expressions of the people who lost their loved ones but survived all because they didn't glow blue. "This..." He took a breath to recompose himself. "These are things I've done before."

Maya looked up at him and sat straight.

Jace removed his arm from her shoulder. "Back in the day, I was the bad guy. I've always been the bad guy. Even when I was a kid. That is, until I had some anchor to tie me back down and get my shit together."

Unable to keep his composure while looking at Maya, Jace diverted his gaze to the sky. "Did I ever tell you the first time I watched the clouds? Like *really* watch them, much like you and I do? It was with Jessica back when I was a kid. I never really saw shapes in the clouds before she showed me. And we spent days and nights watching the clouds or staring up at the stars."

He fell silent for a long moment, remembering a day when he and Jessica sat on the edge of the orphanage wall to watch a sunset and saw his first shooting star. Retreating into his memories, he whispered what she told him that night. "Make a wish, tit-face."

When he snapped out of his memories, he found himself smiling, and Maya sitting and staring at him in both a confused but interested way. "It's nothing. Just... Just a memory."

"Did I ever tell you about my secret training spot at SOC? I don't know if you were around when they tore out the backwoods, but I found this spot deep in those woods near the back wall. I used the money I got from fighting to build this little training facility where I'd do sit-ups and push-ups and beat on a punching bag." He shook his head from the stupidity. "Gah, I was so angry back then. I saw some kid abusing Jessica and Claire, and I stepped in. We got into a fight." Using the phrases that broke the kids down into age groups, four years per floor, Jace said, "The kid was third floor while I was first. Just a punk who had no idea how to move in a fight, but I had no idea how messed up I'd be if that kid ever got his hands on me. Claire and Jessica were so impressed, and they asked where I learned to fight. So I showed them my secret hiding place."

"We were so deep in the woods, Claire thought we were lost. But when I showed them, Jessica took a keen interest and watched me almost every day I trained. Claire went to the city library and took out books on other forms of fighting. Until then, I only used my fists, like a boxer. But then she showed me these books on how to grapple and kick and such. I remember them being a game-changer. I wouldn't be as good at fighting if it weren't for her. Who knows where I'd be without her?"

Jace paused for a moment, and he sniffed. For a moment, he felt like he was about to cry a little, but his eyes were too dry.

Maya wrapped herself around Jace's arm, and she put her head on his shoulder. Even in some of his darkest times, she always made an effort to make him feel better. And it almost always worked.

After a small but genuine smile, Jace stood up. "Come on." He extended a hand and helped her to her feet. "Let's go find Brian."

Without a second thought, Maya lifted her arm and pointed behind Jace. When he turned to look at what she pointed at, he saw his exotic blue car parked in the parking lot.

He lumbered to the driver-side door and peeked inside. Brian slept in the reclined seat.

Jace tapped on the window.

Brian's eyes shot open, and he looked around, as if confused for a long moment. Then he took his glasses off the dashboard and got out of the car. "Hey." He adjusted his glasses. "You good?"

Jace nodded. "Yeah. I think so. I just needed-"

Maya put a hand on Jace's arm.

"Listen, Jace. Believe it or not, we're in this together."

"Yeah, I know." Jace put a hand over Maya's and gave a half-smile at her.

"We can talk about things later. Come on."

Jace blinked in confusion for a moment. "Where are we going?"

"Breakfast." Brian grinned and handed Jace the keys.

After a moment, Jace returned the grin and nodded. Breakfast. That did sound good.

CHAPTER TWENTY-TWO

AFTER BREAKFAST, THEY WENT TO THE POLICE STATION SO BRIAN could fill out a report, which took hours. Once done, they went to the one place they had left—the warehouse.

As Jace pulled up to the security gate, it automatically slid open, and closed when Jace drove through. Even the garage door automatically opened and closed behind when the car rolled inside.

Maya stood by Jace, and the two looked around in awe. The place looked nothing like when they first arrived. It reminded Jace of Brian's house, with technology and light everywhere.

"I know, right?" Brian approached and stood next to Jace. "This is like a headquarters now."

Jace's eyes locked onto some devices that reminded him of her office. "Erica is going to love this. Hey, when is Brittaney due in?"

"Tomorrow afternoon. Come on." Brian took a few steps forward. "Let me show you around."

The warehouse had everything Jace thought he needed, and even more of things he never thought about: mini-apartments for everyone with a full kitchen, bathroom with showers, a laundry room, a fully stocked medical area, a ton of machine stuff, and more.

Brian led them to a room attached to the main warehouse, where a circular table took up most of the space. "And this is our center." He tapped the table. It lit up, and a massive, detailed holographic image of the city popped up.

Maya gasped.

Though impressive, Jace half-expected some ridiculousness from Brian.

Brian adjusted his glasses. "And also..." After another tap, the holographic image turned into the warehouse. "We probably have the best security system in the city." The image rotated and moved, showing every inch of the structure.

Jace noticed a bird fly by, making part of the hologram turn orange. "Is this live?"

"Yep."

"Any defenses?"

"All you need to know is we're safe here."

Jace heard that before.

Maya wandered away as Brian continued, "We can plan whatever we want here. Our missions, our shopping list, anything. We could even order a pizza here."

"I don't know, Brian."

"Just..." Brian turned the hologram off. " Just give it some thought."

Jace sighed, then turned around to see Maya playing with something on a table. "Hey, what's up?" He walked next to her to see her looking inside a briefcase that contained the curved blades he got from Beanie. "That... Those are something I got from someone." Jace closed the briefcase. "Come on. Let's go check out that little apartment."

She looked up to him and nodded. She then gestured toward Brian, who sat at a computer before pointing to him.

"I don't know what I'm going to do."

She grabbed his hand and tugged.

"What?"

When he raised a hand, she pointed at one of his fingerless gloves. They weren't in the best shape—holes and cuts, blood spots and dirt.

"Yeah, I have to get some new gloves."

Her eyes went from the gloves to the briefcase, then back to Jace. She smiled.

"Okay?"

She nodded, and the two walked to their apartment.

"Brian mentioning pizza got me a little hungry. How about you?"

She nodded.

When Jace reached their apartment, he reached for the handle. Before he could grab it, the door automatically opened.

"Damn it, Brian. I can open my own damn door."

They walked inside. Obviously, the first thing Maya noticed was the oversized couch as she charged at the furnishing, leaped over the back, and landed in a fwoof.

Jace couldn't contain his smile before exploring the kitchen for some lunch.

———

The following day, Jace arranged a run to the store. With Brittaney's arrival in a few hours, Jace wanted to make sure everything was prepared.

He heard a knock at the door. Figuring it was Brian's grocery list, Jace answered without a second thought.

Brian stood in the entryway, seeming pale and serious. "Hey, Jace."

"Hey." Jace quickly inspected Brian to see if he had some sort of injury. "Everything okay?"

"Yeah. Um, do you have a minute? I've got something to show you."

Jace eyed him suspiciously. If it were some technological babble, Brian would be excited and ranting along. This was different. "You sure everything's alright?"

"Yeah. Just... Come on." Brian led Jace from the warehouse to a backroom. "So, I was doing some tests on those daggers. I guess Maya watched me and, um... She walked up in a huff and, um..." When Brian opened the door, blinding red light beamed from the portal.

Jace lifted a hand to guard his eyes, feeling heat pour from inside.

Brian stepped aside, letting Jace walk inside. He only took a single pace before he stopped in alarm. Two massive bipedal flame-shapes almost twice his height stood in the middle of the room. Their burning tendrils licked the ceiling but didn't burn the paint. What could be considered their eyes were fluctuating orbs of yellow and red.

Fire elementals. Living embodiments of nature with wills of their own.

Jace knew of elementals, but didn't expect to see one, much less two, standing casually inside Brian's place.

Two things were out of place, more so than having a staring contest against nature itself. Inside the chest of the flaming figures were the shapes of the daggers. Those oddities paled in comparison to the fact that Maya stood between them, standing calmly as if it were just another day.

Not understanding what was going on, Jace tensed up, going into a slight crouch to prepare to spring into action. But what could he do? Two fire elementals flanked his sister, and he didn't have his guns on him.

After a moment of panic, Jace took a breath to steady his nerves. He needed answers. "Maya, are you okay?"

She nodded, then looked up at one of them and pointed to Jace.

The beast on the right spoke in a slow and dull tone, with pops behind its voice like a log in a fireplace. "Youuu...aree this ooone's...guuuuardian?"

As much as he appreciated Maya's wellness, he still wasn't any closer to figuring out what the hell was going on. "Of course I am. She's my sister. I'll protect her no matter what."

The elementals groaned in unison. Were they protesting?

"Very well," said the right flame.

"Choooose your vessel," said the left.

None of this made sense. "Maya, what's this about?"

Maya turned and grabbed something off a table. Then she lifted two big, bulky yellow gauntlets that reminded him of those shows she watched on TV.

"Sooo beee it," one groaned.

The flames began to lash and flail as the elementals turned into a tornado as a strange warm wind blew from every direction. They shifted toward the cartoon gloves Maya held and began to shrink, as if they were being sucked in them. A few seconds later, the heat and winds vanished, and the daggers that floated in midair fell to the ground, clanging on the tile where they smoked and sizzled.

Maya stood with a great smile on her face, as if she deserved praise and thanks.

Brian called from outside, "Are they gone?"

"I think so." Jace took a few steps forward as she presented the gloves. "What's going on, Maya?"

Her answer was more forcefully presenting the oversized cartoon gauntlets. They were no longer yellow, but an almost-black-red color.

"Hey, Jace. Check this out."

Jace looked to see Brian pick up one of the knives from the

floor with a towel. The blades were charred and cracked while continuing to smoke. "Where did they go?"

Maya stomped her foot, getting the attention of Brian and Jace. She continued to present the gloves, her expression showing she's obviously no longer entertained.

Brian stood and adjusted his glasses. "Hey, didn't you get those at that convention? What happened to them? Why did you take them out of the package?"

She lowered her hands and rolled her eyes, then she tucked the cartoon gauntlets under her arms, grabbed one of Jace's hands, and began to take off an old, worn glove.

"What are you doing?" Jace recoiled his hand.

"I think she wants you to put them on."

Maya shrugged with wide eyes, as if to say, "Duh."

Though unsure what was going on, Jace's gaze briefly went to Brian, then back to Maya, and he hesitantly removed his gloves. "What's this all about? What happened?"

"Hold on." Brian grabbed another towel and picked up the second knife. He set the towel-covered knives on a counter and unwrapped them.

Maya grabbed Jace's bare hand and started to put on the cartoon-like gauntlets. Again, Jace felt uneasy, but he didn't know what to do. Decline Maya's strange gift? He had to hand it to Maya. The glove fit perfectly, even if it went almost entirely up to his forearm and had some crazy two-inch spike sticking out at the elbow. It even seemed to conform around his arm, flexing and shrinking, and even felt warm to the touch. As soon as it slid on, the canyons of the rough leather pulsed red. Jace had to consciously hold himself back from retracting his arm.

Brian grabbed a spray bottle and shot the knives. They gave a faint sizzle. When Brian turned to face Jace, he had that look in his eye, like when he was about to go off on a rant about some sort of techno-babble. He took a step toward Jace as Maya put on the second gauntlet. "Hold out your hand."

Jace complied.

Brian sprayed the glove.

It glowed blue.

Jace uncontrollably recoiled.

That seemed to get Brian very excited, and he smiled. "Holy smokes, Jace!"

"Maya..." Jace glared at his little sister. "What's going on?"

She took a step back, visually inspected him, and gave a smiling thumbs up. Then she started to walk toward the door.

"Wait, where are you going?"

Maya pointed toward the wall, as if indicating their apartment.

"Hey, Jace. How do you take them off?"

Jace paused, and he stared at the oversized ridiculous looking gauntlets. "I don't know." He gazed up at Maya, but she was already outside. "Hey!" With no reply, Jace turned to face Brian as he tried to take the gloves off. "What the hell is this? How am I supposed to go grocery shopping with these things on? Are these fucking things glowing?" He brought them to his face. Though it was barely visible, he saw red between the nooks and crannies of the leather. "They are!" He glared toward the door. "Maya!"

Jace heard a whisper and he gazed up at Brian.

"Do you..." Brian, adjusting his glasses while leaning forward to get a closer look, kept an obvious two-pace distance from Jace. "Do you feel any different?"

"What's that supposed to mean?"

"I don't know. It's just..."

Again, Jace tried to tug at the gauntlets. They seemed fixed to his skin. Or maybe his bone? He couldn't tell. But he began to panic. "How do I get these fucking things off?"

"At the convention, there was some button or something on the wrist."

Jace looked but didn't see anything. He began to blindly press his thumb against his wrist. "Nothing's happening. Nothing—"

The gauntlets eased up a bit from his arm. He tossed it to the floor, then removed the second one.

Brian knelt and inspected the gloves. "This is fascinating."

"Fascinating?" Jace snapped his arm out toward his apartment. "Are you not even questioning what the hell that was all about? Or how Maya even did that?"

"I don't know. Maybe Ruth taught her?" Brian picked up the gloves and put them on the counter. "These don't have that strange writing on them."

"What writing?"

"Here." Brian showed Jace one of the charred daggers.

Even under the messed-up metal, Jace could make out the strange etchings in the blade. "Oh yeah. That. I saw that a few times."

Brian put the dagger down and presented a gauntlet. "But these don't have them."

"Huh." Jace remained clueless.

"Here, put it back on."

Jace recoiled. "Hell no!"

"Come on."

"No."

"Just do it!"

Jace eyed the possessed glove for a long moment. "Alright." He took the glove. "But you're doing the grocery shopping for the month."

"Deal."

After wondering what the hell he was doing, Jace slid on the gauntlet. Again, it tightened around his hand, wrist, and forearm, and continued to be warm to the touch.

"Here." Brian handed Jace the other glove.

Jace sighed, then slid on the second one.

"Maya's right. You look awesome."

Jace scoffed. "I look ridiculous."

"Try to throw a fireball."

"A what?" Jace shook his head. "You sound like an idiot."

"No, no. It's in Maya's show. These gloves have lasers or something in the palm."

Jace looked at the palm. "There's no laser here."

"Okay, how about forming a sword?"

Jace nodded. "Yep. You're an idiot."

"No, no. Just hear me out."

"Beanie didn't shoot fireballs or laser beams. He threw knives at me." He picked up one of the charred daggers for emphasis. The gloves gave a gentle pulse of red under the cracked leather, and the hilt of the knife broke from the blade. Jace paused, looking at his hand as he released the mangled metal from his grip.

"Jace, what was that?"

"I don't know." Jace looked around for an explanation, eventually staring at a wall clock, as if the moving second hand would somehow provide an answer.

"Okay, okay." Brian reached behind the bench and grabbed some thin foot long pole. "Catch." He tossed it.

Jace caught the bar. The gloves pulsed again, and the bar bent.

"Jace..." Brian leaned forward, looking totally astonished. "That bar is rated at 350 lbs."

"It's what?"

"And you just bent it in half like a paperclip."

Again, Jace stared at the glove and the twisted piece of metal in his hand.

"Jace, I hate to say it..." Brian gave a huge smile. "But you're a superhero!"

"Don't be dumb." He tossed the metal aside. It clanged across the floor.

"You're a superhero."

"Stop saying that." Jace brought his hands to his face, and he stared at the dark red leather for a long moment.

Brian, too, closely inspected the gloves. "You want to see what else you can bend?"

"Hell ya, I do!"

———

After spending an hour bending and breaking some things at the shop, Jace, Brian, and Maya climbed into Brian's aero-vehicle to go to the store, leaving the oversized cartoon gauntlets at the warehouse.

Very few cars were on the roads. Ever since the lockdown of the city, going out to get supplies was a dangerous task. Looters, muggers, thugs, zealous defenders, and scared citizens, they were all unpredictable. It's no wonder people have been leaving the city.

Jace leaned forward to look at the store parking lot, if it could be called that anymore. Because of the temporary wall and armed personnel guarding the area, a checkpoint would better describe the parking lot. "This place would be screwed if Nick wasn't able to get an outside supply chain going."

"Yeah." Brian pressed a few buttons on the control console. "Even if the supplies are rationed, time and time again, he saves the city."

Maya peered over the side from the window. Jace wondered if bringing her along would be safe. Again, for a moment, he wondered how she was able to do whatever she did with those elementals.

Brian continued, "And when word got out about The Order's attack on the York's house, people exploded. Tensions are high right now. Did you hear about the brawl outside of the warehouse fence? It went from a couple of people to a full-on neighborhood battleground."

That confirmed it. The safest place for Maya would be at his side. "Will Brittaney get to the warehouse alright?"

"Yeah. She has a shuttle service from the airport."

Brian landed his aero-vehicle and used the ground mode to drive it to the checkpoint. After a few questions, they gave him a flyer of guidelines and limitations while at the store and let him through.

After parking the car, the three got out and stared at the store. People rushed in a panic to get in and out. A few people shouted at one another in the parking lot, and armed security guards quickly intervened.

Jace didn't like what he saw. "Let's not spend a lot of time here."

"I agree. Here." Brian began to jot down some notes in his notepad, then tore the sheet out and handed it to Jace. "You get these things. Maya and I will get the rest."

"I don't want her to leave my side."

"It'll be fine, Jace. There's a ton of security." Brian gestured toward the arguing people in the parking lot. "Didn't you see how long it took for that to get broken up?"

He did have a point. Jace hesitantly conceded. "Alright, fine. Don't let her out of your sight."

"You got it."

The group entered the store and split up. As Jace wandered the aisles, he wondered why they had to split up in the first place. It would only be a few minutes longer if they stayed together.

The sound of glass shattering put Jace in a defensive stance. Another pair of citizens argued over a broken bottle on the floor. A moment later, security was there to break up the pending fight.

Brian was right. Security didn't waste any time. Still, with people's nerves on edge, he didn't feel right. He decided to seek out Brian and Maya on the opposite side of the store.

He eventually found them, but not in the area he thought. Jace peeked around the corner to see Maya holding a bundle of flowers and with Brian helping her pick something out in the card section. That's when he realized she wanted to surprise him.

Jace sighed, feeling like an overprotective asshole. He turned to return to his side of the store.

A few aisles over, he heard the distinct voice of Brian shout, "Hey!"

Jace turned and rushed over to the card section. When he turned the final corner, he saw a rope dangling from the ceiling and the hulking figure of Roberts. His hand covered Maya's face as he finished injecting something into her neck.

Roberts seemed not to notice Jace as he stared at Brian. "Don't interfere. Don't follow." As Maya went limp, he flung her over his shoulder. "Or the little one will pay."

As Jace took a single step forward, Roberts grabbed the rope, and he was quickly hoisted into the air through an unseen section in the ceiling.

Jace stopped next to Brian, and he stared helplessly through the hole in the ceiling. "Is there a roof access?"

"I don't know."

Jace leaped onto a shelf and climbed to the top just as security converged around the aisle. "There!" Jace pointed at a door that led to the back.

Brian started to run toward where Jace pointed, as Jace leaped down to follow. Security stopped them.

"You have to help," Brian said. "That guy took his sister."

With no further questions, security started to scramble, and Brian and Jace sprinted toward the back of the store.

Unorganized and cluttered.

Jace couldn't see past the piles and piles of boxes of varying merchandise and supplies. "Damn it."

"Try outside. He has to have some escape plan."

Jace turned and rushed back through the store, leaping over carts, dodging pedestrians, and nimbly getting through every obstacle that blocked his path. Eventually, he got to the front of the store, where he turned to look toward the roof. No aero-vehicle.

Brian eventually caught up. He panted and adjusted his glasses.

"Go that way. Look for anything out of place."

Brian nodded.

Jace and Brian split up, each going toward the opposite ends of the store. As Jace turned the corner, he found Roberts as he climbed into his big lifted SUV. He wouldn't reach the truck in time, so Jace ran toward Brian's aero-vehicle and jumped in the driver's seat. He stared blankly at the dozens of buttons on the control panel, the switches and knobs, light-up displays, and the strange steering device in front of him.

"Shit." He got out and shouted, "Brian!" He spotted Brian at the store and waved him over. Then he watched the lifted SUV plow through the exit point. "Brian, hurry!"

Eventually, Brian got to the aero-car.

Jace scooted to the passenger side, and Brian climbed in. "Follow him!"

Security surrounded Brian's car. "Get out of the vehicle."

Jace looked over at the exit once more. "Erica. Ruth. Claire. There's no way in hell I'm losing Maya."

"Don't worry," Brian said. "Ever since she started following you on your jobs, I planted a bug in her shoe."

Jace snapped a glare at Brian. "You what?"

"Yeah." Brian put up his hands, and he slowly opened the door.

Jace turned to see the security guards approach with weapons drawn. He nodded. "Okay, good idea." Jace, too, raised his hands and opened the door.

CHAPTER TWENTY-THREE

AFTER BEING ALLOWED TO PASS THE STORE CHECKPOINT, BRIAN AND Jace flew back to the warehouse, going well over the recommended airspeed limit.

Jace mumbled to himself while he shook his head. "I fight them, they take Erica and murder Claire. I leave them alone, they take Maya." He clenched his fists. "Fine."

"Fine, what? What do you want to do?"

"Brian, this changes things."

"How?"

Jace glared at Brian. "What do you mean 'how?' They have Maya."

"What I mean is..." Brian adjusted his glasses. "What is the next move?"

"I'm done going easy. I'm through playing around, and all bets are off. How much special ammo do we have?"

"You have a lot of bearing and webbed rounds."

"The other ones."

That seemed to catch Brian off guard. "You mean the lethal rounds?"

"Yeah."

Brian sighed. "I don't know, Jace... Well, I got rid of the plasma and explosive rounds."

"Damn it."

The aero-car pulled up to the warehouse. "You might have some regular rounds in the trunk hidden storage."

When they landed, Jace bolted out and went to his car while Brian went inside the house. Jace started to gear up, putting on the armor, reload harness, and his backpack. He even put on those cartoon gauntlets. And as he went through the hidden compartment in the trunk, he found some regular ammo and a couple of color-tipped ones. He picked up the two bullets. A couple of explosive rounds won't do much, but they were better than nothing. He tucked them in an inside pocket of his jacket and began loading the harness.

A couple of minutes later, when he finished getting geared up, Brian came out with two massive cylinders tucked under his arms.

"Okay, I tracked Maya's location. She's still in the city."

"Where is she? And what's that?" Jace gestured to the cylinders.

Brian put the cylinders in the trunk. "I'll explain on the way. You ready?"

Jace closed the trunk. "You coming with?"

Brian nodded and adjusted his glasses. "I have to."

Not having any time to question or argue, Jace nodded, and the two got into the car. As he pulled out of the warehouse, an aero-vehicle flew in. Jace stopped as Brian leaned forward to get a better look. "I think that's Brittaney."

A moment later, Brittaney climbed out with a couple of suitcases.

Brian got out of the car. "Brittaney."

"Damn it, Brian. We don't have time for this."

"Hold on." Brian rushed to Brittaney. After a few seconds, her expression and posture went serious. She nodded and ran into the warehouse, leaving her suitcases outside. Brian returned to the car and got in. "Okay, let's go."

Brian guided Jace as he drove through the rotted and empty city streets. From time to time, they would see some people outside, but who knew what they were up to?

"Where is this place?"

"It's a small, private airport. It was used to fly people to and from the dam while it was under construction. Now it's basically abandoned. Jace, I've been thinking about it. What if The Order operates the dam?"

That idea didn't sound good. Jace took a moment to think. "If they destroyed the dam, would it wipe out the city?"

Brian shook his head. "No. Well, it might do some damage, but not a lot. The designers planned for any failures in the design of the city."

"Good."

So I have a plan." Brian turned on one of his portable computers.

"Does it have to do with those cylinders you put in the trunk?"

Brian grinned and nodded.

————

Brian and Jace stayed in the bushes just beyond the simple wire fence perimeter. Brian put a camera on a tripod and fiddled with the computers inside the cylinders.

Jace scanned the area through binoculars, seeing the lifted SUV parked next to a small water tower just outside a hangar. "There are cameras at every corner. And I think I see some flying vehicle on the other side of the hangar. Looks like a flying van or something."

"Those cameras probably have motion sensors, but that won't matter."

Jace lowered the binoculars. "Of course it matters. With how far the fence is from any building, I can't get in without being detected."

Brian grinned and adjusted his glasses. "You leave that to me." One of the devices began to light up.

"Turn that off. They'll see that."

"No, they won't."

After a brief pause of blank blinking, Jace shrugged and returned to the binoculars. "If I can just get to the wall, I'll be able to climb it. But to even get onto the property, I'll have to cut through the fence. And I bet that'll probably trip some sort of alarm."

"Don't worry about that."

Again, Jace lowered the binoculars. "Damn it, Brian. This is serious stuff. If I'm spotted, then Maya will be in even more danger than she is now."

Brian carefully clamped about a dozen wires to the fence, which sparked on each touch. "Because they won't even know we're here."

"Are you kidding? They probably know already."

"Trust me." Brian worked on his computer. "They won't know we're here until it's too late. Okay, start cutting. And make a hole big enough for this." He pointed at some computer device.

Though Jace knew the fence was electrified, he trusted Brian. He went through his bag to grab his wire cutters, then cut a fence wire. Not a spark. "Not bad."

When Jace finished cutting the hole, he shoved aside the section of fence, and Brian pushed some computer equipment through. "When I give the signal, you run in. The battery won't last long, though." More typing. "So I can only get you to the outer hangar. The rest will be up to you."

"I don't get it. How is this going to get me through undetected?"

"Because these are the key components to the holographics I showed you earlier. You know the one that simulated touch?" Though everything began to make sense to Jace, Brian continued, "The camera scanned the area so I can emulate the terrain, the holograms will hide you from the cameras, and the sensory signals will scramble any motion sensors. I'll even put an animal crossing, just in case."

"And the fence?"

"A simple signal reroute. Come on, Jace. I thought you were good at this."

Jace grinned and shook his head. "Brian, you're a fucking genius."

He smiled and adjusted his glasses. "When the hologram is up, it'll feel like you're running into something. But keep going. Ready?"

Jace nodded.

Brian tapped at the computer. The second device lit up. "Go."

As Jace went through the fence, reality warped in front of him. The ground shifted and bent. Shadows twisted and contorted. The air grew thick, like some unseen gel was holding him back. Regardless of what his senses told him, Jace plowed through the invisible force. Finally, he skid to a stop at the hanger wall. Not wasting any time, Jace grabbed a handhold, wondering if the clunky gauntlets would get in the way. But he found himself climbing with ease, hoisting himself up effortlessly. Before he knew it, he had climbed the entire wall.

Jace looked down toward the fence he ran through. Brian, the equipment, or even the hole in the fence, wasn't there. Did he get turned around? He confirmed his steps, tracing it back to where the hole in the fence should have been. Nothing was there.

Brian spoke over the com. "The batteries are running low. I hope you're out of sight."

"I am. Where are you? I'm on the roof, and I can't see you."

"Behind a holographic wall. Go on. This won't last forever."

Jace nodded, then he heard Brian whisper something. "What did you say?"

"What? I didn't say anything."

Jace blinked a moment, wondering what happened.

The sound of screeching metal caught Jace's attention. He turned and silently moved to investigate. When he looked down, he saw Roberts walking out of the main entrance, inspecting the area suspiciously. Though Brian's technology was enough to get him to the wall, apparently it wasn't enough to get him through totally undetected.

As Roberts grew closer to Jace's position, Jace's anger grew at a rate he didn't expect. Instead of shooting Roberts from a safe spot, Jace's rage got the best of him, and he leaped down to attack. While somehow detecting the attack, Roberts hopped to the side as Jace crashed hard to the ground, his fist hitting the dirt and blasting a hole in it.

Roberts visibly scanned Jace. "I knew you were alive, runt."

Jace spat, "Where is she?"

"She's here." Roberts smiled. "But you're mine now, runt. You've got nowhere to run. And now you will die knowing you can't save it."

"Her name is Maya!" Jace charged.

Roberts didn't move.

Jace gave a hard right cross, red flames trailing his fist. The impact blew Roberts off his feet through the water tower. Water gushed out, covering the entire area and converting the dirt to mud.

After a moment of angry heaving, Roberts emerged from the hole and ripped a pole from the ground. "You're stronger than I remember. No matter." Roberts threw the rod at Jace like a javelin. Jace dodged and was met with Roberts charging. Roberts wrapped Jace in his arms and slammed him to the ground. The impact should have injured Jace, but the hit seemed to have been diminished.

Not taking the time to question his fortune, Jace broke through the grab and wrapped his arms around Roberts' head, and the two exchanged punches against their bodies.

Roberts broke Jace's grip and pushed him off, and the two got to their feet to square off once more.

"I get it now." Roberts grinned and tapped on his arm. "You got support equipment."

Jace took a step to attack. Roberts gave a brutal front kick. Jace caught the leg and spun around, throwing Roberts into his lifted SUV. The door bent on impact, and it slid back a couple of feet.

Jace began to press the advantage, but Roberts grabbed the SUV wheel and ripped it from the chassis to throw at Jace. It was too big to dodge. The hit knocked Jace off his feet and pinned him under the wheel. Roberts stormed forward, leaped into the air, and landed on the wheel. Jace felt the wind blow from his lungs.

Roberts leaned forward to look Jace square in the eyes. "After I kill you, I'll rip that fetus from her womb and squish it beneath my boot."

When Roberts got off the wheel, Jace tossed the tire aside. Roberts kicked Jace in the face. Jace fell to his back, blood and mud covering his face.

"And when I'm done destroying your bastard child, I'll make sure to peel the skin from that creature you hid from us."

Roberts grabbed Jace by the arm and pulled, as if to take off the glove. Instead, he just lifted Jace to his feet.

Jace wrapped his arms around Roberts. "I told you, her name is Maya." He lifted Roberts and squeezed.

Roberts tensed and stretched, eventually breaking free from Jace's grip.

The two exchanged one brutal punch after another, each hit an agonizingly painful jolt to Jace's body. He felt himself begin to weaken and slow from the injuries.

Roberts grabbed Jace and threw him against the SUV. The impact stunned him as his vision blurred for a brief moment.

Roberts grabbed Jace's jacket to keep him on his feet. "When I'm done with you..." A hard punch landed on Jace's face. "No one will remember who you were." Another punch. "Not even the fallen traitor you are."

Jace intercepted the third punch with one of his own. The two knuckles collided, but it was Roberts' wrist that gave out.

Jace grabbed the wrist, leaped into the air, spun around, and gripped Roberts' arm in an elbow lock.

The two struggled for a moment, Roberts trying to break the lock, Jace trying to break the elbow.

Slowly, Jace gained the upper hand, but not in the way he expected. Instead of breaking the elbow, Roberts' entire arm was ripped off from the shoulder.

Blue liquid burst from the wound. Roberts growled in rage. Or was it pain?

Was that his blood?

The two got to their feet.

Roberts brought his other arm forward, but not to punch. His forearm separated, and the barrel of a gun suddenly appeared.

Jace leaped to the side, bouncing off of the wheel that pinned him just as a loud boom erupted from the weapon.

Jace grabbed the wheel and got to his feet as he saw Roberts pump a fist in the air. Maybe to reload?

Just as Roberts pointed his arm-gun at Jace, Jace threw the oversized wheel at Roberts. The wheel hit the arm, redirecting the attack. Something exploded from behind Jace.

Jace grabbed his own weapons and shot at Roberts. Most of the bullets clanged on impact, seemingly ineffective against the armored cyborg. At least until Roberts fell to a knee.

He pressed the advantage and charged Roberts while putting one of the guns back in the harness. Just as the arm-gun was aimed, Jace swatted it away with his armed hand and gave a hard punch to the face with the other.

Roberts fell to the ground, seemingly dazed from the barrage.

Jace stood over him, stepped on the arm, and shot at the shoulder joint. After a few rounds, he saw the burst of blue he looked for.

"You messed with me for the last time." Jace put the gun away, grabbed the arm with both hands, then ripped it out of Roberts' torso.

When Roberts tried to sit up, Jace laid him to the ground with a punch. He knelt on top of Roberts, who continued to try and get up. "You took Erica from me." He punched Roberts. "You killed my friend." He hit him again, the shape of his face starting to give from the impacts. "You kidnapped my sister." He punched him for the third time. Roberts collapsed hard to the ground.

Jace stood and took a step back to catch his breath.

Roberts rolled over and began to feebly make his way back to the hangar.

Jace walked up to Roberts and put a boot on his back. "You never should have touched my sister." Jace punched hard against Roberts' back, piercing through the armored chassis, gripped the spine, and yanked as hard as he could. After a cry from Roberts, the armor tore away, and Jace stood straight, holding the head, neck, and spine of the dangerous and brutal cyborg in his hand. He swung it hard to the ground like a sledgehammer, then stomped on the skull, crushing it beneath his boot.

Fitting, since that's how he threatened his and Erica's unborn baby.

Jace stood straight, the adrenaline from the fight quickly wearing off, and the injuries he incurred began to kick in. He held his arm and chest while favoring his left leg. His face felt like hell. When he wiped his eyes, he didn't know if it was mud or blood he wiped away.

Brian called from afar, "Jace!"

Jace turned to look at Brian, who ran toward him frantically waving over his head. Then he pointed away from the hangar.

Jace followed Brian's gesture to see someone he hadn't seen in a long time.

Sir Dunemore—with his stupid mustache, cloak and sword and all—carried Maya under his arm, and he got in the back passenger door of the parked massive aero-vehicle. Inside the driver's seat, Dame Moon.

"Maya!" Jace started to make his way toward the aero-vehicle.

Dunemore set Maya down and turned to face Jace. He shook his head, but Maya seemed to stir a little.

"Maya!" Jace pulled out a gun, but he couldn't shoot. Not when Maya was in the vehicle. If he shot down the aero-car, she could get hurt.

Maya looked up toward Jace.

The aero-vehicle lifted from the ground.

"Maya!"

The sound Jace had never heard before, he never thought possible, made Jace pause, and his heart skip a beat. Maya shouted, "Jace!"

Then, from a clear sky, a lightning bolt arced from the horizon and struck the aero-vehicle.

He looked up to see Dunemore grabbing some passenger handle and backhanded Maya. At that moment, another bolt of lightning struck the hangar.

Jace was blown off his feet from the structure's explosion, and he slid across the mud. He rolled over, coughing and gasping, watching the smoking but still functional aero-vehicle fly off.

After a couple of moments, Jace regained his senses. He slowly got to his feet, then turned to find Brian, who got tossed to the side. He rushed to Brian's aid.

"Hey, are you okay?"

"Yeah, I think so." Brian sat up with a groan, his face smeared with dirt and mud with some scratches and cuts on his cheek and neck. "What was that?"

Jace looked toward the direction the aero-vehicle flew. "I don't know. Did you hear her?"

"Hear what?"

"Maya." Jace stood, staring at the smoke trail. "She screamed my name."

CHAPTER TWENTY-FOUR

EVEN BEING IN NO CONDITION TO DRIVE AND IGNORING BRIAN'S protests, Jace took the wheel and sped toward the dam, with Brian giving directions. He did his best to ignore the aches all over his body. There was no time for pain. Not with Maya in danger. And he didn't know if it was him thinking to himself and the fight with Roberts scattered his thoughts, but the whispered, "hurry" or "time is short" kept echoing in his mind. Those whispers would be quelled by the mental image of Maya reaching for him and screaming his name.

His stomach growled. While Brian fiddled with the many buttons on the dash that Jace never touched, Jace gestured to the glove box. "Hey, reach in there and grab some things for me."

Brian handed Jace the requested granola bar, some muscle relaxers, and a bottle of water. He took the pill and began to eat. Each bite and every chew hurt his teeth. Never mind the mixture of blood in his mouth. He rolled a window down, grabbed a bottle of water to rinse his mouth, then spat a stream of red out the window. He leaned back against the chair in a groan as he rolled up the window.

"Mr. York," Brian said.

The voice of Nick came through the stereo speakers. "Hello, Mr. McGuen. Pardon me for not providing any video. I'm still in the hospital."

"We're in trouble here. The Order took Maya."

Nick groaned and cursed under his breath. "What is their purpose?"

"We're working on that."

After a brief pause, Nick said, "I heard about a fire at the eastern airfield and an aero-vehicle making an emergency landing at the dam. I assume that's your work?"

"Yes. Well, Jace's, mostly. He's hurt, but we're chasing them to the dam. That's where Maya is."

Jace rolled his eyes. "I'm fine."

Nick said, "What an interesting location to flee toward. Hold on."

Jace rubbed his jaw, feeling the swelling already beginning. After witnessing the lightning shooting across the horizon from a clear sky, he thought of other times unexplained events occurred—the bonding of fire elementals, and her ability to remove the poison from his body. What else did she do? Did he even notice? But she audibly called out to him. And when she did, that's when all hell broke loose. Was that why she never said anything? Too afraid? Couldn't control her power?

A distant memory came to mind. The voice of Xin sounded in his thoughts of being told a story while going through his briefings.

Fear and anxiety began to build in his gut as timelines started to form in his head.

"Hey, Brian, can you look up something for me?"

"Sure, Jace." Brian extended something from the dash and began working on it. What else did Brian do to his coveted car? "What's up?"

"Do you remember that huge storm back at SOC? Maybe nine or ten years ago? The one that knocked all of those trees over."

"Yeah, kind of."

"Look up other weather events at that time."

Brian glanced at Jace. "What's up?"

"Something... I don't know yet."

A few moments later, Brian said, "Okay, I found something. It looks like there was some tornado or something that landed... Holy smokes, Jace. This was nearby!"

His worries thickened, stretching from his gut to his chest. "Does that article say anything about some town or village?"

"Umm..." Brian tapped more. "Not that article, but I found another one. The storm seemed to have exacerbated a sinkhole. I remember reading about this."

"Could it be?" Jace removed his foot from the accelerator. He began to think about the details of what Xin said. The scream. Dunemore covering her mouth.

"Mr. McGuen," Nick said, snapping Jace from his thoughts. "I have discovered that The Order owns the dam."

Brian smacked the armrest. "I knew it!"

With renewed determination, Jace slammed on the accelerator. "Hey Nick, I have a couple of quick questions. I'm guessing you know about Atmos."

"I do."

"What is it?"

"I'm not entirely sure. I remember my mother telling me Atmos was the tether to another world."

Jace gulped and licked his dry lips. "What would The Order do if they found Atmos?"

"Again, I'm not sure. I do know the world, as we know it, would be in danger."

Brian chimed in, "I don't get it. Why is that?"

"We don't have time to discuss ancient religions."

"Humor us," Jace said.

Nick sighed. "Very well. When something major happens in the world, it is usually because The Order captured Atmos. Revolutions, shifts in global power, great catastrophes, they can be linked to Atmos. But like I said, we don't have time to talk about ancient religion. I have to go, but I shall reach out to my sources to try to get you some reinforcements. Be careful."

"Thanks." Brian pushed a button, then looked toward Jace. "What's that about?"

"We have to find her, Brian. If we lose her now, who knows if we will ever find her." Jace rinsed his mouth again.

"I know we do. And we will. But what can we do when we get there? If Mr. York is right, then we're running straight into a base."

"Won't be the first time." Jace grabbed his backpack from the backseat and handed it to Brian. "This is going to be dangerous. Are you sure you want to come?"

Brian started to reload the harness. "You said it yourself. If we don't get Maya now, who knows what'll happen."

They turned the final corner and drove toward the dam.

Smoke rose in the distance.

Jace gestured to the smoke. "There. You see it?"

"Yeah. But do you see that?"

In the road ahead of them stood a guard station and a crossbar. "Hang on." Jace floored it. The acceleration from the car pushed Jace back into his seat. They blasted through the wooden bar with shouts from a guard fading from behind.

"We won't have long." Jace took the last bite of his snack and tossed the wrapper into the back seat.

"Hey, check that out."

They pulled up to the supposed crash site, which they discovered was on some sort of landing pad in the middle of the dam.

Jace stopped the car near the aero-vehicle. After they got out, Jace pulled out a gun and approached the smoking vehicle. As they walked around to the other side, Jace was stunned with a hit to the face. Brian groaned, and Jace heard him hit the ground a few feet to the side. Before he could react, something swatted his hand, knocking the gun from his grip.

Dame Moon stood before him, holding her side. Her hair, usually in a bun, was messed up. Dirt, broken glass, and blood covered her face.

Jace didn't feel like he was able to fight, so he pulled out his second gun. "Where is Maya?"

"You're too late, fallen." Moon took to her fighting stance. "You should run while you can."

"Not without Maya." Jace fired some rounds at her.

Moon took cover behind the aero-vehicle.

"Brian, get up." Jace scuttled to Brian.

"What happened?" Brian looked dazed as he picked up his glasses.

"Get up. We have to move." Not wanting Moon to throw one of her poisonous needles at them, Jace shot the aero-vehicle a few times to provide cover.

Brian got to his feet, and the two took a few steps back. Jace grabbed the dropped gun on the way toward their car.

Moon broke cover with a weapon of her own, a strange, oversized rifle with a massive clip.

Before Jace could give suppression fire, Moon opened fire. Each round blew holes in the street as Jace and Brian hid behind the car. It rocked from each hit from Moon's gun. Glass shattered. The tires went flat.

"Fucking hell, Brian. Isn't the car supposed to be bulletproof?

"It is."

"What kind of gun is that?"

"I don't know." Brian kept his back against the car, and he looked left and right, as if seeking a solution to the problem. "Maybe an automatic rail gun?"

"They make those?"

A particular hit made the car spark, then began to smoke.

"Apparently," said Brian. "Though I've never seen a railgun that small."

Seeing liquid drip from under the car, Jace's heart sank. It would be a long time before Brian could fix his beloved sports car.

Jace couldn't sit idle any longer. "Stay here."

Brian nodded as he covered his face from the windshield exploding.

Jace reloaded his handguns while moving toward the back of the car. Hearing the attack focused at the front, Jace broke cover and shot at Moon.

She hid behind her own cover, Jace's bullets hitting the downed aero-vehicle.

Jace ran toward the aero-vehicle, firing at Moon and keeping pressure on her until the slides of his guns came back. He returned the guns in the harness just as Moon broke cover to return fire. Jace collided with Moon, and he grabbed her weapon. The two struggled to control the automatic railgun for a moment as it fired wildly at the aero-vehicle and the street.

Jace felt a few hits from Moon's kicks. He elbowed her across the face, the two-inch spike slashing deep into her cheek, then lifted her from the ground and pinned her against the aero-vehicle.

Moon wrapped her legs around Jace, and she reached into her hair.

Jace caught her arm as she stabbed down at him with one of her deadly hair sticks.

She headbutt him.

Dazed, he took a step back from the aero-vehicle but kept his hold on Moon's arm and the railgun.

A quick hit from Moon had Jace feel a sharp pain in his throat.

Jace wrapped his arm around Moon, and the two embraced in a mutual lock.

Moon whispered, "This time, I won't be merciful." Jace felt

something sharp attempt to pierce his armor at his side, just under the ribs.

Jace gave her a bear hug.

He heard the groans from Moon, but her unknown attack kept going, moving around to find an opening from his protective gear.

Jace growled as he gripped harder.

Moon struggled and squirmed, and her strange stabbing kick at his side grew more desperate. She wriggled an arm free, and she began to wrap Jace's neck with some cord.

The sudden lack of oxygen had Jace loosen his grip.

Moon wiggled out of Jace's grasp and nimbly pivoted on his back.

Jace gripped the cord as he fell to a knee, still holding on to the railgun. His head pulsed with pain as the blood built up in his skull. A couple of heartbeats later, his eyes began to bulge out of their sockets, and he found himself unable to take a breath. He tried to stand, but a hit behind his knee prevented him from getting to his feet.

His hearing became muffled tones, and he began to pass out.

All he could do was shoot the railgun. And his only target was the aero-vehicle.

Jace pulled the trigger, blowing holes in the crashed vehicle. The aero-vehicle caught fire.

A muffled shout, then the cord released from his neck.

Jace collapsed to the ground in a cough.

On his side and gasping for air, he saw Brian grappling Moon, holding her from behind and lifting her from the ground. In front of them was the broken computer Brian used to operate the holograms, and one of the needles from Moon next to it.

Jace struggled to his hands and knees, grabbing the needle as he regained his composure.

He looked up to see Moon break free from Brian's grip and deftly beat the shit out of him.

Jace crawled for a bit, grabbed Moon's leg, and plunged the needle into her calf.

Moon looked behind her and backhanded Jace across the face. He fell to his back.

Moon stepped forward while grabbing some sort of blade from an inner pocket of her clothes. Then, she paused, and her eyes went wide. She staggered a step, then fell to her knees as her arms dropped down, as if going limp.

Jace rolled to his side as she grabbed the railing of the dam before collapsing to the ground. They looked eye-to-eye at one another.

"How does it feel?" Jace grinned. "To know that you lost, and all you can do is lie here helpless while your limbs rot away from the inside?"

"This..." Moon gasped. "Isn't over." She visibly struggled, which was more than he could do after being injected by her needle's venom.

"No, it's not." Jace got to his knees.

She seemed to shift more, as if resisting the poison. Maybe she built up a resistance? Maybe she has some antidote?

Knowing she wouldn't hesitate to kill him, Brian, or Maya, Jace pulled out one of his guns. "Hey, Moon. Block this." He fired.

The back of her skull exploded on impact, and she lie lifeless at the edge of the dam, a throwing needle falling from her grasp.

Brian stumbled over to Jace and went to a knee. "Holy smokes, Jace."

"Yeah." Jace put the gun away, fighting back the feeling of shame, dread, and guilt from taking another life. "You alright?"

"I will be." He looked down at Moon's body. "You killed her."

Jace heard sirens from a distance.

"She would have killed us. Probably would have, too." Jace rubbed his throat as he nudged Moon's hand with a boot to point out the deadly weapon. That's when he noticed a drop of blood on the ground, but it wasn't from either of them. The trail went from the crashed aero-vehicle down a set of stairs. He gestured to the drop. "Look. Come on. We have to keep going."

The two climbed over a waist-high fence and made their way toward the stairs. After they got a few steps down, the entire landing pad exploded, and Jace and Brian were tossed into the handrails. As they looked behind them, they saw a section of the dam give way. Part of the landing pad, the aero-vehicle that exploded, and Jace's exotic blue sports car, toppled over the side, crashing into the dam wall on the way toward the ground. Jace's eyes followed the tumble of his beloved car as it bounced once, twice, a third time from the curved dam wall, eventually hitting and destroying some structure that covered the water, finally submerging and being swept away down the river in flames.

As they stared at the river below, Brian eventually put a hand on Jace's shoulder. "Come on. We have to go."

Jace's gaze remained at the splash point for a few moments longer before nodding. It was time to save Maya and save the world.

CHAPTER TWENTY-FIVE

EACH STEP, EVERY BREATH, WHATEVER SOUND THE TWO MADE echoed down the concrete tunnels. They had no idea where they were going, as the blood trail vanished soon after going through the door. Some corridors and halls had Brian hunch over. Jace, being much shorter, had no problem traversing the arched passages. Some paths led to dead ends, while others had them look out a window that overlooked the river far below.

Eventually, Brian gave a futile gasp and put his back against the wall. "Okay, that's enough. I need a break."

Jace felt exhausted, too. But with Maya in danger, he didn't want to stop. "Come on. We have to keep going."

Brian panted as he hunched over, hands on his knees. "No, no. Just...give me a minute."

"We don't have time for this."

Brian looked around, as if visually scanning the area. "We're going down the length."

"Yeah. So?"

"Do you think they took Maya this far down? Or did we miss an elevator or stairs or something?"

That gave Jace pause. He was so focused on finding Maya that he didn't realize he wasn't thinking rationally. He looked back the way they came. "Shit."

"Now, now." Brian hoisted himself from the wall. "We can go back without going back."

"Make sense, Brian."

"What I mean is..." Brian gestured toward the way they came. "We know Maya isn't down there. But what about down there?" He pointed at a small turnoff where narrow spiral stairs led up and down.

Jace nodded. "Alright. Let's give it a shot."

They went down the spiral stairs to the next landing and eventually found a tiled hall. Jace patted Brian on the shoulder, and they peered down the passage.

They started their way down, eventually turning right at a crossway, taking a few turns as they went. Finally, they found their first room since they stepped foot in the grand structure. A low hum sounded from the massive space as it opened up to the right. A dozen paces away were metal handrails. When Jace and Brian reached the rails, they found themselves above a humongous hall. Heavy equipment, some strange drums, and cranes were all over the place, but the funny-looking cylinders sticking out from the ground caught Jace's eye.

Brian pointed at one of the cylinders. "We're in one of the generators. That's the maintenance floor below. But this doesn't look like any of the ones I worked on. Those pipes are not supposed to be there."

"What do you think it means?"

Brian shrugged.

"How many of these rooms are there?"

Brian brought up his hand to indicate the amount. "Two. One on the east end, one on the west."

"And you've worked in both?"

Brian nodded.

That was strange.

Below, a few armed people in hardhats walked from under their balcony and got into a mobile cart.

Jace and Brian flinched and took a step away from the handrail. Jace said in a near whisper, "Okay, Brian. You got us here. Now what?"

Brian replied in an equally quiet tone, "There has to be some sort of control station nearby to monitor the readings. Come on."

Brian led the way to some stairs, down some passages, and eventually to a security door. "There we are." He inspected the keypad. "Print encryption with digital—"

"Can you open it?"

Brian gave a slight smile. "Easily."

A noise caught Jace's attention. A couple of people in white coats turned a corner and eagerly walked away from them down a hall before turning another corner. "Hey, hold off on that a minute."

"What's up?"

Jace gestured with his head toward the lab coats. "When was the last time you saw scientists eagerly walk around a dam? Hold on. I want to check something out."

With Brian in tow, Jace turned the corner where the white-coats went to. It led to another security point. "Open this one."

Brian nodded and went to work.

Jace peered around the corner to look for any visitors.

A moment later, a beep sounded from the door, and Jace turned around.

The double doors slid open to a hallway with privacy-striped curtains blocking the view. When Jace and Brian walked through the curtains, they stood in awe at the sight they beheld—a hallway of massive vats that lined the walls, each connected from pipes and cables that trailed the ceiling. Inside each was a child hooked up to hoses and wires, and they floated motionless inside the liquid. Each of them was scarred, some with fresh stitches from some horrifying experiment.

The disgust had Jace mindlessly walking down the middle of the hallway, looking left and right from one unfortunate victim after another. None of them seemed any older than twelve.

"Jace," Brian gulped. "What is this?"

"I don't know." Jace approached one of the vats and put his hand on the glass. He would have thought they were dead if it weren't for the familiar-looking monitors that showed vital signs on each vat. He clenched a fist, scraping his fingernails against the glass. "We have to stop this."

Brian called with a whisper from down the hall, "Jace!"

Jace rushed over to him. He paused as he saw the one inside. "Is that Ruth?"

Brian didn't answer but began inspecting the machinery. "We have to get her out."

"We will." Jace put a hand on Brian's shoulder. "We're going to help everyone here."

After a sigh, Brian put down some cables, gave Jace a nod, and the two continued their trek down the hallway.

Eventually, they ended up at a door and some operator at a computer. Jace went first, taking out a gun, and walked next to the operator. "Where does that lead to?"

The operator flinched, his chair rolling back a bit, and looked up in fright at Jace. "You can't be here."

Jace, unable to control his rage, swatted the butt of his hand cannon against the side of the man's head. He fell to the floor. "Neither are they!" He gestured to the victims in the tubes. "Now, what is behind that door?" He brought the barrel of the gun to the operator's knee.

Brian sat at the operator's seat. "How about I just open it up, and we can take a look for ourselves?"

Jace's eyes went from Brian to the operator. "That works." He took off his backpack and began to restrain and gag the operator.

When he finished, Brian said, "I'll be working on getting these kids freed while you're checking the room out. Ready?"

Jace put his backpack on, approached the door, and nodded.

The door slid open to reveal a viewing room. To his left was a small control panel. To his right, a window to some operating room and a door to the opposite side. Inside the operating room were the three lab-coats he followed, and one other, surrounding a table. What caught his attention was something casually tossed over a table—a hoodie.

He found her.

Jace rushed over and slammed the door open. "Maya!"

The lab-coats turned to face Jace, but the unseen one, the one who faced away from him, kept on working. Then she stood up straight, removing a vial of blood from a syringe, dark skin and blonde hair in a tight ponytail. Jace couldn't help but gasp.

"Erica?"

Erica turned to face Jace. "Oh, it's you." She lifted a hand, as if to have Jace stop in his tracks.

"What are..." Jace stumbled with his words.

"Finish up and call the transport." Erica went toward a back table with vials of chemicals on it as the lab-coats returned to the figure on the table.

"What are you doing here?"

"Working, of course." She put some of the blood in a small vial with some strange mixture and swished it.

"Working?"

Jace couldn't comprehend what was happening, so he asked again. "What's going on? Why do you have all of those kids in tubes?" His focus, shattered by Erica's presence, once again went toward his little sister, who laid on the table. "And what are you doing to Maya?"

One of the lab-coats looked up. "Dr. Patel, we should have him removed."

"It's okay, Dr. Haruss. Just finish your work, then leave us be.

All of you." Erica walked around the table and approached Jace. It was the first time he was able to get a good look at her. Knowing what he knew, he saw the small bump on Erica's stomach. "Sir Dunemore wants to kill you. You should go."

"Not without those kids."

"Then take them."

"And you?"

She shook her head.

Two lab-coats began exiting the room through another door. And even though he clearly saw his little sister lying on a table under bright lights, all he could think about was Erica and everything that had to do with her.

"I thought you left The Order. You left to be with me. What about us?"

"Us?" Erica scoffed. "There never was an 'us.' I never left."

Jace couldn't believe what he was hearing.

"Your blood had a mystery I needed to solve. And when you vanished after the hotel ambush, I thought you died, and my mission had failed." A smile crept on her lips. "Imagine my surprise when you strolled back into my life."

"Your mission?"

"The magic in your blood."

He did remember her taking more of his blood than anyone else.

"And if posing as your girlfriend helped me achieve my mission, that was a sacrifice I was willing to take." Some device around her wrist beeped. "Speaking of which..." She inspected the vial. The blood visibly turned a semi-transparent blue. She grinned. "Confirmed."

His heart sank, and he felt the blood drain from his head. "What... What about our child?"

"This?" She patted her stomach and started to walk toward the operating table. "As soon as I get home, I'm going to terminate this thing. It'll only get in the way of my work."

Jace was still too stunned to move. He couldn't think clearly, and his grief, anger, sorrow, pain, every emotion got in the way of his rationale.

Once the initial shock wore off, things started to make sense to him—how The Order could find them, all of the isolated attacks, and Roberts. Roberts wasn't going after him. Roberts was there for her. She led Roberts to them. Was she responsible for everything that happened? The kidnapped children? The siege on Brian's house? Even Claire's death?

He gritted his teeth, bearing through the denial that tried to block his vision.

Erica said, "We have the subject prepared. Process it for extraction."

"That's my sister." Jace was about to take a step forward as the last lab-coat went through the door but paused when Erica shot a glare at him.

"This thing isn't your sister. It isn't even human."

"She's my sister. You know that."

Erica scoffed. "You're so pathetic." When Erica gestured to Maya, he caught a glimpse of metal in her hand. That meant Erica had Maya held hostage. "Don't you know what this means?"

If The Order needed her alive for whatever plans they had, they wouldn't dare kill her just to stop him. But he couldn't take that chance. Jace had to make a change to try to get an advantage. "That you're not the kind, loving woman I thought you were."

"This is Atmos, Jace." Erica glared at him while continuing to aggressively gesture to Maya. "This is the answer to our problems. We can eradicate The Evolved. We can develop our world far beyond what we know. This is a huge step for humanity!"

He had no immediate reply. Ever since the conversation in the car, Jace heavily suspected Maya's identity, but to hear a confirmation shook him to the core.

"And we wouldn't have found it if it wasn't for the mysterious magic in your bloodstream."

Jace's gaze wandered to the floor at that revelation. No, Roberts wasn't there just for Erica. Roberts was there for Maya. Even The Order's attacks on the neighborhood were to find her. And since he led them to Maya, he was responsible for her capture. He was responsible for putting her in danger. He was responsible for everything—even Claire's death.

He found his mind spiraling out of control, and guilt piled up into his chest. He had to find a way to center his thoughts. He had to make things right. "And the kids in that room?"

Erica shrugged. "I have no use for them. Take them. They're doomed anyway."

Jace shook his head.

Erica sighed and relaxed her arm but stayed near Maya. "You know, Sir Xin requested that I give you one last chance to rejoin our ranks. You have a talent that can't easily be replaced."

"No." Jace began to reach behind him and pulled a gun. "This is *your* last chance. Hand over my sister."

Erica shook her head. "You're hopeless." She waved dismissively and turned to continue her work. "He's all yours, Sir Dunemore."

A hand grabbed Jace's shoulder and spun him around, and a massive fist crashed against Jace's jaw. Jace lost his grip on the gun and staggered into the viewing room.

"You're a foolish boy." Dunemore stood, blocking the door back to the room.

Though the hit should have been devastatingly brutal, Jace hardly felt a thing. Perhaps he was able to go with the punch just in time? Maybe the blow wasn't a solid of a hit as he thought. Regardless, with him still recovering from the brutal battle from Roberts, and the near-death experience from Moon, Jace wondered if he had the strength and energy to stand a chance against Dunemore.

CHAPTER TWENTY-SIX

WHISPERS ECHOED IN JACE'S MIND, REACHING THROUGH THE RINGING in his ears.

"Save her."

"Stand up."

"Fight back."

Were the repeated hits in the head making him crazy? Maybe he did hear something. And if so, what? Or perhaps the sudden punch from Dunemore dazed him more than he thought, and his mind and thoughts were scattered.

Jace began to get to his feet before Dunemore slammed his boot into his chest. His back crashed against the wall. The lights in the viewing room flickered, then went out. That's when Jace noticed his cartoon-like gloves glowed red.

"I don't know what Sir Xin saw in you." Dunemore picked Jace up by the jacket. His feet dangled off the ground. "But I always thought you were an arrogant child unworthy of your title."

Unlike in the mountainside structure where Dunemore used some restraint, Jace knew the attack was at full strength. And if it weren't for his backpack, he'd probably have broken bones. But for reasons Jace couldn't explain, the kick only kind of hurt. Like it wasn't enough to even knock the wind out of him. On top of things, his aches and pains were going away. It was about time the muscle relaxers kicked in.

Jace, finally recovering from the surprise punch, lifted his head to look Dunemore in the eyes. "One problem, though. I know you're cheating." He grabbed Dunemore's wrists, the gloves gently pulsing with light, and he slowly began to overpower the might of Dunemore.

Dunmore's eyes locked onto Jace's gloves. "What's this?"

"Payback." When Dunemore's grip released Jace's jacket, Jace used the momentum of the fall to throw Dunemore over his shoulder. Glass from above crashed down after his boot hit the ceiling, and Jace threw him hard to the floor.

Jace punched down hard at Dunemore. Dunemore rolled to the side. Jace's fist slammed on the floor, cracking the tile.

As Dunemore stood, he backhanded Jace. Jace staggered back a few steps.

"Though you've gotten stronger, you still can't win."

Dunemore stepped forward for his assault. Jace blocked one attack after another, each blow slightly lifting him from the ground or shifting him to the side. He may have the mystery strength of the cartoon gloves, but his light frame could still be knocked over or pushed aside. However, regardless of how hard Dunemore hit, Jace only felt a fraction of the pain. And if he could be knocked over from being so light, maybe Dunemore could be knocked over from being hit so hard.

Jace took a chance to go on the offensive. He swerved a jab and gave a punch with all of his strength. It hit Dunemore square in the chest. He was launched back off his feet and into the wall before falling to his hands and knees.

That seemed to do it.

Jace glared. "Stay out of my way."

Before he could turn to retrieve Maya, Dunemore stood

straight and tall, brushing the dust from his cloak. "You still don't get it? You have a lot to learn, boy." He charged, the bulk of his massive frame taking up the whole hallway. There was nowhere to move. He plowed into Jace and crushed him against a wall with a shoulder ram.

With limited mobility, Jace struggled to find a way out of Dunemore's crushing force. His hand found its way to Dunemore's face. With no accurate angle to attack, Jace did the only thing he could. He grabbed Dunemore's mustache.

Dunemore winced and wavered. That was enough for Jace to push himself to the side and out from the wall.

Dunemore swatted down at Jace. Bad move. Jace was knocked to the side, but his grip held firm. Dunemore growled. A decent-sized chunk of Dunemore's upper lip was torn, and a patch of skin was missing. Jace shook his hand, removing the hair from his fingers.

The voice of Brian called out from behind Jace. "What's going on?"

"Brian, stay away. Keep working on freeing those kids."

"They're already out."

"Then get them out of here."

"Got it."

Dunemore wiped away the blood that dripped down his lip. "Your efforts are for naught. With Atmos in our possession, we win again. They'll all die soon, anyway."

"Not if I can help it." Jace closed the distance.

Dunemore, too, charged. He wrapped Jace up in a hug and plowed him into the back wall, then tossed him to the side. Jace slid on the tiled floor that led to the hallway of imprisoned children. Dunemore took a few quick strides toward Jace and kicked him in the gut. Jace flew a few feet into the air before sliding against the smooth tiled floor.

Even though the hits didn't hurt as much as they should have, Jace found himself spit up some blood. He stared at the pool of red and wondered why. If the hits didn't hurt, if something, probably the gloves, protected him somehow from the blows, why was he spitting up blood?

The whispers came back. "Return to her. Protect her."

Jace growled and slammed a fist into the ground. "I'm trying, damn it!" He looked around, seeing the empty vats, and felt a hint of relief that at least Brian got them out. Now it was time to deal with Dunemore.

Dunemore approached as he reached to his side and drew out his sword. That's when his eye caught something. Dunemore's belt! That's his enhancement. That must be why and how he was able to brush off the blows he had received. However, the presence of a sword changed the rules in the fight.

As Jace got to his feet, the two squared off for a moment.

Dunemore began to ramble off some edict as he brought the crossguard to his face. "By the power and authority granted to me by The Order, I, Sir Dunemore—"

"A little dramatic. Don't you think?"

Dunemore pointed the blade at Jace. "You are accused of conspiracy against humanity."

"Don't give me that."

"Accused of murder."

Jace swiped his hand out to the side. "As are you! Don't spout off some hypocritical bullshit."

"The death of Dame Moon and Sir Roberts is on your hands." Dunemore took a fighting stance. "I find you guilty and sentence you to death."

"You are so full of yourself." Jace took a stance himself, reaching back to grab his gun. It felt like something pinched at it, as if catching on something as he tried to take it out. After a moment of struggle, he finally drew the gun, and he pointed it at Dunemore. "What was the saying about a knife to a gunfight?"

A moment later, red strobe lights turned on from the ceiling.

The whirring sounds of some gizmos or gadgets were heard, then something lowered from all over the ceiling.

Turrets. Not good.

Jace turned and ran just as the turrets began to fire. Glass from the vats shattered, the ground split and cracked from the bullets, and the world around him exploded, piece by piece.

Jace peeked over his shoulder to see Dunemore giving chase, not caring if any of the bullets hit him. In fact, he hardly seemed to notice.

After feeling a punch in the shoulder, and one in the side, Jace turned the corner to escape the hallway of death.

More turrets lowered from the ceiling.

Dunemore took the corner, not far behind Jace.

"Not good." Jace continued his retreat, eventually finding his way to the maintenance floor of the generator room.

More turrets lowered from the ceiling.

Soldiers or guards started to come in, armed and pointing their own weapons.

Jace took cover between the wall and a generator.

He was pinned.

A chill on his arm caught his attention. Jace looked down to see a dark red stain in his coat. When he looked underneath it, he saw a hole through his shoulder and one at his side.

At that moment, he felt light-headed and leaned against a barrel. He tried to take off his backpack, but it caught on the destroyed reload harness. Not being able to get it off, he disconnected the harness and tossed it, and the backpack, to the ground.

Whispers. "Hurry. Save her."

Jace growled. "Shut up!" His fingers shuffled through the crushed and broken items in his backpack until he found Brian's gunshot wound kit. He leaned back against the generator and shot the foam into his side, then his shoulder.

As he allowed himself a moment to relax, he noticed the

cracked plastic box of the earpiece stuffed to the side. Jace opened the box and put in the com device and pushed the button. "Brian, can you hear me?"

A moment later, Brian replied, "Jace. Are you okay? I've been trying to get a hold of you."

"Oh, I'm wonderful." He tossed the empty canister of the gunshot foam aside. "Some sort of internal defense system kicked in. They have guns on the ceiling all over the place."

"Okay, okay. Hold on."

Dunemore called out, "You lose, boy. Come out now, and I shall give you an honorable death."

Brian said over the com, "Okay, where are you?"

"I'm pinned in that generator room. The one with the cylinders."

"Okay, okay. Hold on."

Jace dabbed at his side, feeling the foam thicken. "By the way, your armor doesn't stop those bullets."

"They don't? Wait, you've been shot?"

"Yeah. I used that foam, so I'll be fine."

"Remember, that's a temporary solution. And you shouldn't move too much. But you'll need to go to the hospital as soon as possible."

Jace picked up his gun from the drum. That's when he noticed a red and yellow label, indicating fire and explosive. "I'll be fine."

"Holy smokes, Jace. There are a ton of people in there."

Jace looked around, as if he had x-ray vision to find Brian through solid steel and stone. "Where are you? Are you and those kids okay?"

"We're okay. Hang on."

"Last chance, boy. I'll give you a count of three."

Brian said, "Okay, I got you covered. When I say go, make your move. You won't have a lot of time."

"One... Two... Th—"

"Go!"

Trusting Brian with his life, Jace broke cover and charged.

The turrets on the ceiling opened fire, but not at Jace. Soldiers began to scatter for cover, many falling to the ground in a bloody heap.

Though holes were blowing into Dunemore's clothing, he stood in the gunfire, as if it didn't faze him one bit.

Jace charged Dunemore, who stood stoically, raising his sword over his head.

The whispers came to Jace's mind. "Free our brethren."

With his arms up, Jace saw his target. Jace aimed and fired at the belt.

Finally getting some reaction from Dunemore, he took a step back, guard broken, and brought his arm forward to block the gunshots.

Jace shoulder-slammed him. He heard Dunemore drop the sword as Jace lifted him into the air and slammed him against the wall. The two engaged in a brutal punching contest, trading one punch for another.

"Jace," Brian said over the com. "I'm losing control of the defense grid."

With him running out of time, Jace threw his punch, but redirected his movements and grabbed the belt. Dunemore grabbed Jace's hands to try to prevent him from removing the belt, and began pushing Jace, sliding him across the floor.

Jace used that momentum and performed a belt throw, tossing Dunemore over his hip and into the generator. It cracked, and sparks flew from the energy-gathering cylinders. Jace covered his eyes, and the lights in the room went completely dark. But only for a brief moment as emergency lights turned on.

He couldn't get the belt off, but Dunemore didn't move from that hit.

Brian said, "Nice job, partner. I think that stopped the defense grid, but I don't know for how long."

Jace groaned as the burning agony in his side broke through

whatever stopped him from feeling pain. He held the wound, feeling the blood ooze from between the foam and his injury. "I have to get Maya."

"Now's your chance."

Whether Dunemore was stunned or killed, it didn't matter. Not taking the opportunity for granted, Jace started to run back to Maya. It was time to get his sister and get the hell out of there.

———

After knocking out a few guards, Jace finally returned to the hallway where the children were being held. Brian sat at the control panel intensely leaning forward and looking at a computer screen.

"Brian."

Brian didn't look back. "I'm here. The defense grid is starting to come back online. It looks like someone is redirecting power. The security door is closed. I'm working on getting it open now."

Jace, holding his side, leaned against the control panel next to Brian. "Where are those kids?"

Brian turned to look up at Jace. "They're sa-holy shit, Jace!"

"What?"

Brian stood up, a lot more than a hint of concern in his expression. "Are you okay?"

"I'm fine."

"You don't look it."

"I said I'm fine." Jace gestured with his head toward the locked door. "Get that open. We have to save Maya."

Brian briefly hesitated before sitting back down. "Okay, okay." As he worked, he gave one more glance toward Jace.

Did he really look that bad? He went toward some polished surface to see into a reflection. Yeah, he really did look that bad.

His face was swollen and discolored, bloodied and bruised. He hadn't taken many shots in the eye, so it didn't seem like he would lose his vision. At least a dozen lacerations were all over his face, and blood covered almost every inch of his skin.

"I think I got it, Jace." Brian tapped a few more times before the door cracked open.

Jace grabbed the door, using the slight opening for a solid grip, and pulled the door open. Then he charged through, traversing the dark hallway, looking through the broken window that led to the room. Thankfully, she still lay on the table. When he entered, Jace paused as he spotted the two defense turrets—one pointed at the door, one pointed at Maya. He stood still for many heartbeats, his eyes locked on the gun aimed at his sister.

They didn't move.

Convinced they were still shut down, Jace rushed to her side and began to unbind her, ripping out tubes and cables as he went.

A sharp pain came from his wound. Jace's muscles tensed up, his muscles convulsed, and he collapsed to the ground.

Erica stood over him, a high-powered taser in her hand. "You're not going to get in the way." She pushed him aside with her foot and began re-attaching whatever was on Maya. "You look terrible. You know, if you returned to The Order, we could get you healed up in a few hours. And with Atmos in our possession, you can be stronger than ever."

"Arise," said the whispers. "Free our savior."

The feeling began to return to his limbs. As Erica moved to the opposite side of the table, Jace stood up, trying to keep his balance to appear strong to his unfortunate adversary.

Erica paused as she gazed up at him. "Well now, you recovered much faster than I thought. Then again, you've always been a mysteriously fast healer." She turned a knob on her taser and brought it close to Maya. "I wonder if this creature had something to do with it."

Again, Jace was stuck. With Maya in immediate danger, it would be too dangerous for him to make a move. "What do you want?"

"I already told you. Or has Sir Dunemore messed up your head?"

A beep sounded, and a man spoke on an intercom. "Dr. Patel, an aero-vehicle is approaching."

"Excellent." Erica stared at Jace with a grin. "Our transport is here."

For a moment, Jace considered the situation. He could lash out at Erica and get her away from Maya. But with the taser so close to Maya, there was no guarantee that she wouldn't get shocked.

As he stared at Erica, the woman he felt a deep connection to, the woman he loved, the woman who bore his child, doubt arose in his mind. Even if he physically could get to her before she had a chance to shock Maya, even after everything she had done, could he actually will himself to lay a finger on her?

"Jace," Brian said over the com. "That big guy is coming back."

The ceiling turrets whirred as they seemed to reactivate.

That answered every question he had about what he should do. He hesitated too long. He lost.

"I see her. Hold on."

A turret rotated.

Jace raised a hand. "No!"

A single round was shot from the turret. Erica was slammed against a table, and she fell to the floor, knocking all sorts of vials and medical equipment over.

"No!" Jace rushed over to Erica and turned her over. Blood pooled under her body. Her lab coat and shirt were soaked in red. "Damn it, Brian." Tears began to form in his eyes as he held Erica in his arms. He couldn't move. All he could do was hold Erica as he felt the warmth drip down his hands. His eyes went to her stomach, and he placed a hand on his unborn child. Even after everything she put him through, he still cared for her. He whimpered, "Damn it, Brian."

Brian ran into the room. "Jace, we have to hurry. That big guy is coming."

His heart ached, and tears dropped onto her cheek. He gave her a last kiss on the forehead, gently laid her down, and put a cloth from the floor over her face, keeping his hand on her stomach for a moment longer before standing up.

He didn't know what to feel. Angry? Sad? Disappointed? Everything was going too fast for him to emotionally process.

Brian's words broke him out of his trance. "Come on, Maya. Wake up."

"Maya!" Jace turned and focused his attention on his sister. Brian had detached all of the hoses and tubes from her.

Glass crunched from the observation room. Jace looked up to see Dunemore making his way toward the room.

How on earth was he supposed to win Dunemore in his current state? A thought of rationale rang in the back of his mind. He can't.

"Take Maya and get going." Jace closed and held the door with his back.

Brian did as requested, taking Maya into his arms and going through the side exit as Dunemore pounded on the door.

The sharp blade of Dunemore's sword pierced the door, cutting into his armor. He flinched as he realized the strike. He was relieved when he saw no blood.

The blade retracted from the door.

Jace leaped to the side just as another thrust of the blade plunged into the door, an attack that would have pierced the middle of his chest. Not having any more time, Jace followed Brian, fleeing through the side door as well.

CHAPTER TWENTY-SEVEN

JACE HELD HIS SIDE AS HE FOLLOWED BRIAN, WITH MAYA ON HIS back, from one corner after another. Eventually, they made their way back to the control room just before the hallway where the kids were found.

"Brian, what are we doing back here?"

"We can't leave them here." Brian knocked on the door in a one-three-two pattern. A moment later, the door opened.

They entered, closing the door behind them, and Jace looked upon dozens of kids around Maya's age standing shoulder-to-shoulder in a room filled wall-to-wall with computers and controls. Brian sat Maya in the operator's chair as Jace leaned his back against the door, his hand holding his side.

"Let's take a small break here." Brian adjusted his glasses and leaned at one of the computer terminals.

Jace scanned the room, seeing the children wide-eyed and frightened. Who knows what The Order did to them? And how would they be able to look past this nightmare to live out their lives?

"We got a problem. It looks like some aero-transport just landed with reinforcements. A lot of them."

Must have been Erica's ride.

"What about those internal guns?"

"They're offline."

"Figures." Jace glanced at his blood-covered hand. Even with such a severe wound, Jace didn't feel much of the pain. Still, he wasn't in any condition to fight. He looked over the room once more, his eyes locking from one tortured kid to another. "Is the aero-transport taking off?"

"No."

"Then that's our way out." Jace thrust his hips to push him from the door, staggering a step from a hint of dizziness. "Brian, get us to that transport."

Maya stirred awake, and she groggily lifted her head. Her eyes bulged when she spotted Jace.

"Hey." Jace knelt in front of her. "Are you okay?"

Even under such sedated conditions, Maya sat up and put her hands on Jace's cheeks. Her touch made his skin go from numb to cool and soothing.

At that moment, things made sense. How her every touch made him feel better, and how he healed so much quicker than usual, even without Erica's goo. "My recovery was your doing. Huh?"

She nodded, then gently placed her hands on Jace's shoulder.

Jace could only smile and shake his head. How stupid had he been not to recognize all she had done for him. If only he had known who she really was. He would have gotten her to safety and hopefully made the world a safer place. Not just for humans, but for everyone.

"I'm sorry I wasn't able to protect you." Jace held Maya's hand. "But I promise I'll do everything I can to get you out of here." He gestured to the children. "All of you."

Maya nodded, a half-smile rising in the corner of her lips.

"I think I figured out where we're at." Brian adjusted his glasses, and he pointed at a computerized map of the facility. "See, this is a generator unit underneath the main generator stations. I guess to power..." He gestured to the room. "This place."

"So you know how we can get out of here?"

"Almost. This place wasn't in the original blueprints, but I think I'm figuring out where to go. Uhh, Jace, we have to go." Brian stood straight, eyes staring at a screen. "That big guy is coming right for us."

Jace stood. Maya tried to stand with him, but she slumped back in the chair. She was in no condition to run. "Take it easy for a bit longer." He went next to Brian. "Do you have a route?"

"I think so."

"Where?"

Brian placed a finger on the computer screen to a large room. "We have to go through the generator room. A stairway will lead us to an escape route, which will take us to the top."

"No other way?"

"Nothing nearby. At least not that I saw."

Jace cursed under his breath as his gaze remained on the map.

"Jace, that big guy is in that crazy hallway."

He didn't have time to think. Didn't have time to plan. This would all have to be done on the fly. First things first, make sure Dunemore didn't find Maya. "Okay. Once I leave, wait two minutes, then take Maya and lead everyone out of here."

"What about you?"

Jace scoffed. "I'm fine. You remember the tower job?"

Brian slightly shook his head. "This is nothing compared to that."

Jace patted Brian on the shoulder. "Two minutes."

Brian returned the shoulder pat.

With a plan set and with renewed energy, Jace exited the room and ran down the hallway to intercept Dunemore. Just as the door to the hallway opened, Jace paused, and the two stared off once more. Dunemore's clothes were riddled with holes, and he held his sword to his side.

Jace grinned in a cocky fashion. "Do you still think you can win?"

"Don't play games with me, boy." Dunemore swung his sword, apparently not in the mood for chitchat.

Jace leaped back, the tip grazing his armor, and he turned and ran. As he had hoped, Dunemore followed, his heavy boots thumping against the tile.

One turn after another, Jace led Dunemore on a chase through the hallways, eventually going to the natural-looking tunnels they had arrived in. He thought he had a decent idea where everything led, so Jace confidently played the mouse, ensuring the cat stayed in step.

Then he took a corner, ran twenty feet, and he found himself at a dead end. "Shit!" He put his hands against the wall, feeling more out of breath than usual. This was supposed to be an open passage. Perhaps he took a wrong turn somewhere.

Dunemore caught up, slowing his charge as he huffed behind Jace.

Jace turned to face Dunemore and ran his fingers through his sweat-soaked hair.

"End of the line, boy." Dunemore pointed his sword at Jace. "Nowhere else to run."

"Doesn't matter." Jace grinned, scratching his head. "Maya's safe. You lost."

Dunemore took a step forward and adjusted the grip on his sword. "I know what it looks like. I know who it is."

Jace shook his head. "You'll never find her."

"Oh, I will, boy. And when I make my report to The Order, they'll hunt it down to the very ends of the earth." He dramatically clenched a fist. "To the very edge of existence!"

Jace considered Dunemore's words very carefully. Who knew Maya was Atmos? Erica did. What about those lab-coats? Then he remembered seeing them leave while he and Erica talked. Who else knew? "So you're the only one that knows."

"It's time to die, boy. Prepare yourself."

Jace knew the last of his bullets from his gun wouldn't hurt Dunemore, though he didn't know how. If bullets couldn't stop him, he knew he'd need something heavier. More powerful. However, Dunemore's clothes had a ton of holes in them. And that would be his tactic.

Before Dunemore could lunge forward, Jace grabbed his gun from his belt and fired. Two rounds near the hip, hitting the belt. He aimed at the clasp of his cloak and fired a third round, but the shot went wild as he had to dodge a thrust. His back smacked against the wall.

Dunemore brought his sword back for the killing blow. That's when his pants fell from Jace shooting out the belt buckle. They didn't fall far, but enough for Dunemore to pause a moment and look down.

Jace made his move. He stepped forward, giving a punch as hard as he could, landing his fist squarely into Dunemore's jaw. Dunemore's head slammed to and bounced off of the rugged wall, and he crashed to the ground.

He leaped over the body of Dunemore to the hallway, reached into his coat to grab one of the rounds he found in the trunk of his car, and loaded it into the gun chamber.

Dunemore stirred, slowly getting to his feet.

"If bullets can't stop you..." Jace fired. The confined space increased the loud boom as the specialized bullet hit just above Dunemore. It exploded. And like a stick of dynamite, parts of the ceiling began to collapse, crashing on top of Dunemore.

Jace covered his face as a wave of dust and dirt blew his way. A moment later, the dust settled, and all he could see was a pile of rock from the cave-in.

That would do.

Rocks began to slide from the cave-in as Dunemore's hand reached out from the rubble.

"Maybe not," Jace mumbled to himself.

He looked down the hall. It was time to get back to Maya.

————

Jace eventually found his way to the balcony that oversaw the secret generator room. This was where Brian said he'd have to go to escape. He hoped the armed guards didn't find them first.

A moment later, he heard the stomping of many feet.

Did the reinforcements arrive?

From behind, Jace heard Dunemore call out, "I'm coming, boy!"

"Shit!" Jace looked down the vast space, seeing what his options were and thinking of his next move.

A moment later, Brian, with Maya and many kids in tow, ran through the generator room.

"Brian!"

Brian paused and looked up. "Jace!"

Jace leaped over the balcony and prepared to roll with the fall. Once he hit the ground, he immediately regretted it.

"What the hell, Jace?" Brian, along with everyone else, ran up. Brian knelt.

Jace groaned. "I normally roll with the fall."

"You could have used the stairs to the side. What was that?"

"Not rolling." Jace, with Maya and Brian's help, got to his feet. To his surprise, there was no pain. He could have sworn he twisted his ankle or something. He didn't question it.

"Jace, are you okay? You're looking pretty pale."

"I feel fine. Where to?"

"Up ahead is the ramp that leads outside. I think we can avoid a lot of internal security by going up the hiking path. Did you hear that explosion?"

"Yeah, that was me."

"I figured it was."

"Keep moving." Jace looked over his shoulder at the balcony, where Dunemore was to make his appearance soon.

"Jace..."

Jace gazed toward Brian, and he stared at his side. Jace looked down at the massive amount of blood that soaked his clothes. "Geez."

"You're not okay, Jace."

The heavy footsteps of Dunemore echoed through the room. He called from the balcony, "I got you now."

Jace looked toward the balcony as Dunemore leaped over the side. Unlike Jace's graceful crash, Dunemore landed in a kneel.

"Brian, take everyone and go."

Before Brian could protest, Dunemore stood and drew his sword from the sheath, slashing at the draw in a single motion.

Jace leaped back, and he held his arms out to push everyone behind him. "Just go!"

An icicle flew by Jace and crashed into Dunemore, who didn't even seem to notice. Next, a ball of fire, and a bolt of lightning. The small army of adolescent Evolved used their powers to attack, each of them chanting, waving their arms, or performing gestures. Dunemore stood valiantly, brushing away each hit like it was nothing.

A kid from behind called, "Freeze him!"

The ground turned to frost, and shards of white whizzed past Jace.

Dunemore, seemingly not fazed by the attacks, swung his sword. Jace took another step back, keeping everyone behind him as best as possible.

Another swing, but Dunemore's footing slid ever so slightly. Jace, taking any advantage he could, leaped forward to close the distance. Dunemore didn't seem to be as off-balance as Jace thought, and he gave a back-handed slash. Jace caught the blade between his arm and his side, hoping the armor would soak the damage. Jace gripped the edge and kicked Dunemore's knee, almost slipping himself, and gave a feeble punch to Dunemore's side.

Dunemore gave Jace a hard right cross. Jace crashed to the ground and slid across the ice, eventually hitting some machinery.

Jace couldn't figure out how many seconds passed before he could move once more. Brian and Maya were at his side while ice slowly encased Dunemore from one attack after another from the dozens of Evolved.

The ice shattered from the top as Dunemore struggled, but he seemed to be trapped. At least for a moment.

"Come on, Jace. Get up."

After a few blinks, Jace gathered his senses enough to roll on his side and get to his hands and knees. That's when pain shot all through his body, and he curled up into a ball with a growl. Then he realized one of the gauntlets was missing. It had been cut off. Where it should have been was a huge gash that ran the entire length of his forearm. Jace's left arm heated up, almost unbearably, and parts of his body began to grow numb. Maybe with the glove's effects, he could move. When he put weight on his leg, he almost collapsed. "You need to get out of here."

"You said that already." Brian wrapped Jace's arm around his shoulder and, with Maya's help and regardless of his protests, they hoisted him to his feet, where he favored his left leg. "Let's go."

Again, the top of the icy tomb broke. This time, a couple of the kids got smacked with chunks of ice.

Shouts came from the balcony. The reinforcements had arrived.

The Evolved turned their attention toward the balcony and shot their magical abilities at the soldiers. Seemingly caught off guard, the soldiers took cover.

"Brian, you have to get them out of here. Quick, before the reinforcements start shooting back."

"I can't leave you."

Jace removed his arm from Brian's shoulder, almost collapsing from the agony that raced through his entire body. His left arm pulsed with heat, and he winced in pain. But at least the rest of his body continued to numb. "You can, and you will." With his breath short and with a racing heart, Jace stood as tall and as strong as he could but found himself leaning against the wall. "Look." He gestured toward Dunemore and the balcony as some soldiers began to return fire. "These kids are in serious danger."

The ice cracked once more on Dunemore's tomb.

"Maya isn't safe here. If you don't get her out of here, they'll catch her again. If that happens, the world will be fucked. You get me?"

Brian frowned. "No. Not like this."

Jace put a hand on Brian's shoulder. "Remember the tower mission?"

"This isn't anything like that damn mission." Brian wiped away a tear.

"Maybe not. But it was still a miracle I made it out." Jace looked at Maya, who let her tears fall freely.

"We can still get you—"

Jace shot a glare at Brian. "Don't you get it?" He pointed to his wounds, where the blade of Dunemore cut deep into his side, and where the gunshot wounds began to flow freely. "I know the symptoms of bleeding out. I see the signs. I'm not getting out of this one."

Maya put her hands on Jace's wound.

Some gunfire came from the top, and some machinery inches away from Brian's head sparked. The three crouched, but Jace's legs couldn't support him, and he slipped on his butt, putting his back against the wall.

A kid cried out in pain. Then another.

Jace looked squarely at Brian. "If you don't go, they die. You're the good guy. Remember?"

Brian returned the gaze, then gave a slight nod. He put a hand on Jace's shoulder. "Yeah."

Jace tried to lift an arm to put a hand on Brian's shoulder but found his right arm not willing to move. He instead smiled. "Take care of yourself."

Brian nodded, patted Jace's shoulder one last time, then turned to help the kids.

Maya didn't move. She stared hard at Jace, tears flowing freely down her cheeks.

The burn in his left arm grew more intense, and he grimaced in pain. "You have to go, too."

After a moment, Maya wrapped him in a great hug. To Jace's surprise, with a rasp and coarse tone, Maya whispered in his ear in a broken voice, "You can't."

Jace's heart melted, and he felt a tear fall down his own cheek. "You have a pretty voice. You—" His side pulsed, and his body tensed. The numbness began to wear off. "You were the best thing that happened to me."

Maya sniffed and buried her head in Jace's shoulder. "You saved me," she replied, keeping in a coarse whisper.

"You can't control your powers. That's why you don't talk."

She nodded, her head still buried in his shoulder.

More gunshots and another kid shouted in agony.

"Maya, you have to go. It's not safe."

"I can't."

The ice continued to crack on Dunemore's prison.

"You have to." Jace gave her the best hug he could, wrapping his only good arm around her.

Maya gave an audible whimper. The ground shook, and an alarm sounded.

"Go." Jace removed his arm.

Maya stood up and stared down at him.

He gazed up at her, smiling as best as he could. There stood his beautiful, sweet little sister. The salvation of humanity. The entity he hunted for his entire career with The Order. Atmos. Though he still had no idea what or why she was who she was, Jace knew her safety was paramount.

Brian shouted from the far side of the room. "Maya!"

She paused, continuing to stare down at Jace. Then, with what looked like a smile on her lips, she mouthed, "Goodbye," then ran through the battlefield.

Jace watched as she grabbed an injured kid and dragged him to safety. He grabbed the gun from his belt, set it in his lap, and took out the last special bullet in his jacket. That's when he noticed his hand, the one with the gauntlet on, had turned black. Probably from the magic being pumped into him. Or maybe it's being burned or killed off?

The ice shattered to Jace's right as Dunemore broke his arms free of his prison with Jace loading the round in the chamber. One swipe after another, and he removed almost every piece of ice that held him.

Dunemore approached, and the soldiers made their way toward the maintenance level. Dunemore looked unhurt from the barrage of attacks. "How the mighty have fallen. Such a sad state you're in, boy."

Jace's eyes went toward the soldiers as they drew closer. It was almost time. His gaze returned to Dunemore. Then he asked the question he always wondered. "Why a sword?"

"What's that?"

Jace winced from a pulse of pain. "Out of all the things in this world, why a stupid sword?"

Dunemore looked at his blade. "I've had my blade for over a century. Like my belt, an elemental is bound to it. It can cut through almost anything and is indestructible."

"Your belt and your sword. Magical." He coughed, blood spitting from his lips. "I knew it."

Some soldiers ran by. He was out of time.

Dunemore lifted his weapon, ready to stab down at Jace.

"One more thing. One last question."

Dunemore nodded. "I shall grant you that."

For the sake of humanity, the safety of his sister, and the future of the world, Jace raised his hand, his thumb unlocking the gun's slide to load the round. "Can you breathe underwater?" Jace fired. The bullet struck a barrel of petroleum, and it exploded in a deafening roar. A ball of blinding light flashed as a cloud of fire rushed toward him. Soldiers flew to the ground, and Dunemore staggered a step, and he looked behind him. Through the flames, a wall of broken stone and water raced toward them.

Jace took a deep breath and closed his eyes with a smile on his face.

For Maya.

For humanity.

EPILOGUE

News of The Order's doing spread quickly as the survivors from the dam told their stories. They'd been kidnapped and tortured, tested, and experimented on. They never knew if, when they were awakened, that would be their last day alive.

Over the next few years, Nick York became a leading figure in the dismantling of The Order, working to bring them to justice for their heinous crimes. But The Order's roots remained deep in the world's governments. No matter the evidence presented, it would be belittled and downplayed, often saying they were flat-out lies by the Evolved. A trick to fool the common people to bow down to a race of monsters.

So people grew divided, building off of hate, jealousy, and prejudice. One side against the other.

During that time, Maya worked with many Evolved, learning to control her powers and helping her learn how to talk. Though it was a painful and frustrating experience, she eventually learned how to have a conversation like a normal person without the ground splitting or a tornado forming.

One day, Maya pulled her tiny car up to the apartment

complex, opening her hand to check the holograph Brian had sent to confirm the directions. Feeling confident, she parked and exited the car. She walked on a path, looking at the maintained lawn and bushes of the apartment complex, walking around a pool, and eventually making her way to some stairs that led to a second floor. There, she knocked.

After a moment, the door opened. A woman with auburn hair answered, her gaze scanning Maya head-to-toe. "Yes?"

Maya smiled. After all of her searching, she had a feeling this woman was the right person. "Hi there. Did you know a kid named Jace in SOC?"

The woman seemed surprised at that. Almost scared, but her blank expression and diverted gaze told Maya she was going back in a distant memory. "Jace?" The woman opened the door a little. "Holy shit, that's a name I haven't heard in a long time. I always knew that shit stain would come back to bite me in the ass. Who are you? How do you know that little fucker?"

"I'm Jace's little sister." When the woman gave a questioning glance, Maya added in, "Adopted." That seemed to answer her untold question. "Did you know he searched for you almost his entire life?"

The woman scoffed. "He did? Why? That asshole told the fuckheads about what happened."

Maya shook her head. "No. He said the same day Claire was adopted, you vanished."

The woman angrily glared at Maya. "I didn't vanish. I..." She stared at nothing over Maya's shoulder. "What did he tell you?"

"He spent hours telling me stories of you and him. About some special room you, Claire and he had. About how you and he would lie on the grass and stargaze. And so much more." Memories of when he and Jace laid on the grass and stared at the clouds made her smile.

"Really? You mean he didn't tell anyone?" She opened the door wider. "You mean this entire time... Gah, those fuckers!" She smacked her hand on the doorframe, then peeked her head out the door to look around. "Speaking of ass-hats, where is he?"

Maya's heart skipped a beat. It was her turn to divert her gaze and to hold back the emotions from her chest. "I'd like to talk with you. Do you have some time?"

The woman's voice grew solemn, as if detecting the bad news from Maya's reply. "Uh, yeah. Sure." The woman opened the door, inviting her in.

"By the way, my name is Maya." She extended a hand.

The woman shook her hand and gave a crooked smile. "Jessica."

———

Don't miss out on your next favorite book!
Join the Melange Books mailing list at
www.melange-books.com/mail.html

THANK YOU FOR READING

Did you enjoy this book?

We invite you to leave a review at the website of your choice, such as Goodreads, Amazon, Barnes & Noble, etc.

DID YOU KNOW THAT LEAVING A REVIEW...

- Helps other readers find books they may enjoy.
- Gives you a chance to let your voice be heard.
- Gives authors recognition for their hard work.
- Doesn't have to be long. A sentence or two about why you liked the book will do.

ABOUT THE AUTHOR

J. P. Edgar is an American author who was born in Sacramento, California in 1980. He went to college to obtain his Associates Degree in Information Technology, and then got his Bachelor's Degree in 2010 in Game Design. A man of many faces, J. P. Edgar is a musician, a technical artist, a game designer, and a computer programmer. Now, he is working on the Bloodlines of Atmos series, expanding his web of talents to the art of story writing.

www.jpedgar.com

ALSO BY J. P. EDGAR

Bloodlines of Atmos, The Story of Jace, Book 1 – Sanctuary

Bloodlines of Atmos, The Story of Jace, Book 2 - Savior

Bloodlines of Atmos, The Story of Jace, Book 3 - Redemption

www.ingramcontent.com/pod-product-compliance
Lightning Source LLC
Chambersburg PA
CBHW020556260626
47157CB00003B/729